...een publishe... *Granta*, *Playboy*, Oxford *American*, *New Haven Review*, the *New York Times* and many others. He lives and writes in Southern Indiana. This is his first book.

'An astonishingly powerful debut book … It's a brutal rabbit punch of a book – a shotgun blast in the chest of literature and a crystal meth hit to the reader … It blends the most violent and disturbing storylines, and a genuine empathy for the worst low-life characters, with a wide-eyed, downhome, acid-tongued lyricism. This is not shocking violence for the sake of it, and is a million miles away from so-called "torture porn". Instead, Bill and his contemporaries are channelling age-old storytelling from down through the millennia and placing it in the context of a very real and very desperate modern America, where times are hard and the people are harder. The best stories here have a timeless quality to them … This debut is remarkable.'

Doug Johnstone, *Big Issue*

'Frank Bill's *Crimes in Southern Indiana* should feature high up on your New Year's book buying list … 17 unbelievably violent, often heartbreaking stories in this amazing collection … It's all overshadowed by a Southern Indiana landscape that proves eerily ideal for guns, hunting, secret meth labs and the casual infliction of terrible pain. 270 pages of gripping and harrowing shitloads of it.'

Dazed and Confused

'There's a whiskey-gargling swagger to [Frank Bill's] Cormac McCarthy-style prose, and each noir tale is savagely addictive.'

Shortlist

'Surely everything that can be tried has been tried in the field of crime fiction, down to the last bullet and falling body? Not quite, as Frank Bill's *Crimes in Southern Indiana* satisfyingly proves … You are doing yourself a disservice if you avoid the book; this really is something new and exciting in a field that – it appears – is still capable of renewing itself … The dramatis personae whose paths cross dizzyingly in this fizzing book is a memorable one … Perhaps the most striking characteristic of Frank Bill's magnum opus is the surprise that the reader will feel when discovering that − however outrageous that tale we have just read − the author is able to top it with the next one. It's not a book (as they used to say) for the squeamish, but readers of gamey, pungent crime writing will be in seventh heaven.'

We Love This Book

'Good Lord, where in the hell did this guy come from? Blasts off like a rocket ship and hits as hard as an ax handle to the side of the head after you've snorted a nose full of battery acid and eaten a live rattlesnake for breakfast. Seriously, I'm warning you in advance: take your heart medication and strap yourself to your bar stool for one of the wildest damn rides you're ever going to take inside a book.'

Donald Ray Pollock, author of *Knockemstiff*

'What can I say about this book? This: planning a summer trip north from Mississippi, these stories caused me to reroute to avoid southern Indiana. Frank Bill knows his people well, and writes like they live − on the edge of the edge. Just plain unforgettable fiction.'

Tom Franklin, author of *Crooked Letter, Crooked Letter*

'Take the bark of a .45, the growl of a rusted-out muffler, and the banshee howl of a meth-head on a three-day bender, and you approximate the voice of Frank Bill, a startlingly talented writer whose stories rise from the same dark lyrical well as those of Daniel Woodrell and Dorothy Allison.'

Benjamin Percy, author of *The Wilding* and *Refresh, Refresh*

'Dark, grim, and achingly beautif
most original and compelling voic
crime writers.'

John Rector, autho

'These stories form the ideal nex
pulp fiction: beautifully crafte
and addictive as crystal meth.'

Pinckney Benedict, autho

'Some serious hillbilly-noir that l
end. Open the first page … and d
Craig Clevenger, author of

'Frank Bill's characters all seem to
an hour down dead end streets,
passage is vivid and unforgettal
amphetamines, but the voice is u
William G

Crimes in Southern Indiana

Stories

FRANK BILL

Designed by Jonathan D. Lippincott

Printed and bound by CPI Group (UK) Ltd, Croydon, CR0

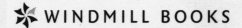

WINDMILL BOOKS

Published by Windmill Books 2013

2 4 6 8 10 9 7 5 3 1

Copyright © Frank Bill 2011

First published in the United States in 2011 by Farrar, Straus and Giroux
First published in Great Britain in 2012 by William Heinemann

Windmill Books
The Random House Group Limited
20 Vauxhall Bridge Road, London SW1V 2SA

Addresses for companies within The Random House Group Limited can be found at:
www.randomhouse.co.uk/offices.htm

The Random House Group Limited Reg. No. 954009

www.randomhouse.co.uk

A CIP catalogue record for this book
is available from the British Library

ISBN 9780099558446

The Random House Group Limited supports The Forest Stewardship Council
(FSC®), the leading international forest certification organisation. Our books
carrying the FSC label are printed on FSC® certified paper. FSC is the only
forest certification scheme endorsed by the leading environmental organisations,
including Greenpeace. Our paper procurement policy can be found at:
www.randomhouse.co.uk/environment

This first one is for John and Ina Bussabarger,
who raised me in the ways of the old. And my rock and
my center, my wife, Jennifer.

CONTENTS

HILL CLAN CROSS

Pitchfork and Darnel burst through the scuffed motel door like two barrels of buckshot. Using the daisy-patterned bed to divide the dealers from the buyers, Pitchfork buried a .45-caliber Colt in Karl's peat moss unibrow with his right hand. Separated Irvine's green eyes with the sawed-off .12-gauge in his left, pushed the two young men away from the mattress, stopped them at a wall painted with nicotine, and shouted, "Drop the rucks, Karl!"

Karl's towline arms contorted in a broken epileptic rhythm. Dropped the two heavy military backpacks to the carpet. Irvine stood with his chest rising and falling in a hyperventilated rush and, sounding like a southern Indiana hick, he said, "This here is our deal."

Behind Pitchfork, big brother Darnel kicked shut the motel door and corralled the two buyers to the right of the bed, into the nightstand, slapped a leather blackjack down onto Dodo Kirby's widow's peak. Helped his knees discover the cigarette-holed carpet. Dodo's little brother Uhl stepped forward, and his checkered teeth of bad dental mouthed, "What the shit, man, you can't—" Darnel obliged Uhl with the blackjack. Beat his nose into chips of flint. Mashed his lips into blueberry stains. Slid the blackjack into his bibs, pulled a small coil of fence wire from his other pocket. Shook his head and said, "Can't what? We never gave the go for this deal. We's taking back what's ours."

Pitchfork and Darnel had found several of their storage drums coming up short in the weight department after they'd been scaled for a customer who'd rescaled them and was none too happy. They'd their suspicions of who'd skimmed the dope, considering the hands to be trusted were a select few. They passed the word to the Harrison County sheriff, Elmo Sig, who'd been on their payroll for the past ten years, letting them use the only motel in town to do their trade. The man also gave the DEA leads in other counties, detoured their noses out of his own. Sig had his own eyes and ears, who went by the alias AK, running through the surrounding counties. AK delivered some chatter that he'd overheard about two twenty-somethings with some primo weed. Needed to turn it to cash quick. Wanted to set up a deal at the same motel where they'd watched Darnel and Pitchfork make theirs.

Darnel kneeled down. Pushed a knee into Uhl's blue flannel spine. Started weaving tight figure eights with the wire through Uhl's wrists. Pulled a pair of snips from his back pocket. Cut the wire.

Sweat bathed the garden of red and pus-white acne bumps across Karl's forehead as he yelled, "We helped harvest, dry, weigh, and package them crops when you all was busy! We deserve a piece of the profit."

Pitchfork's briar-scarred right arm pulled the Colt away from Karl's brow an inch. Thudded the barrel into his forehead. Karl hollered, "Fuck!" Pitchfork told the boy, "You deserve what you earn."

Behind Pitchfork on the other side of the bed, Darnel finished with Dodo's wrists. Stood up. Told Karl, "You'd been a smear on your mama's leg I hadn't wanted me a boy to carry on my line. Course, I don't know if you deserved that."

Darnel stepped toward Karl and Irvine, said, "Turn around. Tired of lookin' at all your stupid." Karl and Irvine turned around, faced the yellowing wall. Pitchfork slid the Colt into his waist. Held the sawed-off down at his side. Shook his bone-shaved skull, told the boys, "Two shit birds didn't even check the parkin' lot for extra men. This time a night they coulda rushed you like we did. Hell, we's sittin' over off in the shadows in the '68."

Karl turned to Irvine and said, "Told you we shoulda checked the damn lot."

Pitchfork stepped away from the boys, watched Darnel coil the wire over and under Irvine's wrists, and Darnel asked Irvine, "Who vouched for these two scrotums?"

From the other side of the room Karl whimpered, "Eugene Lillpop."

Darnel laughed his carburetor laugh. "That inbred shit has got one hand in his pants, the other up his mama's skirt. His word ain't worth the phlegm he lubes his palm with."

From the floor, with hair matted to his face, Uhl whimpered and spit from swelled lips turning purple. Talked in his toughest tone. "Sons of bitches best let us be. Know who our ol' man is?"

Pitchfork stood disgusted by Dodo's question. "Sure I know backstabbin' Able Kirby. Shoulda been buried beneath an outhouse for rattin' out Willie Dodson years back. Course you all run in a different county. Shit like that don't fly 'round here, your kind is used for fertilizer."

Uhl coughed and protested, "Our daddy's a good man. Didn't never rat Willie out."

Darnel finished with Karl's wrists. Put the wire and snips back in his pocket. Grabbed the two rucks Karl had carried in. Slung one over each shoulder. Smelled that honey-thick odor. Told Uhl, "Son, I know for a fact it was your ol' man 'cause Willie worked for me. Crossed counties to meet with your daddy and some of his people way down in Orange Holler. When the shit went down your daddy walked away clean as cotton."

Pitchfork laid the sawed-off on the floor. Opened Uhl and Dodo's ruck. Reached in and dug through the bundles of bills, all Benjamins banded around identical-sized blank cutouts on the bottoms. Then he felt the weight of steel, pulled out two nickel-plated .38 revolvers. Looked at the boys and said, "You two dick stains didn't even check to see if they's packin' heat or the right amount of cash? Fuckin' greenies."

Darnel dug his hands into Karl's and Irvine's hair. Told them, "Could at least used a different motel room or another county. Don't matter no way. You two got a lesson to learn." Then he guided them to the door by their greasy heads of hair. Opened it.

Pitchfork put the two .38s back in the leather ruck. Slung it over his shoulder. Grabbed the sawed-off. Pulled Dodo to his feet. Then Uhl, who begged, "Let us go. We won't say shit."

Pitchfork stared through Uhl and questioned, "Keys?"

Confused, Uhl said, "Keys?" "Motherfucker, how'd you get that rape van out yonder, hot-wire it?" Uhl stuttered, "F-F-F-Front pocket." Pitchfork patted Uhl's front, pulled the van keys from the pocket, sneered, and told Uhl, "And we know you ain't gonna say shit 'cause where we gonna take you, won't nobody hear a word."

Darnel loaded Uhl, Dodo, and the ruck of dollar bills into Irvine and Karl's Impala. Pitchfork loaded the boys and the rucks of marijuana into the bed of his '68. Left Uhl and Dodo's van with the keys in the ignition, payment beneath the driver's seat for Sheriff Elmo to scrap over at Medford Malone's salvage yard. Then they drove to the Hill Clan Cross Cemetery. A place where bad deals were made good and lessons were buried deep.

The two vehicles were silent except for the crack and pop of night air cooling the engine blocks. Headlights from the Impala and '68 Chevy outlined the profiles of Dodo and Uhl, their features now wet and swollen hues of yellow and purple turning darker with the night. Blood peeled like three-day-old biscuits. The shovels they'd used to dig the eight-by-eight grave left their hands unsteady at their sides as they stood looking down into their handiwork.

Pitchfork stood behind Dodo and Uhl, the .45 pressed into one head, the sawed-off into the other. Karl and Irvine kneeled off to the left, taking in the three silhouettes. Behind them, Darnel made his cigarette cherry with a final inhalation as he flicked it to the ground and told Pitchfork, "It's time."

Pitchfork asked the two buyers, "How old you say you was?"

Dodo slobbered, "We didn't." Hoping the nightmare would end and they'd be released, he said, "I's thirty-five, Uhl's—"

Pitchfork cut him off. "Well, least you ain't gotta worry about cancer or achin' bones like your mama." Then he squeezed the .45's trigger. Dodo's skull exploded into the beams of light, disappeared into the air. His body thudded forward into the grave.

With Uhl's ears ringing, his crotch found warm fear as he screamed, "No, no! Oh God, please! Please!"

Pitchfork said, "Ain't you the whiniest chickenshit I ever did hear."

Darnel said, "His ol' man was the same way, don't you remember that time over at Galloway's fish fry? Grabbed Galloway's daughter's ass. Got all wet-eyed when Galloway was gonna stomp him into cornmeal."

Pitchfork said, "Sure I remember. Galloway's daughter was only fourteen at the time." He told Uhl, "Your ol' man's 'bout a sick son of a bitch."

Uhl's face contorted. If skin could chatter, his would have. He said, "Let me go. I can pay triple."

Pitchfork growled, "With what? You knock over an armored vehicle full of one-dollar bills?" Shook his head. "Ain't just about money. It's about blood."

From behind Karl and Irvine, Darnel said, "These two boys need to know they can't steal their own kin's means to provide. Two of you was packin' heat, I know you'd have done somethin' just like this to them in that motel room we hadn't showed up. Tonight everyone's got a lesson to be learned."

Karl and Irvine watched with their faces damp. Their wrists were free but aching from the wire that had cut into their skin.

Uhl's weakness turned brave as he spun around, knocked the sawed-off out of Pitchfork's left hand, only to have the .45 add another split of pain to his head. Uhl fell flat and mumbled, "You bastard." Pitchfork pressed his boot down into Uhl's neck, pointed the pistol at his head, said, "Didn't think you had any fight in you, kinda impressed." Then he pulled the trigger. Uhl's complexion disappeared across the soil. Pitchfork slid the .45 into his waistband, kneeled down, and rolled Uhl's body into the grave.

New tears warmed Karl's and Irvine's cheeks. Pitchfork stepped away from the grave and sat on the Impala's hood.

Darnel's hands gripped Karl's and Irvine's sweaty hair. Pulled them to their feet. The boys' insides tightened while their minds burned with a revelation: never steal from your father and uncle's harvest to sell on the side, because in the end, whether it's spilled or related, blood is blood.

Stopping the boys in front of the grave, Darnel reached into his pocket and gripped the Colt. Raised it. Dropped Irvine, then Karl, in quick succession. Listened to them hit the bottom of the grave.

To Darnel's right, Pitchfork leaned off the car hood and asked, "Think they broke anything?"

Darnel shoved the pistol into his pocket, turned and walked over to Pitchfork, said, "Hope they did."

The '68's truck door squeaked. Pitchfork reached inside, pulled a couple of iced bottles of Falls City from a cooler. Handed one to Darnel, asked, "How long you think it'll take 'fore they wake up?"

Darnel pulled a chipped red Swiss Army knife from his pocket, used the bottle opener. "Don't know, but we got plenty beer till they do."

Taking the opener from Darnel, Pitchfork said, "Just hope they learned their lesson."

Darnel turned the bottle of beer up and crystallized foam burned his throat like acid as he swallowed, then he said, "Yeah, I'd hate we had to kill our only two boys."

THESE
OLD BONES

It was as if God himself had shot the son of a bitch from the sky. But the good Lord had done no such thing to Able Kirby.

His body lay facedown, ears still ringing from the small-caliber gunfire that dotted his upper back, chest, and gut. Blood etched a path behind his work boots, leading all the way to the flaked wooden screen door of the house from which Able had stumbled.

He pressed his palms into uneven earth. Steadied himself. Tried to push his chest up as if doing a push-up only to fall flat, smelling cinder and soil with a sideways glance, remembering all the bad he'd done in this life.

He'd burned his father's home for insurance money. Shot Esther MacCullum's dog dead in front of him for a debt he owed. Forced himself upon Needle Galloway's fourteen-year-old daughter. Opened Nelson Anderson's skull in the Leavenworth Tavern with a hammer for saying he'd ratted out Willie Dodson on a cross-county dope deal, even though he did it for the local law.

And today he'd sold his granddaughter, Knee High Audry, to the Hill Clan to whore out. Needing the extra cash to help pay for his wife Josephine's cancer medications. Yeah, he thought, I's a son of a bitch.

Josephine stood in the kitchen smelling the spoiling skin that hung loose and gray like dry rotted curtains on a rusted rod, wishing she'd stopped Able before it got this far. Thinking of how she lay in bed, night after night, listening to him worm from beneath the cloth, cross the floor, the squeak of hinges to the bedroom where their granddaughter slept. Jo would work her way out of bed, inhaling hard and grunting, and Able would be in the kitchen getting a sip of beer by the time she passed Knee High's bedroom and made it to the kitchen. Seeing her, Able would say, "Couldn't sleep, needed me a swallow." That's why she began sleeping with the Ruger beneath her pillow. A .22-caliber pistol she'd wielded to remove varmint and snake from the chicken house and garden. She knew she'd grown too weak to physically do damage.

Over the years Jo pretended not to notice the glints Able made at county fairs or the grocery, eyeing the young and their parts that had taken shape. He started with Knee High while she prepared supper, did dishes, fed the chickens and gathered eggs. Jo would question him about staring and he'd told her, "She's just become womanized awful quick like. Remember a time when you's that pretty."

His tone had bored a lump of disgust in Jo's gut, making these comparisons of the flesh. Then came the rumors about Galloway's daughter.

Fearing the answer, Jo questioned Able about the girl. He didn't deny his actions. Reaffirmed his motivations. "Shit you think, woman, girl like that, man such as myself. She was lookin' to me first. I's just offering is all. You bein' the shape you're in, man's got needs you can't possibly meet."

Thirty-five years of matrimony and his words carved into the bone, panging worse than her cancer. With age, the man had been molded into a sickness she'd ignored far too long, didn't know how to deal with. And moments before, Able had come into the bedroom with a devil's grin igniting his chicken-neck face. He laid a small brown sack loaded with crumpled bills on the bed. In his crusted eyes was a wilted cellophane glow. Their granddaughter had supposedly ridden to town with him to run an errand, and she asked, "Where's Knee High?"

Standing, Able rubbed his palms together, a trickle of sweat spitting from his brow. He tongued his lips. Looked Josephine in the eye, said, "Hear me out, Jo. You and me been strugglin' here with your cancer meds and the boys disappearin'. Knee High needed to put more of her fair share in the coin jar. So I hocked her for cash to Pitchfork and Darnel to help pay for your meds. Let her work off the cash. Come home when all is square. Didn't see no other way 'round it."

Josephine's jaundiced eyes cleared. She pulled out the Ruger, fingered the trigger, and buried a round in his belly.

Should have done this long ago, she thought, could have protected her own. Her mind wondered about consequence for a split second, too late, and realized this was his and her consequence. Short of breath, propping up her old bones from the bed with the ping of joints and the lactic ache of muscle, Jo quipped, "No other way around it? Oh, they's ways around it, only I waited too long for direction."

Able tried to stand but hit the bedroom's hardwood in shock. Stumbled to his feet. Josephine fired a round into his shoulder. Then his chest. Able fell into the dresser, screaming. "Crazy ol' bitch!" He turned away with his hand pressed into the wet heat of his belly, the other steadying him into the next room.

Josephine's feet found her unlaced boots, disregarded the folding wheelchair leaned against the wall. She wheeled her oxygen tank into the next room, where Able's body fell into the living room wall. She lined the pistol up with his chest, her grip unsteady as her vision. She pulled the trigger. "Shit!" he squealed. Another circle of red pressed through his white T-shirt, with the wall guiding him into another room.

Now she balanced herself on the silver oxygen tank's wheeled frame. Inhaled air from the clear tube that forked into her nostrils from the fire-extinguisher-size tank and asked herself how Able could sell their fourteen-year-old granddaughter to the Hill Clan like livestock. Sell Knee High to the likes of those two cutthroats, Pitchfork and Darnel Crase.

Able and she had just lost their two sons, Dodo and Uhl, Knee High's daddy. They'd run off, always up to no good. Left the house late one evening months ago. Never returned. Neglecting responsibility. Leaving Able and her to raise Audry, who would now be forced to offer her teenage self with womanlike curves to wasted feed sacks of broken-down men for dirty wads of paper.

Josephine steadied her sunken yellow eyes, squeezing the handgrip of the Ruger in her right hand, knowing in the back of her mind she needed to get out that damn door and end Able's sickness before it ended her.

One of the shots bounced around inside Able till it severed a nerve, caused his legs to lose their flow.

Behind him he heard the creak of the screen door. Lungs clawing for air. Wheels and boots scraping the ground. Josephine's voice. "Hope you find the good Lord's soil comfortin', 'cause that's the only comfort you gonna get."

Trying to contract his leg muscles, Able's body throbbed cold. He gritted his teeth. Blinked tears from his eyes, "Dammit, Jo, hold on. We need that money. Once she's worked it off we'd get her back."

Josephine's movements grew in pitch till her syllables towered over Able. "Get her back? She's our grandchild. A human bein'. Unlike yourself." Able dug at the soil, twisted his neck, made out Josephine's outline, and he begged, "Help me, Jo, can't even feel—"

Tiny flashes of fire erupted around what Able believed to be Josephine. His mouth moved but his words were unheard within his head. Cramps bounced up his back, into his neck just like the black that replaced feeling inside his body. Josephine stood with the gun empty, tiny brass scattered around her. Seeing no movement from Able, knowing he was dead, that she'd ended the sickness she'd ignored far too long, she'd no idea how to get Knee High back home.

ALL THE AWFUL

One of the man's hands gripped Audry's wrists above her head. Forced them to the ground. She bucked her pelvis up. Wanted him off of her. The other hand groped the rounded shapes beneath her soiled wifebeater. Her eyes clasped. Held tears. The man's tobacco-stained lips and bourbon breath dragged against her neck.

"Like that . . . don't you?"

The man's name was Melvin. He'd the scent of coagulated chicken swelled in three days of hundred-degree heat. He'd paid four hundred crumpled bills to the Hill Clan for three hours with Knee High Audry.

Knee High lay between the rows of corn that shadowed her goat-milk complexion. Unwashed shoulder-length hair the hue of burned tires fanned out in matted clumps. Melvin grunted. Knee High's thoughts darted to how her ride with Able to run an errand had been detoured to seeing men about money in another county. Where a man named Darnel laughed, told Able, "Ain't you a taste of treason. Sell out your two boys, this girl's daddy and uncle, to Sheriff Sig. Now you's swindlin' your granddaughter to us. Shit, you've pretty much snitched out half the county for Sig."

Able nodded, said, "Need money, cancer meds ain't cheap for the wife."

Darnel passed a sack to Able and told him, "Nor is your taste for the booze."

Knee High watched Able thumb through the brown sack of bills. Trying to decipher Darnel's words, not realizing what was transpiring, her brain ignited with confusion and anger. Her daddy and Uncle Dodo had run off. The only speech she could muster wasn't to Able, it was to Darnel, and she shouted, "Where's my daddy and my uncle?"

Darnel chuckled, his sight boring into her like two hollow points, and he said, "Dead and buried."

She looked to Able to correct this. He stood silently holding the sack of money, digging his hand into it, and she demanded, "What'd you do, Granddad, what'd you do?"

It was Darnel who responded. "He did the same to them that he's done to you." Knee High reached for Able, wanting to shake answers from his hide. He stepped back, still counting the money as she questioned him. "What's he saying, Granddad?" And before she could wrap her mind around what was transpiring, Darnel's talcum grip restrained her. She twisted away from him and he backhanded her and said, "He sold you to me and my brother to satisfy the men of our county."

She tongued blood from her lip as he drew her to a room where wallpaper was smeared by tea stains and soured skin. The last thing she saw before the door slammed and bolted shut was Able turning his back, walking out the same way they'd entered.

She beat on the pine door, trying to fathom these things Able had done, trying to understand what Darnel meant, saying Able had sold out her daddy and uncle to Sheriff Sig. And why Able had traded her for a sack of money to pay for her grandmother's cancer medications. The man named Darnel told her it was "to satisfy men." She understood she'd been sold for sex. But her grandmother Jo would never have agreed to such a thing.

Her arms and fists swelled and hardened as she sat barefoot on the floor, crying, a broken-down mattress quilted by a sheet once white lying gray and sticky behind her. She held her knees and rocked back and forth for what seemed like hours, realizing her daddy and uncle were dead because of Able. Then came the roar of a vehicle's engine outside. The slamming of a door. Men speaking, saying, "Four hundred. She's in yonder. Take your time. We got people to tend." Feet trampled out of the house, an engine fired up and became distant. The sound of metal unlatched on the bedroom door's opposite side. A towering stranger entered. Kneeled down in his cutoff red flannel, smiled with teeth caked by tobacco, and ran a finger tainted by motor oil down her cheek, told her, "Call me Melvin."

He grasped her firm arms, lifted her to her feet, guided her backwards toward the bedding. In his eyes she made out the same sick lust she'd tried to ignore in her grandfather over the months as she did chores around the house, and she pleaded, "No." He slapped her. She turned with the strike, dodged his reach, and ran out of the room to the entrance and then out of the house.

Melvin followed, tackled her down in the field between the rows of feed corn. Punched her, tore her shorts and panties from her. Unbuckled his pants, made the grainy earth their bedding.

Now all she wanted was to survive, but he was bigger than she was, stronger. She had to pretend, to be a chameleon. Thought of men and women. Affection and a neighbor boy who'd kissed her, brushed his tongue into her ear. Remembered the spark and chill that ran down her spine and dimpled her body from this gesture. She wiggled her tongue into Melvin's ear, tasted the disgusting flavor of a toad floured in fresh manure. His lips forced into hers, busted and bloody. "That a girl." He released her hands. She crimped her eyes closed, groped Melvin's bare bushy ass. Wanted to vomit as his heated breath in her ear moaned, "Oh pretty." She tickled a path with her left hand down over the hump of his bareness. Felt the waistline of his pants, followed the leather belt to the hard handle he wore on his side. Thumbed the snap loose. Unsheathed a wicked curve of steel.

Knee High's mouth engulfed Melvin's ear on one side. She dug the blade into his neck on the other. Pulled it out as her teeth ripped tissue and cartilage from skull. He jerked into his shoulder, shouted, "Little fuckin'—" She didn't allow him to finish, drove the knife into his throat. He gargled. Collapsed atop her like warm molasses. His breathing slowed to a stop. Her fingers pulled at the earth. Dragging herself from beneath the degenerate beast, she stood, spat out Melvin's ear. Her chest and legs blood-covered and vibrating. Bottomless, she ran down the row of corn toward the house she'd escaped from. Hoping Darnel and Pitchfork were still gone, hoping their business wasn't finished.

She wanted to go home. Tell her grandmother Jo all the awful Granddad Able had done. How he'd sold out her daddy and uncle to Sheriff Sig, gotten them killed. Do the same awful to Able that she'd done to Melvin.

Corn leaves like miniature razors cut her face and arms. Her bare feet pounded the row's soil. Met the green grass.

Yellowed heat from the sun led her to the house's fly-decorated screen door. Karl, one of the Hill Clan's boys, stood on the other side, surprised Knee High—she'd not seen him when she'd arrived earlier—and he screamed, "The shit?"

Karl pushed the door open. Got his left leg out. Knee High dropped the weight of her body against it. Trapped him in between jamb and door. He hollered, "You bitch!" Fell backwards into the house.

Knee High turned in a panic. Ran toward a weathered corncrib where wood was split and piled. Heard the screen door slam behind her. Felt boots on her bare heels. Nearing the split wood, Knee High was grabbing for a piece when she saw the handle. Both hands met it just as Karl's words struck the rear of her head. "Gonna beat and fuck your ass all in the same—" Knee High hefted, whirled around with the double-sided axe that was almost as long as she was tall. Finding the left side of Karl's rib cage. Cutting off his words. The sound the axe made going in was godawful, but when she pulled it out to finish him, the sound he made was damning. Like a dog chasing and biting at a passing car's tires only to have its bark replaced by the crunch of its skull between rubber and pavement. He dropped to his knees in shock. Knee High stepped back. Swung. Karl fell wordless to the warm earth.

In the house she trembled. Irvine, the other son of the Hill Clan, was gone. Knee High was blood and stink from head to toe. The bones of her crusted hands jumped as she fought the moisture that bubbled in her eyes and shock that rifled through her mind. In a panic she searched for clothing to cover herself with. Discovered an old dress scented with mothballs in a closet, worked it over her battered body.

Outside she found Melvin's keys in the ignition of his

red Dodge truck. Magazines lined the floor with photos of young girls. Wadded rags and paper. Crunched cans of Miller and empty pints of Wild Turkey. Knee High turned the key. The engine coughed to life. She shifted into drive. Stomped the gas.

What the Hill Clan found at the house was Melvin between rows of corn. A mess about his neck, knife protruding from it. Karl out by the pile of wood next to the corncrib. A bloody axe. His head an unrecognized shade of dead. To them it looked as though they'd paid for the Wisconsin serial murderer Ed Gein's daughter.

Now, pulling down Able Kirby's long gravel drive, Pitchfork chewed on rage. His brother Darnel wanted to watch Knee High bleed and beg. They rounded the curve, saw Melvin's red truck.

"Told you the cunt got nowheres to go."

"We kill her we out of thirty grand."

"Able still got it."

On the creek-rock steps, flies shared the bloated corpse of Able Kirby. Several buzzards circled overhead.

"So much for Able."

"Must've pissed off Jo."

"He's plenty dead."

The inside of the house sat silent as a child in sleep. Pitchfork's and Darnel's tones echoed from vinyl-papered walls and ceiling. Nothing in the kitchen, or the dining room. The upstairs was devoid of sound or body. Knee High's room, untouched. Just framed black-and-white family photos of times past. Men, women, and children. Able, Jo. The two Pitchfork had murdered. They walked through the living room. Pitchfork carried a .45, Darnel a blackjack. Darnel stepped toward two wooden doors that connected in the center. Reached to divide them, slide both doors open. Called out, "You in there, Knee High, you gonna pay us back double in front of Jo. One after the next."

The doors parted. Josephine sat in a tarnished chrome wheelchair. A clear hose wishboned into her nares, offering air from a nickel-colored cylinder on the floor beside her. The barrel of a Remington 11 semiautomatic was leveled not even ten feet from Darnel's chest. Her one eye closed, the other open, the two men in shooting view.

Knee High stood beside Josephine, trying to steady the 4-10 she'd locked, cocked, and readied to fire while the horror of what had happened rattled her nerves.

Darnel raised the scarred flesh of both hands, palms facing the females, the blackjack held by his thumb. "Hold on, you two—"

Josephine skipped not a syllable. "You hold on, Darnel. What you done is devilry."

Darnel said, "Wasn't just us—"

The next sound deafened even God himself. Jo's bones splintered from the .12-gauge's kick. Darnel's right knee segmented into red-white jelly chunks slung about the hardwood. Pitchfork dropped his .45 and caught Darnel, who dropped the blackjack.

Josephine rasped, "You's right, it was the whole Hill Clan."

Darnel slobbered and gritted his teeth. "Your Knee High killed my boy."

Knee High leveled the 4-10 down to Darnel's face with

a slight jerk. "That'd make us almost even." She paused. Shifted her eyes toward Jo. Swallowed. Continued, "Seeing as you all killed my daddy and my uncle Dodo."

Hearing Knee High's words, Jo's finger pulsed against the .12-gauge's trigger. Her vision blacked everything around the men who'd killed her two boys that she'd believed to have run off. Bringing all their awful to fruition.

Not knowing if she would, Knee High said, "Let it be, Grandma Jo, let it be."

THE PENANCE
OF SCOOT
McCUTCHEN

Wire springs poked through the worn vinyl front seat like he imagined the mattress of a jail cell's bed would, pricking his conscience as he sat within his personal purgatory. His memories from that last day and every day since. Fingering the keys dangling from the ignition, so tired of the searching, of the running, he'd come to terms with his decision. His only task now was waiting for the man. Glancing out his driver's side into the window of the Mauckport town marshal's office, he watched some woman carry on a conversation with what must have been Dispatch. But Deets didn't need Dispatch. Glancing down at the head shots, a shadow of a wanted man, rolled up and tied by twine in the passenger's seat, he needed the marshal, so he sat and waited and let his mind wander.

It seemed long ago, but still so clear in his mind, the scene from that last day. That even with a pillow covering her waxy face, it didn't make it any easier. Not seeing her face. Not hearing her jumbled tones, which scratched his conscience like the rake of fingernails down a chalkboard. The pressure of her touch. He closed his eyes, still feeling the buckle of the seat as he imagined her final expression. So permanent, so final.

Like a jolt of pick-me-up kettle coffee, it was the first thought Deets acknowledged every morning and pondered all day, till it tucked him into bed. Haunting his dreams with the tossing and turning of "How could I not have known?"

He must have driven for days afterward. Finding that first town in Tennessee that wasn't on the map. So small the town paper was a single page, front and back with an obituaries column no bigger than a Bazooka Joe bubble gum comic strip. And it was here that Deets Merritt would try to begin anew, searching for his self, an identity. But even after finding a job, trying to start over, he discovered he couldn't outrun the shadow and guilt that haunted him. A decision that was nothing more than a two-sided coin with fate on each side of the flip. A piece of his existence gone. Something he could never get back, only carry on his conscience. Life would never be easy again. The only time life is easy is childhood, but by the time a person realizes this, it's too damn late.

But still, he never gave up. Kept searching. And every new town meant another trade. Another new job. He'd worked construction, framing and building houses. Flipped burgers at greasy-spoon diners in towns whose populations were less than the price of an oil change, towns so small if you blinked between the post office and the police station, you thought you'd made a wrong turn because of the town's sudden disappearance in the side mirror.

There wasn't a day that passed by that he didn't miss her. But he didn't want to go back. He'd do it all over again even if the outcome would be the same.

Now, as he sat waiting in his '61 International Scout four-wheel drive, the sun lowered at the breech of the town's street. Dust was a Van Gogh landscape etched across his windshield, adding to the crawl of the oncoming evening. Discovering the darkness that was night.

He remembered how it all began. How he'd bought the Scout its first year of production. His father had driven him into Indianapolis, from their small town of Corydon. He'd bought it with money he'd saved from his childhood, working his father's hog farm, then the money earned in his job at Keller's, the local furniture factory, manning the band saw to rip the wood that was honed into furniture. He'd seen more than his fair share of fingers removed by that saw, never replaced.

So proud of his purchase, he'd cruised through town, and that's when he saw her walking along the town square that first time. He slowed down, pulled up beside her. Asked if she needed a lift. As she turned to him, her smile was misleading; her lips told him to eat shit. She'd not need another useless shade of man catering to her. She'd been married once already, to a boozing pugilist who eventually ran off with a younger woman and several warrants. He'd left her not only paying for the divorce but several dozen or so debts, and the last mistake she wanted was a ride home from a strange man. After that he'd framed her in his mind not by images but by her words, her simple yet harsh construction of language that she'd offered to him.

Her words were honest.

He apologized and drove home, knowing he'd met his future wife.

Every day after work, with his face stained by sweat and sawdust peppered in his hair like lice, he'd see her walking. And every day he'd ask her if she needed a lift. He told her someone as easy on the eyes as she was shouldn't have to walk, let alone work. And she told him to mind his own, as he could find cleanliness with a bit of bristle lathered by lye. And he laughed at the directness of her tongue.

But finally she broke down, and he gave her a ride. She gave her name: Elizabeth Slade. Like a felon ignoring the wanted posters hanging from the post office walls of a town, Deets threw caution to the wind, asked her out for lunch. She was hesitant at first. Then she accepted. They had coffee and apple pie at Jocko's Diner on the corner of town, where she told him she worked at Arpac, the local poultry slaughterhouse, slicing the necks of chickens. He questioned how something so fragile with beauty could earn a wage doing something so violent. And she explained it was the only decent-paying job for a woman with cutlery skills.

One date led to another until he visited her parents to ask permission to marry Mr. and Mrs. Slade's daughter. The Slades had not seen her this happy since she was a child, so they gave their blessing to Deets, as did his own parents, and he proposed. She moved in with him, living in the log cabin he'd built by hand from the ground up on some fifty acres. He told her he'd plenty of money. There was no need for her to work if she didn't want to. So she gave her notice to Arpac, and they consummated their vows two weeks later.

In five years they had a bond that most marriages didn't share even after three kids and twenty years of loyalty. They'd no children, only the bliss they found in each other.

He'd work during the day, coming home some evenings to help her in the garden they planted every summer. Even with all the work she did—picking and breaking beans, shucking ears of corn, digging potatoes and onions, all of the canning for winter—how her hands felt against his flesh. Soft as a baby deer's tongue, the warmth of innocence.

Her shoulder-length locks were like her eyes, stained like a walnut, and her flesh was colored by the sun as she worked in the garden, where she went barefoot in cut-off jeans and one of his old worn-out Hanes T-shirts tainted by the heat from a day's worth of work.

Other evenings after work he hunted to keep their freezer full of meat. Used the double-barrel .12-gauge his granddad had left him. It had a firing pin that sometimes misfired on the right barrel. All one had to do was pull the hammer back and try again.

But it was that one evening he came into the cabin with several rabbits gutted and skinned, ready to soak in saltwater, that he found her on the kitchen floor. Meeting her cheek's flesh with the back of his hand, he discovered her dampness from a fever. As if he had stepped into a hornets' nest, Deets was stung by a swelling panic as he phoned Dr. Brockman for a house call. Then he undressed Elizabeth and placed her in their bathtub. She didn't agree with standard medication nor the county hospital. But she did agree with the old ways. It was how her parents raised her. Lye for soap to wash off the sawdust and sweat of the factory. A hot toddy sipped to break the mucus of a head or chest cold. Bacon for a bee sting until the stinger showed enough to be tweezed free from the flesh. Fresh-squeezed tomato pulp with canned pickle juice and a shot of Everclear to nurse a hangover. And if she had a hound who'd not received his vaccination quick enough but instead acquired parvo, she'd end his suffering by placing the barrel of a gun to his skull to prepare him for burial. She'd helped her daddy do it more than once.

Deets had been raised by the same old ways. He crushed large squares of ice and packed them into the bath. He held warm Jell-O in a coffee cup to her lips to help keep her hydrated and break the fever. The fever that would last longer than the labor of a child. Days, not hours.

At first he feared her brain would be damaged. He'd heard the stories his mother had told him as a child, men and women whose fevers weren't broken quickly enough, held for too long, their brains frying like the rabbits he coated with buttermilk to stick to the wheat flour, then placed into a skillet of lard and fried to a crisp.

Once her fever broke, she was unable to remember names and faces, places and times. Her speech was slurred for a while, as though her jaws had been pistol-whipped by the butt of a .38.

But Brockman prescribed his vitamins and assured Deets that Elizabeth would recover. And as the days added up on the calendar, she gradually returned to being the same woman he'd married some years before.

But what he later told himself was that he shouldn't have trusted him with her. Shouldn't have trusted Brockman with his wife. But he had.

The woman talking to Dispatch came out onto the sidewalk, wobbled to a pace, disappeared down past the Dollar Store, around the corner past the bank. But the marshal hadn't shown up. He was what Deets's daddy would have referred to as so poke-ass he was probably late for his own conception.

But he'd wait. One thing Deets had was time. He'd passed through so many towns he couldn't remember if this was his tenth town or his twentieth job. They were all the same. What he could remember were the four characteristics that built a small town: a post office, a sheriff or marshal's station, a bank, and a graveyard. He'd always check the post office, pulling the wanted posters of a man who haunted him, collecting them from each and every town. An identity that wouldn't let him forget. That wouldn't let him start over.

By day he'd pass the bank, the marshal's station, and at night he'd walk the graveyards, wondering how the dead had passed. By accident, sickness, or the hands of their loved ones, their kin.

He'd been down as far south as Greenville, Alabama. Traveled back through Dayton, Tennessee. Manchester, Milan, and Dyersburg. Crossed over into Poplar Bluff and Garwood, Missouri. But he'd backtracked over the years through Illinois, Indiana, and back into Kentucky. Through Owensboro, Elizabethtown, Bardstown, Mount Sterling, traveling into the polarization of the hills. Traveling to Morehead, then back into Pine Ridge, Campton, Jackson, Hazard. And Whitesburg, where everybody knew your kin's family tree, fished with dynamite, and hunted with a double-barrel .12-gauge. Your daddy either owned a lot of land or worked a coal mine in a surrounding county like Harlan that paid well. You always attended church on Sunday, and no matter how much you did or didn't contribute to the offering plate, it was a place where people lived a simple and straightforward life. And it was here that Deets realized he'd traveled so long he'd forgotten who he was, and what he was running from.

From town to town some had heard the story. Had read

it in the papers if they could read or heard it on the television if they owned one with an antenna. Had seen the features of the young man he once was, clean-shaven and baby-faced, now covered by age, the look of tires run on back-road gravel, blanketed by remorse and regret that had left his features thick with the shadows of barbed-wire whisker and uneven locks of hair. His mane, coarse as a horse's tail, braided down his spine. The person on those posters on the passenger's seat and the man who collected them were two identities with the same torment.

Deets sat fighting the tears of memory. He wiped snot on his flannel sleeve with one hand while the other pulled a fresh Pall Mall from his pack, then placed it unlit onto his lips as he thought. He should have seen it, acknowledged its presence. Her love was a cripple fighting frostbite. As her feeling was permanently lost, all he could do was watch, because there was no cure for frostbite.

He should have noted her appetite disappearing along with the meals she no longer prepared, the garden she no longer kept, beans no longer broken, corn no longer shucked, potatoes no longer dug.

Everything gone to waste. Spoiled. She said she felt too weak. Said she was too tired or she lost track of time. That daylight was too short.

That's what she'd told him after that first discovery of her slip on the kitchen floor and the fever that followed. And as they lay in bed at night while he ran his hands over her warm outline, tracing her beauty, her words exchanged with his, how she'd maybe try tomorrow, she just needed her rest, to lie with him, to lie with this shade of skin. This man. Her husband.

But then he came home from the factory one evening, found her feeling weak on the couch, as she'd discovered another slip. A jarring of her brain. She'd crawled to the phone and called Brockman, who said it was probably her blood sugar. But after that more stumbles followed as her balance was no better than a square dancer with a crooked limb or a clubfoot. She'd lost her posture, her rhythm, and her balance when moving across the cabin's hardwood floor, no longer recognizing the upright position.

Deets trusted Brockman; so did Elizabeth. But then came her confusion and uncontrolled outbursts of emotion. She believed one of her ears was bigger than the other. She asked him to look. To compare. To see what she'd seen in the bathroom mirror every morning. During simple conversations she'd cry inconsolably about the beauty of the day or how the outside air felt against her features, dried the tears that shadowed her cheek line. He'd see nothing, and like her, he understood even less.

And the visits from Brockman and his vitamin treatments began to add up. They had become similar to visits from the Reaper—your soul was the toll and all you could do was wait.

Finally Deets had lost his trust in Brockman and his vitamin treatments. He forced Elizabeth into his Scout, made a trip to the county hospital, where he explained her fever, her stumbles and tumbles, along with her confusion over the ear and her emotional outbursts. They admitted her. Took X-rays. Ran blood tests. Discovered an imbalance in her mind that was so far beyond treatable it was incurable. Her mind had fermented into soil that enriched a tiny crop of malignant ginseng spreading and rooting in her brain.

Afterward Deets asked himself what he had done, trusting Brockman, waiting too long, putting it off. He blamed himself.

What she had would deteriorate her to a plot of loose earth in six months or less. And it began tearing her numbers from the calendar, stealing what days she had left, taking with it the bond they once shared. He'd come home from work trying to comfort her, wanting to lie with her in bed, feel the warmth of her outline next to his. Wanting to bathe her and cook and feed her. He hoped for a miracle, but she'd given up on what he couldn't let go of. She'd mumble pleas, telling him she was like a hound with parvo, she was suffering, she'd lost her quality of life and needed to be put down. It was a choice a husband didn't want to hear about, let alone carry out.

Now, seated in his Scout, he remembered that scent as he flicked his Zippo lighter. It was that familiar sparking of the flint, so identical, coaling his Pall Mall. Only that day, entering the home, it was like a Zippo that wouldn't light. That flint being flicked over and over without any fuel. No butane, just the spark of sulfur. He remembered coming home early, wanting to surprise her with flowers. And there sat Dr. Brockman's Cadillac in the driveway. With a sprinter's heart, Deets dropped the flowers, entered their home. The slamming of the wooden screen door, hinges squeaking, needing oil, drowned out the loud blast, leaving only that aftereffect in the air. A scent that he followed through their home into the bedroom. He found Brockman sitting in a chair next to their bed, blocking his view of Elizabeth. He grabbed the doctor's shoulder, spun him around, revealing what he hadn't noticed at first, that what had stained the walls had stained the bed. It was the stain of what was missing—part of his wife, who was somehow still alive, her hands fumbling with the doctor's hand as if playing a clarinet, the hand that had either helped her hold the double-barrel .12-gauge to her mouth or tried to stop her from pulling the trigger that had taken the right side of her jaw. Had they planned this? Or like Deets, had the doctor walked in on the attempt?

Weak, her hands trembled and slid, from her failed attempt to end the suffering. Her suicide. Something Deets would never accept.

She grunted, gargling and blowing bubbles, as her thumbs tried to push the hammer back on that misfiring pin on the right side. Adrenaline took over, and Deets lost control of his temper, unleashed a fit of rage that led to both of his hands becoming a vise around the old doctor's windpipe. Brockman lost his grip on the shotgun as Deets squeezed until he had the doctor on the floor, slamming his skull to the hardwood surface, screaming, "What have you done, what have you done?"

And by the time he'd realized what he'd done, the old doctor was limp in his grip but his wife was still alive, trying to produce syllables with her split tongue and chipped teeth, her complexion half removed. And seeing all of this, he'd no other choice.

That discomforting warmth of a memory, of that final day, was what accompanied Deets, haunted him in every town and every motel room or rented farmhouse's bed. He could strip the sentiments, but still the guilt of his actions was there. Rooted in his mind. An incurable disease still pricking his conscience after all the time passed, all the distance traveled. What he missed most were her words, which once formed her outline next to his. That warmth of completion, now gone.

Watching the marshal enter the station, Deets stubbed out the cigarette in the Scout's ashtray and grabbed from the passenger seat the head shots of a wanted man. The history that wouldn't allow him to run or hide anymore.

With the scent of fresh-brewed coffee and a hint of Old Forester thick in the marshal's office, Deets threw the head shots onto the desk. Sipping his coffee, the marshal smacked his lips, savoring the caffeine and bourbon with a late-night smile, and asked Deets, "Whatcha got there?" He removed the twine, unrolling the head shots, the wanted posters that Deets had collected from all the small-town post offices over the years.

Deets told the marshal, just up Highway 135, five years ago in the small town of Corydon, a husband walked into his home, walked in on another man helping to hold a shotgun for the husband's ailing wife. What he believed was the unfinished suicide of his wife. The name of the man who held the gun was Dr. Brockman. And in a fit of rage, the husband murdered the doctor with his bare hands. The husband was then left with his wife, whose face had been partially removed on her right side, as one of the shotgun's barrels had misfired. The husband didn't murder his wife, but he'd no choice with his wife's mutilated profile. She had reinforced her pain rather than eliminating it. And swallowing the lump in his throat, the husband placed a pillow over her face, hiding what was left of her, and helped her hold the shotgun, helped her push the hammer back, felt the trembling of her hand atop his, guiding his hand to the trigger, hooking it. He turned his head away from her, feeling her trembling and pressing his finger until his shoulder buckled and her trembling ended. The wife destroyed the tiny ginseng root in her brain that didn't offer energy but robbed her of it. The husband buried his wife in the garden that she once grew, but left the doctor limp and lifeless on the bedroom floor. He then packed up and ran away from what he had done. The partner he'd lost. Traveled from one small town to the next, searching for the identity of Deets Merritt. The surname of a deceased man he'd come across in a small Tennessee town's obituaries. He couldn't forget who he really was, Scoot McCutchen, the wanted man whose head shots the marshal was holding.

The marshal, whom everyone in the town of Mauckport called "Mac," took several deep breaths and laid the head shots back on his desk, pulled a Lucky Strike from his pack, lit it with a match, and blew smoke, muttering to Scoot, "After all these damn years of running, you gotta trot in here and turn yourself in."

Mac looked Scoot dead in his eyes and told him, "Guilt's a heavy package for a man to carry. It's wrapped by all the wrongs a man'll do, which are really lessons he learns by living life so he don't do them no more." He told Scoot he knew his story. Had the wanted posters. The all-points bulletins. Had read in the papers about how his wife's body was exhumed. How the authorities contacted her parents, Scoot's in-laws, so they could identify what they thought was Elizabeth. Afterward they placed her back the same way they found her. It was how her family believed. The old ways. Made from the earth, returned to the earth. And they placed a stone over her mound. But he didn't know where they had buried the doctor, only that they auctioned his car, seeing as how he had no next of kin.

The marshal then spoke about the letter left behind by the wife.

Scoot said, "A letter?"

In all the places he'd been, all the stories he'd overheard in passing through towns and truck stops, he'd never heard about any damn letter.

Nodding, the marshal told him there was a letter detailing how she'd hinted to her husband but knew he wouldn't do it for her, put her down like a hound with parvo, put her out of her misery. How she'd decided to try and do it her damn self or that she might ask her doctor to help her do it. He told Scoot he knew, because he knew how much he loved his own wife, loved her more than the beauty that God and nature creates and destroys, more than the two kids he and his wife brought into this world, one by one, to carry on their bloodline. Now, if his wife had gone through what Scoot's did, Lord, what with all of that suffering, knowing every damn day was a countdown to her last, he'd want to make the most of it, not cut 'er short. So to come home, see some man helping her to kill herself, well, he'd have done the same damn thing, maybe worse.

What the marshal wanted was to break the oath he'd sworn to uphold. To hold the head shots over the trash can next to his desk, fire a match, light a corner of the head shots, and tell Scoot that as long as he was the marshal Scoot's identity was safe with him. Right or wrong, the man had suffered enough. But he knew that was no option for Scoot.

To Scoot the letter made little difference now as he emptied his pockets and the marshal led him to a holding cell, locked him in behind the steel bars. He didn't feel the springs of the cell's mattress, but he felt the guilt he'd carried over the passing years dissipate as he awaited his punishment, his penance.

OFFICER DOWN (TWEAKERS)

It was too damn early for this shit, Conservation Officer Moon Flisport told himself as he steered his Expedition down the country road, sweating bourbon through his pores. His heart was pounding in his skull, ready to explode across the front windshield because of the Knob Creek he'd torn into last night after his wife, Ina, had called him a racist.

Moon had told her about the truck of illegal immigrants he'd pulled over for speeding. Told her about the dope he'd smelled but couldn't find on their persons or in their vehicle. Told her how he'd taken everyone's driver's license, knowing all of them were fake. He'd radioed INS. They gave him the runaround, told him he couldn't prove they were illegal. Told him to let them go. They didn't have the room or the time to deal with them. He told Ina one of the illegals had a license with the name Bob on it. And that's when Ina blew up. Accused him of racial profiling.

"Illegals can have American names."

"His license IDed him as Bob Dylan."

Ina told Moon he cared more about his job, hunting, training his coonhounds, and catfishing on the Blue River than he cared about her. Said she was tired of it and locked herself in the bedroom.

Moon went swimming in a bottle of bourbon on the basement couch.

He'd been phoning the house all morning, in between answering calls for trespassers on private property and hunters drinking beer at the Harrison County weigh station. Being a conservation officer during deer season meant that Moon had been busier than a champion mountain cur stud mounting a female cur to pass on his champion bloodline. That's what Ina didn't get, Moon thought, being a conservation officer meant he'd more jurisdiction than regular law, could pull over a drunk driver, answer a domestic dispute, or bust a dope farm or a meth lab.

Now it was near lunch. She still hadn't answered. He knew he'd hurt her feelings, telling her to get a fuckin' hobby. But she'd accused him of being a heartless racist. *Heartless* he could swallow, but not *racist*. In his mind he was a fair man, and it burned his ass to be accused otherwise. Then he came upon a truck in the distance, parked in the center of the road, hazard lights flashing, the grill busted, one headlight hanging down by the wires. He keyed his mic. "Earleen?"

"Go 'head, Moon."

"Looks like I might have a 10-50."

"Another person hit a deer?"

"It's lookin' that way."

Moon pulled off the potholed back road in front of the truck, next to a field of dead grass bordered by a pine thicket. Woods once owned by Rusty Yates. Someone he'd not seen, let alone thought of, in ten years. They'd taken many trips down into Jackson and Hazard, Kentucky, on coon hunts, each of them passing a thermos of Folgers, nipping bourbon, and words on their wives, how each was as stubborn as a young pup. And they wished they could break their mule streaks same as they would a pup. Looking back, it was as if the earth had sucked Rusty up after his wife left him.

Moon got out of his Expedition and realized whose truck it was. Brady Basham was a little colored man who lived on down the road a ways where the mill once stood, now gone because of a fire some years back. Brady was old-school. One of the best carp and cat fishermen in all of the county.

Moon smiled and asked, "Hit a deer?" With curls the shade of a gray squirrel poking out from beneath his black-and-red checkered hunter's cap, he looked up at Moon with eyes cracked by tiny red veins across the surface and big black dots in the center and told him, "The cocksucka 'bout gave my old bony ass whiplash."

He pointed to where it had jumped out, said he'd slammed his brakes. But it took a pretty good dent and gave an even better dent to the front of his rusted Ford Courier, though it was still drivable.

Taking in the damage to Brady's truck, Moon kept noticing the faint scent of cooked bleach in the cold country air. Brady was holding the headlight that hung out like a eyeball, said the deer went down; when he got out the damn deer got up and limped into the field.

Moon nodded. He asked Brady, "Got a question for you. Think I'm racist?"

Brady sucked on one of his four teeth that wasn't black from too much smoking and drinking, running his tongue over his gums, and he said, "Nah, Moon, seeing as we shared the bottle many a night, catfishing on the Blue River. I'd say you 'bout as fair a man as any black blood I ever knowed."

Moon looked into the old man's sour-mash soul, told him he appreciated the kind words, because his wife had called him a racist after he'd told her about a truck of illegals he'd pulled over for speeding. He'd known they were illegal but was unable to do a damn thing about it.

And Brady told him, "Women. Never had much use for one unless we was swapping the spit, you know what I mean." Then he hit Moon on his shoulder with his frail pigeon-wing hand and both men busted up into laughter.

Basham wanted the deer if Moon could find it. He'd had a hankering for some fresh venison. Especially the tenderloin and some ground deer burger to make some homemade summer sausage. He pointed out the direction in which he thought the deer had gone. Moon told him to wait by the truck, he'd give him a shout or come back if he found it.

Moon went out in a field, walking around like a hound that had lost its trail. His head was a throbbing knot even though he'd taken four or five aspirin already. Taking in the patches of briar that ran along the sides of the field, he was reminded of all the rabbit he'd hunted with Rusty years ago, nipping a bottle of whiskey to cut the chill from their bones.

Moon couldn't place what had happened to Rusty after his wife left him. It seemed that with age and a person's job, the responsibilities of everyday life just kind of distanced a man from a friend until he'd not even realized he'd forgotten about him.

Inhaling the cold air through his nose, he noticed the cooked bleach scent was getting thicker but couldn't tell the direction it was coming from. He stood looking around, said fuck it and pulled his cell phone from his pocket, checked his signal, thought he'd phone Ina again before he got too far out of range. Still no answer.

With each step his head pulsed as he searched the earth beneath the dead reeds of grass for a hint of blood, hoping the deer was laid out somewhere close. He thought of all the hit-and-runs he'd worked over the years, and how the deer had never gotten more than a few feet and dropped deader than a doornail. Or on impact. Not this tough son of a bitch. He just kept on running. And Brady wanted it. Snaggle-toothed old crow had maybe two teeth. What the hell was he gonna do, gum him to death? Put him in a blender, suck the pulped venison through a straw?

A few more steps forward and he saw a thick mess of red painting sections of grass in front of him. He swiped it for freshness and it smeared warm. It was injured. Running on adrenaline.

Moon trailed the blood through the field and into a pine tree thicket.

Trees scattered out every so many feet ran all the way up into the dead sky. Vines or plants grew here and there. He stepped into the dank silence, boots cracking the foliage of yellow pine needles splotched by blood. Every step grew louder and louder, breaking the silence of the woods.

He stopped, his head a mess and his stomach in a bind. He was hungover and hungry. He cursed Ina for not answering her damn phone and Brady for hitting the deer. He hoped Ina would cook some fried chicken when he got off work this evening, with mashed potatoes, corn on the cob, rolls, and some fried apples with cinnamon. Damn, that made his stomach ache. To hell with Brady's snaggletoothed ass for wanting this damn deer.

In a few more steps, the blood trail stopped. The smell of cooked bleach suddenly blistered his eyes and nose. Glancing around the deaf woods, he knew from hunting the area years ago that Rusty's farmhouse was on the other side of the thicket. He didn't know if he heard it or felt it first, but an explosion stung his left shoulder worse than a hornet. He'd been shot.

His ears rattled. Adrenaline took over. He hit the ground like a bushel of potatoes. Lay on his back unholstering his .40-caliber Glock handgun with his right hand. Thumbed the safety off. Rolled to a tree. Pushed his back into a pine, taking away his chances of getting shot in the back. Lungs elbowed his ribs to find air, red stained his jacket. The blood weighed down his left arm. His left shoulder had been separated by a shotgun slug. Could be a hunter mistaking him for a deer or just some crazy son of a bitch.

Laying his pistol down, he tugged his radio off the side of his stiffening arm, keyed it. "Earleen? 10-78. I been fuckin' shot. 'Bout one mile from where I's parked on Rothrock's Mill Road. Takin' cover in a pine thicket on Rusty Yates's property."

"Sit tight, Moon. Another conservation unit, county K9, and state police are on the way."

Moon picked his Glock up from the ground. Adrenaline turned to panic. Footsteps crunched. Moon looked about the trees, saw no movement in the open silence. He wondered what direction the shot had come from, remembered he was on duty, and yelled, "Stop fucking shooting, I'm Conservation Officer Moon Flisport!" Before he could finish a voice screamed, "Fuck you, squirrel cop!"

Just what Moon needed, he thought, some crazy-ass redneck. He hoped Brady's frail ass didn't try walking into this mess, having heard the shot fired, thinking Moon had found the deer, put it out of its misery.

He heard twigs breaking around him, closing in, but couldn't see anything. He was becoming light-headed from the loss of blood. His mind played tricks on him—vibrations ran down into the marrow of his sternum.

He was searching for his breath, squeezing his lids over his eyes. He searched through the confusion of his mind for some sense of control. Remembered his academy training. Fight or flight. Moon was a hunter. Who the hell did this crazy ass think he was, shooting a conservation officer. He didn't just check fishing and hunting licenses, arrest poachers. He'd more authority than the town, county, or state police.

Footsteps stomped close, then stopped, and Moon yelled, "You got one more chance to put your damn gun down and—" Disoriented, he saw what he thought was boots on a man dressed down in splotches of puke green, black, and mud brown clothing, aiming the bored end of a shotgun at him. The skin of his face was depressed and scabbed, cleaved by strawberry whiskers, eyes expanding into the red webs that had replaced his whites. The man was Rusty Yates and he told Moon, "Come passin' where you've no business, squirrel cop. Think you gonna bust me?"

Moon thought about Ina, their argument, not speaking with her, and all at once the shotgun blast gripped the air. Moon fell to the left, squeezed the Glock's trigger. Once. Twice.

He lay on his side staring at Rusty on his back, quivering. Coughing. Trying to breathe as his lungs filled with fluid. He was dying. The sound of sirens came from a distance, wavering through the trees. From somewhere behind Moon a voice screamed, "Fuck! Fuck!"

Moon was spent. Rusty had just missed him. But his body felt waterlogged. He couldn't distinguish the cursing voice from the voices yelling, "Moon! Moon!"

He held his pistol tightly, anticipating a slug in the back, watched Rusty's chest heave. Moon had shot him there. Crimson spewed in a spatter-shot pattern from his mouth. Moon wanted to help him, roll him onto his side, but his body snuggled with cold, his hearing flatlined, and the surrounding woods lost its hue.

Moon sat in a wooden chair, his arm stiff from the gunshot wound, his ears ringing from the sound of a .12-gauge slug, his .40-caliber Glock, and Rusty Yates laid out, exhaling his last moment.

He'd flipped the actions over and over in his mind. Waking in the Harrison County ER. Phoning Ina. But just like the nurses who'd phoned her, he never got an answer. He was released the next morning. Fisher, a conservation rookie, escorted Moon to the Sellersburg State Police post for a debriefing of what had happened. A man sat recording the events; Brady, the deer, the charred smell of bleach. The damp silence within. And the pain that ignited his arm and brought the cold.

The Indiana State Police knew Moon had no other choice, ruled it a clean shoot. After the debriefing with the state boys, Fisher escorted Moon home.

Now he was seated at the kitchen table, where a manila

envelope inked with the bold print MOON lay torn open. A letter from Ina, next to his glass, empty like his house. He shook his head, everything gnawing away at him.

He'd done more than shoot a man. He'd killed someone he'd hunted with. An old friend. And for the first time in his life, Ina wasn't here to talk with about it.

Filling his glass with the tea-colored liquid, he sipped the bourbon, tasted the burn that coated his throat, lined his gut. Being a part of the law was all about choices. Moon had made plenty of them, always involving people and their families. The struggles within their trees, the branches, limbs, and roots. They were the community he served. But in a world that took and took from the workingman, Moon guessed there was a breaking point between right and wrong.

He hadn't seen Rusty Yates in years. His wife had left him after he'd lost a good factory job, at a battery separator plant that had sold out, moved to Mexico. Hired a cheaper workforce. Cost a lot of men and women their livelihood.

Rusty owned more than two hundred acres out in the middle of nowhere, needed a way to get by, hooked up with Ray Ray, the other voice Moon heard yelling *fuck*, started cooking crystal meth. And by dumb luck Moon had gotten too close while trailing the deer for Brady Basham. Rusty and Ray Ray had been out in the woods hunting, tweaked out of their minds on amphetamines, and seen him in his uniform, thought he was sneaking in the back way to bust them.

Fisher said they'd caught Ray Ray and sent Brady home without the deer they never found.

In the letter, Ina said she was unhappy, tired of his judging others with racist comments and never giving her the attention she needed.

Walking from the kitchen to the bedroom with his glass of bourbon, he saw that the closets were empty. Ina's luggage was gone. Moon was too ashamed to call the station, post a lookout for her license plate, a description of her '85 Toyota Land Cruiser. Taking a sip from the glass, ice rattling, Moon thought that worst of all, he was too drunk to go look for her.

THE NEED

THE NEED

Speeding into the gravel curve, Wayne lost control of the Ford Courier, stomped the gas instead of the brake. Gunned the engine and met the wilderness of elms head-on. His head split the windshield, creating warm beads down his forehead, while flashbacks of an edge separating flesh and a screaming female amped through his memory.

Blood flaked off as Wayne balled his hands into fists, remembering the need he could no longer contain.

From behind, light chewed through the night and into the Ford. Wayne turned, looked into headlights that tattooed his eyes with black-green spots until he saw the red and blue blinking from above.

The cruiser's door slammed. Boots trailed over the loose gravel. Wayne watched the headlights black out the features of the approaching officer in the driver's side mirror. His right hand gripped the wooden stock of his Marlin lever-action 30-30 in the seat beside him that he had used to kill deer hours ago. The Need square-danced with the amphetamines in his bloodstream, driving the fever in his brain to a boil, and he opened the door.

·

Rookie Officer Fisher keyed his mic.

"Moon, you out there?"

"Just finished with those kids at the mill."

"Close to Wyandotte Road?"

"I'm a few minutes away, whatcha got?"

"Looks like Brady Basham sampled some of his home brew again. His Courier's head-on into a mess of elm 'bout a mile up from 62 on Wyandotte Road."

"Shit. Crazy bastard ain't supposed to drive this time of night. I'm on my way."

Fisher shone his Maglite onto the blue tarp over the Ford's bed, saw the streaks of fluid shading down the patches of Bondo.

The driver's door swung open. A figure stepped out onto the gravel. Fisher shouted out, "You all right, Brady? Looks like you got yourself into a mess back here. Moon's on his way, might be helpin' to sort this—" His Maglite reflected a bone-tight face stitched with every angle of rage imaginable.

The barrel of the 30-30 rifled an orange flame. Separated marrow and meat from Fisher's right shoulder. It felt as though he'd been struck with fifty pounds of pressure from a pickaxe. His light clattered to the gravel and he followed, trying to configure speech. "You . . . you . . . shot me."

Wayne levered the empty brass to the ground. Stood over Fisher, listening to his lungs wheeze from what sounded like a combination of asthma and shock. Fisher tried reaching across his chest for his Glock. Wayne pushed the barrel into Fisher's left shoulder. Pulled the trigger. Earth and bone exploded. Fisher jerked stiff. Wayne levered another empty brass and knelt down. His ears chimed from the gunfire and he laid his 30-30 beside Fisher, whose blinking eyes met Wayne's blank stare. Fisher's mouth began to foam like keg beer as he gasped, "Wayne, w-w-why you d-d-doin' this?"

Wordless, Wayne unsheathed his razored skinner with his right. Pressed his left into Fisher's froth-filled scream. The Need tightened Wayne's grip around the knife. He pressed the blade between damp follicles of hair and ear, finding the soft connection of tissue. Bearded faces stained by war screamed familiar and foreign tongues in Wayne's mind. He cleaved ear from skull just as he'd done in the mountains. Fisher thrashed into a limp state.

The Need made Wayne's insides all pins and needles as he picked up the ear and added it to the other one in his desert-patterned fatigues. Sheathed his knife and grabbed his 30-30.

Behind him the radio attached to Fisher crackled with a static voice. "Fisher, Brady all right?" Wayne knew the name attached to the voice. Moon. Memories from years before he'd enlisted, served in Afghanistan. He and his father coon hunting with the man. Wayne heard the engine roar in the distance. Saw the treetops lighting up like roman candles as he disappeared into the woods.

Tires skidded to a stop. Moon stepped into the dust of headlights, saw the human form laid out on the road.

"Shit!"

Moon's fingers met Fisher's neck. He'd a racing pulse. Wetness spat from his forehead. Moon keyed his radio. "Earleen?"

"Go 'head, Moon."

"Got an officer down. Still breathing. 'Bout one mile up from 62 on Wyandotte Road. Get an ambulance ASAP!"

"It's on its way."

Fisher's right shoulder had a railroad-spike-sized opening. Shot from four to six feet, Moon guessed. Fisher's mouth spewed over like Alka-Seltzer and down into the neck of his county browns. Moon thought Fisher's left shoulder looked as though some son of a bitch had opened it with a small stick of dynamite. Close-quarter shot. Then he noticed all the dampness where his left ear used to be.

"Son of a bitch! You hold on, Fish."

Moon turned around with his hand on his .40-caliber H&K. Shone his Maglite into the woods. Nothing. He searched inside the Ford. A near-empty case of Milwaukee's Best on the passenger's side floor. An empty bottle of Old Forester. A large black canister on the duct-taped seat: a spotlight. A Ziploc spilled over the dash with traces of crushed crystal. It was meth. Moon thought to himself, Brady ain't no damn tweaker.

He shone his light on the blue tarp that covered the bed of Brady Basham's truck. Pulled it back. Fresh venison engulfed him as he saw three outlines. It was early October, deer season wasn't even in and he had two doe, poached and gutted. And one human: a dead friend. Moon pursed his lips, keyed his radio. "Earleen?"

"Go 'head, Moon."

"On top of the downed officer we got two poached doe and a fatality. Brady Basham has been murdered."

"I'll radio a county unit."

Moon studied the contours of Brady's pigment, rough as worn rawhide. He'd slate-colored hair that matted into claws and his eyes were beaten into slits. Brady had flattened cartilage in place of his nose and, like Fisher, was missing his left ear.

One thing was certain, Brady wasn't the one who wrecked his Ford Courier.

Moon could hardly swallow, looking at his dead fishing buddy, and he asked, "What kind of hell did you find tonight, Brady?" Knowing he was deader than the catfish they'd carved and boiled the skins from over many a late night, sipping whiskey in his kitchen, telling stories of women and passing hunting secrets and myths, Moon pressed two fingers to Brady's neck, wondering how warm his body was. Removing his fingers, Moon believed Brady had been killed within the last hour.

Whoever the son of a bitch was that killed him was on foot. Which direction? Moon guessed downhill: easier travel. Moon had just missed him.

Moon keyed his mic once more. "Earleen?"

"Go 'head."

"Wake up Detective Mitchell and County Coroner Owen. Also, radio Sparks, tell 'im to bring his canine. My guess is the suspect is on foot. Armed and dangerous. And send a county unit to Brady's home. He's a daughter stayin' with him. Let's hope she's still breathin'."

Moon flashed his Maglite to check on Fisher. Noticed the glitter of brass beside him. Kneeled down. Warm shell casing from a 30-30. Presumably the caliber that bored out Fisher's shoulders.

Lungs burned and leaves crumbled beneath each step. Wayne's eyes adjusted to the night with the 30-30 strapped across his back, dodging standing trees. Jumping over the fallen trees. He heard sirens, dropped down behind a rotted tree trunk. Watched the red-orange wail of an ambulance and the blue-red screams of two cruisers following behind it, their lights strobing along the trees up Wyandotte Road.

Wayne's heart beat like a mule kicked, hard. He sat catching his breath, remembering the rapping of bone on his camper's door. Opening it to Brady, who stood out in Wayne's father's hay field, a can of Milwaukee's Best dripping cold in his hand. Wanted to go spotlighting, poach a few deer.

Wayne told him, "Sure."

Brady asked, "Could yuh bring that 30-30? All I got packed is a .22."

Wayne grabbed a box of shells and the rifle that lay by his mattress of tangy sheets.

Brady took a sip of his beer, said, "Got a fresh case, and a untapped fifth of whiskey."

Wayne had been up for days. His eyes looked rimmed by bruises. He was trying to numb the Need, chasing amphetamines with bourbon, chain-smoking cigarettes. Every time his high started to taper off, visions came stalking with grunts and shrieks. He'd chopped line after line, inhaled the moist talcum burn that seared his brain, and castrated all feeling of dread and murder.

Coming out of his camper, he heard a screen door slam in the distance, saw a man with age step from the sandstone house Wayne had grown up in. His father, Dennis, let Wayne stay out in the camper they'd used when he was younger, camping out, hunting and fishing. Wayne hadn't slept in the house since coming home from overseas. Since the passing of his mother, Dellma. He never got to grieve, to say goodbye, but he missed their talks when things went bad, her telling him it'd be okay. Everything always worked out. He missed the flannel sheets and hand-sewn quilts, the stews and roasts from the meat he and his father had slain, mixed with fresh vegetables his mother had picked from the garden and canned. All the scents and textures. The woman brought comfort to his and his father's lives, their home. But Wayne had buried all of that in the Afghan mountains forever.

Dennis's hair fanned over his head the shade of a turtle-dove. He stood in Dickies work trousers and a white Hanes tucked in at the waist and asked, "Goin' out?"

He was a Vietnam vet. He understood his son's ways of dealing with what he'd seen and done.

Wayne told him, "I be late."

His father nodded his head, said, "Keep safe." As if he knew that someday the shit would no longer stir, it would be spilled. Wayne saw it in his father's movements. The shuffling of feet with unjudging stares, his hands shoved into the pockets of his faded blue work trousers, it was worry for when his son snapped. Dennis didn't know everything but some he did. Seeing the jungles of Vietnam, he'd taken in a lot of his own bad. Told Wayne therapy might help, though he never had it in his day. No one respected soldiers back when he served. He was expected to come home, pretend nothing had happened, drink himself back into the person he was before he left.

Wayne asked his father, "Would therapy help those that switched sides?"

His father never asked what he meant by that, but he

said, "War's a confusing way to solve a country's problems. Not everyone wants our way of being, but when Uncle Sam gets involved, no one has a choice."

Wayne waved to his father. Dennis waved back and went into the house. Wayne had the last of the meth in his pocket and his 30-30 in hand. Brady never could see to drive after dark, even before Wayne left for the military when he and Brady used to go catfishing down on the Blue River at night, so Wayne took the wheel. They'd cruised the winding back roads down around the old mill that had been burned down years back by kids. Farm fields ran for hundreds and hundreds of acres. All the timber, green, wildlife, and quiet one could want.

Brady's brittle arm had held the spotlight over the harvested stalks that lay chopped and dried about the soil as they passed slowly. Until light reflected eyes scavenging for dropped ears of feed corn. Wayne placed the shifter in neutral, pressed the emergency brake, grabbed his rifle, leaned over the idling hood as the engine missed and adrenaline stoked his tendons and shots opened the night.

The first deer dropped. A hollow shell fell from the rifle, rolled down the hood. Another explosion chewed the night and a second deer dropped.

Wayne had field-dressed each, using his blade to cut from the ass to the sternum. Missing the stomach, then using his hand to dig up into the chest cavity, cutting out the esophagus, and the heart and intestines poured out along with the euphoria that coursed through Wayne.

Wayne had driven back to Brady's graying cabin to quarter the deer meat. Brady's daughter, Dee Dee, had come out to the Ford. She'd prepared a late-night breakfast. Inside, Wayne sat at the kitchen table uninterested in nourishment, telling Brady they needed to take to the meat before it spoiled. Brady waved his worry away, said they'd time to share a bottle of Boone's Farm, what he referred to as Kool-Aid with a kick.

Dee Dee began to flirt with Wayne, tickling his neck with her long nails painted the color of a tongue. Wayne tried to ignore her leaning in front of him while setting a bowl of white gravy down, a tray of towel-covered biscuits and a platter of bacon. Her brown eyes staring, shoulder-length hair black as burned wood. Her shirt loose with toffee-colored cleavage dangling.

Brady's hand wrapped around her arm and he jerked her from the table. Dishes clanged and broke on the pine floor. Brady raised his free hand and Dee Dee begged, "Daddy, no!"

The Need from the mountain villages painted Wayne's insides black as ink. Alcohol and drugs had mutated into wrath. Wayne grabbed Brady's wrist from behind, didn't let the old man strike his daughter, spun him around face-to-face. Brady released Dee Dee. She fell back, watched Wayne hook his fist into Brady's left kidney. Wayne felt the pressure in his bloodstream rising and his ears popped. He seared Brady's vision with his fist and pancaked his nose. Then he dug his hand around Brady's turkey neck, squeezed. Bones gave way like a number-two pencil.

Dee Dee kept screaming for Wayne to stop. Brady was without form. Wayne had crossed over to that other way of being. He unsheathed his knife, pressed the edge to cartilage, and removed Brady's ear. That's when he felt four tiny prongs of steel open a muscle in his back.

Dee Dee had stabbed him with a fork. Rage took over

Wayne's instincts and he backed her into the sink. Her lips pleaded while her eyes watered. "Please, please. I sorry, I sorry." Wayne grabbed her by the throat, squeezed and squeezed as he swam in the memory of men. Locations mapped out in his mind. Coordinates for caves and villages. A man bound, blindfolded, sweating with the shrieks of an innocent female. The tearing of clothing and her foreign voice.

Dee Dee went limp. He'd choked her out. He'd never killed a female, nor would he. He let her drop to the floor, loaded Brady in the truck with the two does. Gathering the dead, that's what they'd called it in the mountains. Piling them, sometimes for burial, other times for burning. He grabbed the Old Forester from the floorboard of the Ford, not knowing where he was going or what he'd do, just driving and drinking the whiskey until everything went black and he found himself on Wyandotte Road pressing the gas instead of the brake. Meeting the elms head-on with the Need still whittling through his insides.

Now a county K9 unit's dog barked, echoed through the woods from which Wayne had just run. Lights opened the darkness, showing Wyandotte Road in the distance. A spotlight prismed between trees in the woods. Wayne's mule-kicking heart returned. He stood up. Ran for the dim light at the hill's bottom where an old shack sat. From behind, growling teeth ripped tendon and ligament, worked up and into his hamstring. Pain was unrecognized as Wayne stumbled; he and the dog rolled down the hill with the 30-30 strapped to his back. Leaves sounded like paper sacks smashing over and over, limbs gave and scraped, until Wayne and the dog leveled out on the hazed dew beneath the humming quartz of the old shack's yard along Highway 62.

Squeezing the canine tight to his wiry frame, Wayne smothered the dog's attack like a vise being tightened around its muscles and bones. Pinched the fur of the shepherd's neck between shoulder and ear. While unsheathing his blade with his right hand, he smothered the animal's snapping jaws, parted fur beneath the neck, forced the knife up into the canine's brain.

Four legs attached to a mound of down lay silent as he removed its left ear and smuggled it into his fatigues.

The conservation officer's and the K9's Expeditions braked to a stop on Wyandotte Road. Moon's spotlight shone upon the wet grass, showing the man who stood in his gray T-shirt and desert camo stained by animal and human blood. Arms and face were chiseled like ice, hard and cold. His blade sparked in the light. Reds and blues danced in the darkness behind K9 Officer Sparks and Moon, who'd stepped from the truck. They were within forty feet of Wayne when Moon drew his .40-caliber H&K and recognized him. He'd hunted with Dennis, the boy's father, and Wayne before he left for the war several years ago. He couldn't remember the details, just as he couldn't believe he was the one who'd murdered Brady, and he hollered, "Drop the knife, Wayne."

Sparks shone his Maglite down at his canine in the distance. The dog wasn't moving.

"Crazy bastard killed Johnny Cash."

Moon kept his H&K on Wayne. Pleaded. "Don't make me do it, Wayne."

Wayne sized up the distance. He'd picked men off in simulations at this range before. He fought the rush of knowing he was in danger, could be killed. Dropped the knife. But that thought pushed him and he turned his back. Half limped, then ran. Felt an explosion nick his left shoulder as he crossed Highway 62. Heard a man yell, "He cut off my Johnny Cash's damn ear!"

Several more rounds exploded, but Wayne felt nothing as he leaped over the guardrail on the other side of 62, falling down into the steep darkness of the hillside. Tree limbs and briars jabbed his body with welts and the faces flared up in his mind again, men in villages. Restrained.

Wayne splashed into the deep current he'd inner-tubed down as a kid. Hit the flat rock bottom. Pushed to the surface. Gasped. Floated down the river on his back like a leaf from a tree, ignoring his splintered insides. His bruised and bloody outsides. Knowing he was only six miles or less from his home, remembering how all his wrongs started with a man. A farmer similar to his father, dressed in fraying brown and gray rags, with stalactite beard.

The U.S. soldiers in Wayne's eight-man unit believed that this man and the men that sat bound against a dirt wall were Taliban, pretending to be farmers, passing information about soldiers and their whereabouts when they were seen crossing the valley below the village.

The farmer begged, told them he was not Taliban. Three of the soldiers called him a liar. Spat on him, made an example for the others to heed. Sliced his elbow flexers and doused him with fuel they'd siphoned from a rusted generator. They did this in front of his wife and daughter.

Wayne argued this wasn't gathering intel.

But it was the five soldiers dragging the females into the back room of the mud structure and the screams that came in foreign tongues with the ripping of garments that forced Wayne over the edge.

He'd rushed over the dirt floor, through a doorway,

only to find one soldier laughing, holding women at gunpoint, inciting them to scream. The other two soldiers held down a younger female and one soldier stood up, dropping his gear and unbuttoning his fatigues.

Wayne grabbed the soldier's shoulder and tugged. The man faced him and said, "You'll get your turn," and started to turn back to the female. Wayne grabbed him and the soldier turned with his grab, spun into him. Drove his shoulder into Wayne's stomach. Pushed him into the wall. Knocked the wind from him. Head-butted Wayne's face. Panting, he called Wayne all kinds of motherfuckers. Wayne felt the warm flow from his busted nose and lips. Listened to the farmer in the other room scream to the smell of his own skin igniting. Wayne reacted.

He woke up with a blade in one hand, 9 mm in the other, a pile of left ears in his lap. The Need in his brain. Every man in his unit, one less ear and matching bullet holes in their heads. The Afghan was burned beyond help. The women horrified, in shock. The rest of the men in the village were rattled by fear but among the living, keeping their distance, looking at him with curdled awe and fear. He helped bury the farmer and burn the seven soldiers he'd murdered, scattering their remains along the valley.

Wayne went rogue. Knowing the U.S. routes in and out of the mountains, he began ambushing his own. He'd been trained by the elite, knew how the Taliban gathered intel. Slow disembowelment. Promises of food, of one's release to get the information, then the beheading. Methods preserved from medieval times. Condoned by holy men. He killed the bad along with the good. Fighting a war within himself for six months in the mountains. Living in that village with those farmers. Trying to make sense of what he was doing. Of what he'd become. Until he realized none of it made sense. But it was too late.

It's what happened when a southern Indiana farm boy scored high on the ASVAB test before entering the military. Could wield a blade better than a Filipino knife fighter. Shoot dead center for the length of cornfields. Had stand-up skills like Ali before the draft. Could track better than a bloodhound. Wayne wanted to serve his country, use his God-given abilities. Unfortunately, God had other plans.

Now, the river carried Wayne down through the dark valley and he remembered when the United States raided the village, found him, wanted to know what he was doing there, where the others were.

They isolated him for two years. Wanted to know what happened over there in the mountains. He told them he couldn't recollect. He spoke with doctors every day. Told them of his rage, the shaking of the earth. The dead he'd seen, the dead he'd created. They medicated him, ran question after question, test after test. They evaluated him as no longer psychologically capable of carrying out his duties and discharged him with a small pension.

Wayne floated atop the warm drift, reached for the roots of a washed-out tree, held on, knowing it didn't matter where or how far the river carried him 'cause the Need would always be inside him, waiting.

BEAUTIFUL
EVEN IN DEATH

With his back to Christi, Bishop stood knee-deep in the bone-stiffening current of the Blue River, clenching his fist around his fishing pole. Christi ran her flower-petal fingertips down his neck again. Instead of jerking from her this time he swatted her away.

"Why you doin' that?" she asked.

"Done told you we gotta quit each other."

"But you came like you have all summer."

Christi lived a mile up the road from the river, walking distance. Bishop and she held a childhood crush that went from flirting to an affair.

"I came to fish, to tell you to quit callin' the house, showin' up unannounced. We're first cousins. Let's leave it at that."

On wobbly balance Christi dropped her fishing rod, forced her lips against Bishop's ruggedly aged warmth. Then she took a breath and pleaded, "Don't do this." He was silent. She continued: "I'll kill her for you. I will. No more Melinda. Just Christi and Bishop."

Her words pulsed a threat within Bishop's forty-plus years of understanding right from wrong. If anyone ever found out about Christi and him, they'd be forsaken by their families, their community. He'd have to use something more than words to end it, because thus far they hadn't sunk into her understanding.

Bishop dropped his pole, exploded his catcher's-mitt palms against Christi's ears. She gulped a scream. His fingers spread into her thick hair of black edged with pine needles of gray. He kicked her balance from beneath her. Guided her under the current and straddled her chest. Christi's legs splashed. Bishop's hands swallowed her clawing hands, which had sorted mail from eight to five Monday through Friday at the post office for twenty years. Pinned them to her throat. Watched bubbles explode into lost breath beneath the cold water, telling himself he'd no other choice, she wouldn't listen.

He heard a vehicle barreling down the gravel road from the valley above. Christi's fight slowed just as the sound of the vehicle did. That damn steering squeak rang familiar, but Bishop could not place it as it meshed with the uneven rhythm that thudded and pulsed within his head. The vehicle sounds disappeared. Bishop kept Christi pressed into the flat river rock with madness chewing through his bloodstream.

A door slammed. But his hearing played tricks with the rushing sounds of his insides and the flowing river in which he sat, and he couldn't place its direction. He heard boots kicking gravel, the snapping of weeds and twigs. He froze, glanced up along the bank, but couldn't locate the source of these noises, nervousness maturing in his ears and the static sounds bouncing off the river's surface.

When the cold current had numbed his grip to an ache and she was passive, he stood with her body floating to the surface. Her pits caught on his damp shins. He saw no movement along the weeded valley road above. He must have imagined the noises. Dragged her to the riverbank. Pulled a tin of Miller High Life from the six-pack that lay along the river's edge. Popped it open. Downed it, wondering what to do with her body.

He smashed the beer tin and opened another. Took a long hard sip, closed his eyes, shook his head, and laughed. Feeling the sensation from taking a life climb through his veins.

Standing over her, he couldn't say she'd drowned, as he took in the cellophane gaze of her open eyes. The shock that filed down her chalk white cheekbones. The bruises already forming like ink smudges around her neck and wrists. The dampness of her flower-print dress with two shapes lying beneath like perfect snowballs. He told himself, "Beautiful even in death."

Bishop stood remembering how his father and he had fished this area since he could string a pole and bait a hook. Remembering all of the largemouth bass, hand-size bluegill, and channel cat they'd caught. He pulled a smoke that wasn't wet from his shirt pocket. Along with a dry Ohio Blue Tip match. Knelt down, flicked a flame. Pulled a coal with his lungs while his eyes followed the current downstream. Exhaling the smoke, it came to him like a vision from his Maker: a pit so deep that even darkness was lost, an unmarked grave for Christi.

He walked up the dirt trail of boot prints that separated the wilted weeds littered with fish bones and rusted beer tins to the gravel of the road where he'd parked his rusted Chevy. He looked down the valley in both directions, saw no hint of a vehicle parked along either side. Started to walk down a ways but stopped. He'd no time to waste.

He opened his truck door, pulled the burlap sacks from behind the truck's seat that he used for keeping the coons, rabbits, or squirrels he shot during hunting season. Grabbed the rusted log chain. Pulled a pair of pliers from the glove box. A length of barbed wire from the floorboard. He looked up and down the road once more, stood silently. A breeze scratched his face, knocked a few loose limbs to the ground from the surrounding trees with leaves turning the shade of pumpkins while his heart punched his eardrums. No one around but him. Back down along the riverbank he filled the burlap sacks with flat flint and limestone. Tied them shut. Forced them beneath Christi's damp dress. Remembering how her skin smelled of apple cider. He coiled the wire around her frame, thinking of the way her shapes bounced and rubbed against his chest in the front seat of his truck, and twisted it tight to her flour-tinted pigment with pliers. The barbs broke her skin open, formed tiny rivers of red, coating her beauty. He reinforced the weight with the rusted log chain he wrapped around her, connecting the hooked ends into each other. He dragged her stiff frame downstream like a small johnboat until he got to the fishing hole from his youth, where Bishop remembered his father telling him, as they stood knee-deep staring into the dark green hole that melded into black, that if someone ever wanted to hide something, this would be the place.

He wiped the wet that sprouted from his forehead, looked at her locks of hair spreading with the sound of the river rushing her dress up her thighs, which he'd run his hands up just yesterday while she unbuckled his belt, their mouths meeting, and he blinked, but her dead eyes did not, they stabbed through him. Tightened around his heart with all of their memories together. When he died, he thought, he'd be judged for what he'd done. And when that time came he'd say, "I felt I'd no other choice." He hoped he'd be forgiven.

He pushed her into the thick blackness. Dived in, guiding her sinking body, the cold water lockjawing his bones, burning his bends and pivots. All the way to the bottom, where his hands felt, pushed, and tucked her away beneath a smooth cliff of river rock. A space made for a human outline. With eyes closed he pushed her body until he felt rock meet his shoulders and face, both arms extended into the unknown void.

He surfaced with his mind aching for air, lungs tight and fast expanding. Feeling as though he were breathing through a tractor's brake line.

Bishop sat on the bank of river sand and scattered flint, clothes dripping in the evening sun. His teeth chattering. Telling himself he had to protect his family from being shamed by his wrongs.

Somewhere up on the road he heard the slamming of a vehicle's door. And the faint cranking of an engine disappearing down the distance of the valley.

Food steamed on the hickory-grained table. Bishop was out of the river stink of his wet clothes, fresh from the shower, spooning baked cabbage. Grabbing a buttered ear of corn. Then forking two fried pork chops onto his plate, wondering if his wife, Melinda, was waiting for him to confess his sins. What he'd been doing all summer after working at the furniture factory. What he'd ended today. The body he'd hidden on the river bottom.

"Run into Fenton while you was wade fishin'?"

"No, why would I?"

Melinda stood next to the stove, twisted the burner knob, and ignited the blue gas flame. Knelt down with a Lucky Strike between her lips and inhaled. Her hazel eyes looked into Bishop's blue ones. He thought maybe she could see the dead female's soul floating within the glare of his sight.

"He's supposed to go fishin' this evening down on Blue River."

"Didn't see sight nor hair one, ain't no tellin' where that boy went fishin'. If he even went. Probably out drinkin' with that Beckhart boy again."

"You're one to talk, you been drinkin' again."

"So I had me a few, I'm forty-four, not twenty and breakin' laws."

"It's the third time this week, used to be on the weekend."

"Why don't you worry about that boy and where he's at? I ain't bailin' his ass out of jail again."

"He should be home anytime, ain't like he'd miss a meal his mother cooked."

As she spoke, they heard their son's truck pull up outside, the wheels skidding, the steering squeak as he pulled to a stop.

The screen door opened and slammed. Fenton stomped into the kitchen with his rusted brown layers of hair peeled back over his head. A face like Bishop's when he was younger. Sanded to a smooth pale-wood finish. Only Bishop's now bore the age of untreated graying lumber; sanding it would only make it age quicker.

"Told you he'd not miss his mother's cookin'."

But her words were lost as Bishop's fork rattled against the ceramic of his plate and his chair scooted backwards, making the wooden leg bottoms scream across the linoleum as he fake-coughed and barreled to the front door. He was up in Fenton's face, straight-eyeing him, twitching with anger. The madness Bishop had discovered at the Blue River grew into a swarm of bees being disrupted from nurturing their nest of honey. "Where you been, boy?" Bishop growled.

Silence, then: "Drivin'."

"Out with that Beckhart boy again, don't you work no more?"

Fenton shuffle-danced around his father, insolently staring back into Bishop's eyes, and his boots trailed mud across the scuffed linoleum to the sink. Melinda shook her head. Fenton turned on the water and began lathering the bar of soap in his quaking hands. He'd watched his father wring many a chicken's neck, shoot rabbit and squirrel. Divide their white bellies with a blade in one hand while the fingers of his other hooked and ripped out their purple and opal guts. He'd done the same with bass and bluegill. Forms of life taken to place meat in the freezer or on the table. He crimped his eyes shut, knowing he'd never seen his father take the life of a person until today. And driving the back roads of the county for the past hour, he tried to make sense of what his eyes had watched his father do, murder Christi.

Between the Formica counter and the pearl fridge, Fenton

said, "I was off from baggin' groceries today. So I went drivin' around the county."

Bishop spoke before he thought and asked, "Where at around the county?"

Fenton hung the towel back on its hanger, imagining how cold that water must have been, blanketing those forty-year-old bones. Watching from the dying weeds had stiffened his own into a totem pole of panic. He turned and stared at this man he'd called "Father" for twenty years, wondering what drove him to kill his own. A disagreement? Money? He couldn't see that, he'd never witnessed a cross word between them. Always laughing and cutting up. Christi was the only female he knew that drank beer, fished, and even went hunting.

At that moment Fenton told Bishop, "I's down around Blue River, stopped to see you—"

And Bishop saw it in Fenton's eyes, fear of what he'd seen his father do, and he raised his voice and said, "Around Blue River? Been out drinkin' and drivin' again, ain't you?"

Melinda stood blank, paralyzed by the tension in the air, closing in and suffocating each of them, and she demanded, "Fenton, you gonna answer your father?"

Not believing the reaction from his mother and father, Fenton stood confused by his own name. His lips formed an expression as though he'd eaten a spoiled piece of fruit that had rotted his insides. And Fenton tried to finish, said, "I seen you down in Blue River dragging . . ."

Stepping closer to Fenton, Bishop focused on the bottle of Early Times behind him on the counter, cut him off again, louder, with "Boy, you are sick, comin' in here liquored up 'fore the sun has even set, ain't learned your lesson yet, have you."

Fenton tried to speak again. "I seen what you did . . ."

Hard and rough as droughty earth, Bishop's palm drew blood from Fenton's mouth. Bishop pinned Fenton against the counter. Ashes and tobacco dispersed as Melinda dropped her remaining cigarette to the linoleum. Bishop reached over behind Fenton to the counter. Grabbed the Early Times. Pushed it to Fenton's face.

"You seen what I did, been nice if you'd helped me."

Melinda shrieked, "Seen what? What'd you see, Fenton?"

"Seen his father bust his ass is what, damn catfish jerked my ass off balance. Near busted my head open. I tole you why I's piss-and-pour wet when I come home. 'Course our boy here was too busy nippin' the bottle to come help his old man."

Bishop inhaled the air from Fenton's busted lip, smirked, and said, "I can smell it on you strong as fresh-spread manure on a field."

And he could. Fenton had tossed down a few skunk beers he'd hidden beneath his seat, trying to calm his nerves after what he'd witnessed his father do. And quick as a copperhead's fangs delivering venom to its prey, Bishop balled his left hand into Fenton's T-shirt. Swung him around in a broken circle and into the kitchen table, which scooted across the linoleum along with steaming food and plates. Melinda screamed, "No! Stop!" Fenton came quickly from the table. Met Bishop's backhand. Fear pushed him out the screen door. Blood warm like bacon grease dripped from his nose. He stepped to the gravel-mortared surface of the sidewalk. Barefooted, Bishop followed behind, cursing, "Run, you spineless son of a bitch, run."

How much had his lazy useless drunk of a son seen, heard?

Bishop twisted the lid from the bottle of bourbon. With a Walker hound's bite he clamped down on Fenton's shoulder, spun him around.

"You wanna drink, then have at it."

Bishop flung bourbon into Fenton's bloodied face, stinging his nose and lips.

From the kitchen, Melinda yelled, "Stop!" Bishop raised his voice, told her, "Stay out of it."

The madness from the Blue River ripped through Bishop's body. He punched Fenton off the sidewalk. In his mind Fenton was no longer his kin, he was like Christi, a threat to his everyday existence. He'd remove his tongue or even kill him if that's what it took.

Bishop clamped his left hand onto Fenton's throat. Slammed him against an elm tree within the yard. Fenton's face boiled red. Air punched up from his lungs, rushed from his broken lips.

Bishop turned the bottle upside down with his right, parted Fenton's lips with his left, emptied the bourbon down Fenton's blinking eyes and spitting mouth.

"Like that, boy? Wanna drink, come home disrespecting me, get your mother all upset. I'll teach you."

"Stop, you bastard."

Bishop dropped the bottle. Pulled his Case XX knife from his pocket. Thumbed the single blade, which had skinned and gutted many a coon, squirrel, and rabbit.

"Say ahhh, boy!"

Fenton's hands channel-locked around Bishop's soupbone wrist while he glanced down at the ground. He saw Bishop's bare feet and he stomped.

Bishop cursed, "Bastard." Dropped the knife. Stepped

backwards, lifting his feet as if standing on molten lead. Fenton followed him like a pig wallowing in shit. Stomping his feet. Drove a fist underneath Bishop's jaw. Teeth gritted and chipped down onto tongue. Bishop spat blood thicker than brown gravy. Fenton grabbed the empty bottle of Early Times. Exploded it across Bishop's face. Dropped him to the ground. Where he hunched on all fours, shaking his head and spitting blood.

Confusion and anger pumped Fenton's heart. He raised his boot into Bishop's ribs. Watched the red spit from his mouth. Fenton thought of the truck he'd parked down from the Blue River at the old barn used by Rudy Sawheaver for sheltering his hay. Then he'd walked down to surprise his father but instead he got the surprise. Seeing Bishop knee-deep in the green river, the surfaced body between his father's legs.

Hidden by the dying weeds, Fenton watched Bishop drag the body to the riverbank. Taking in glimpses of the pale female's flesh, the flower-print dress, drenched locks the color of soot that clung to her face. His vision blinked and pieced together glimpses of their cousin Christi.

Fenton kept driving his boot into Bishop's ribs. The veins in the side of Bishop's neck grew as thick as earthworms discovered beneath rotted wood. He raised a hand to his throat. His face swarmed into a fire barrel of red. He heaved and gasped. Fenton remembered Bishop dragging Christi's body down the river current until he lost sight of him. Fenton stood within those weeds frozen by panic.

Bishop twisted his graying madness up at Fenton, who'd raised his knee. He drove his boot down into Bishop's face, dropped down and knelt beside him, put his mouth to his father's ear and said, "You tell me the truth of why you murdered Christi, tell me."

Bishop's outline was granulated rock, spread out face-down without movement. Blood drew a puddle around the shape of his skull onto the earth. Fenton touched his father's neck, got a pulse but no answers.

From behind him the wooden screen door slammed. A hard thud met the rear of Fenton's skull. Vibrated a black pain throughout. Taking away his sight and kneeling posture. Dropped him to the earth beside his father. It was the butt of a .12-gauge held by his mother, Melinda, who stood questioning what her only child had done.

"It's been over a week and that cousin of your father's is still missin'."

"She's in Blue River somewhere, you'd not even known she was missin' I hadn't told you."

"Boy, we drug that river for two miles up one direction and two miles down the other. Through every bend and split they is. Ain't found shit."

"I watched my father load her body with rock, wrap her with a log chain, and drag her down the river."

"I don't buy that, them two never held a cross sentence to one another. If anyone killed you-all's cousin I believe it was you."

"Why would I kill her?

"Got me. Lust, money. Maybe she seen you do something you wasn't supposed to be doin'."

"Like what?"

"Guess we'll never know 'cause she ain't nowhere to ask.

All I know is when we brought you in, you was whiskey-soaked belligerence. Deputies found some empty beer cans on your truck's floor. Pack of smokes under the seat, same brand we found down along the riverbank."

"Told you, my father poured the whiskey on me."

"Whiskey or beer, don't matter, you had both in you and on you. Your mother's sayin' you come home actin' strange, little drunk. Says that you provoked Bishop into a fight."

"Provoked him? She's crazy, it was self-defense."

"Fenton, my question is if you watched Bishop drag Christi down the river, why didn't you try to stop him? Or come to me?"

"Told you I was in shock, didn't know what to do. 'Sides, all you've ever done is give me a hard way."

"Son, I give you the same respect as you give me."

Fenton stood with steel bars tarnished by the stink of slobbering drunks and wife beaters before him, dressed down in faded black and white county stripes. A bunk attached to the wall. The smell of piss from a toilet behind him.

On the other side stood Sheriff Koons in county khakis. Island of gray hair wrapping around the rear of his head, matching handlebar mustache. He'd time lines pouched across his cheekbones. He looked into Fenton's tired baby blues, told him, "Let me tell you somethin', Fenton, I've know'd Bishop for as long as people have driven automobiles in Harrison County. He's a hardworkin' son of a bitch. You, on the other hand, got caught drinkin' with that Beckhart boy a time or two and recently tore up the BP gas station's bathroom. Got combative with my deputy. Add that to beatin' your father into an incurable polio patient. You're a loose cannon. Your words mean about as much to me as a champion racehorse with splintered joints and a bum hip. They's useless. That's why you're bein' charged with attempted murder."

Koon's words dissolved before entering Fenton's ears as he turned away. Uncaring of the charges against him, Fenton fell back on the mattress that felt like concrete. Cold and hard. He wondered what Bishop had done with Christi's body.

THE ACCIDENT

With the phone in his hand and a dial tone on the line, Stanley's still waking up. Between each ring he's somewhere amid being dragged by a tractor-trailer and a billionaire becoming a street vagrant.

When the doctor's "suck-retary" questions what the appointment is for, Stanley tells her anxiety. Depression. Maybe even shock. Take your pick. Stanley wonders why a patient cannot call his doctor and say, I just feel like shit today.

Suck-retary is what he and his wife, Earleen, refer to as the relationship between the doctor and his secretary.

On the phone, the suck-retary is asking if he has seen the doctor for these symptoms before?

"In his office," he says, "several weeks ago."

Pressing the phone between ear and shoulder, Stanley looks in the bathroom mirror. The corners of his eyes are crusted black punctures. His strings of melted-rubber-like hair push east and west. To think he made fun of people like this when he was younger.

The suck-retary says, "Did he tell you to come back for a follow-up visit?"

Well, he didn't call to talk. Sometimes Stanley doesn't comprehend these people, places, and things. All of these nouns. He doesn't know their definitions.

"Yes," he tells her.

"Name?"

"Stanley, Stanley Franks."

"Date of birth?"

"February sixth, 1970."

"And you're at 337 Kennedy Drive?"

"That's correct."

"Tomorrow, around ten a.m.? That work for you?" she says.

"No, it won't, I need one today."

"Sorry. Dr. Towell is booked for today."

Muffled, he hears her say it's the bipolar.

"What the hell is bipolar?" he yells. "I'm not bi anything, curious or sexual. I'm a homo sapien. A straight white male."

Now she's explaining. "This condition," she calls it.

"Oh, I see, so you think I'm a recluse? A nut bag."

Now she's apologizing, saying, "I wasn't implying that you were a nut bag, Mr. Franks."

"Yes, you did imply that I'm one card shy of a full deck. Look, lady, I don't think I like you very much."

"Well, maybe we can squeeze you in today, Mr. Franks."

"Today?"

"Yes, sir. How about two hours from now?"

"I'll be there."

Thumbing the talk button on the phone to off, Stanley thinks, The things a person must do to get an appointment with his doctor. The next thing you know, he'll end up in some asylum or self-help circle walking around with a Barney bib around his neck, drooling. Plastered on his back will be a name tag: Loser.

Walking through the house, he thinks, the thing about his wife, she's never around anymore. Either she's gone to work before he wakes up or he's in bed asleep before she gets home. Leaving a Post-it for her, he writes, "Earleen, went to the doctor's office. Be home later. Stanley."

Signing in at the front desk, Stanley explains that he's not bipolar or any other type of transgender. Then, in the waiting area, seated next to him, an old raisin of a female says her sphincter muscle has been rebuilt three times. Looking at her he says, "Your asshole has been rebuilt three times?"

"Yes," she says, "my sphincter muscle."

Her face resembles brownies, with enough lipstick and eyeliner to restock Revlon. Her hair has been colored so many times it looks like a safety hazard. He says, "Isn't there a limit or are you giving birth?"

Her rainbow eyelids almost separate from her eyes as she mumbles something and gets up to sit somewhere out of his sight.

There's the weigh-in, checking the blood pressure, and taking the temperature. He's lost weight. No fever, but his blood pressure is a little high.

In a small, boxlike waiting room, with a steel sink and an examining table, he feels as if he's in a prison cell. A quarantine for the sick. Beneath the closed door, outside in the hallway shadows run in and out of the light. Half sentences double as conversation between voices he does not recognize. If only they could close their damn mouths, he thinks. Instead he closes his eyes, grits his teeth, and paces the checkered floor.

When Dr. Towell enters the room Stanley's in such a state, he imagines wrapping his hands around Dr. Towell's neck.

With miniature white scabs flaking his thinning hair, Dr. Towell says, "How are we today, Stanley?" Stanley questions Dr. Towell's ability, asking questions like this. He's in his doctor's office. He is the doctor.

"Since the accident," he says, "not so good."

Gesturing for him to sit down, the doctor says, "What's wrong?"

Staring at Dr. Towell's unibrow, Stanley tells him, "All I think about are people giving me the finger. I even dream about a severed arm dressed in an Armani suit chasing me around the hallways at work. Trying to force me into an elevator. Then I wake up flipping myself off, calling myself a sorry-ass prick."

"How long has this been going on?" the doctor asks.

"Ever since my last visit several weeks ago on the dreams, but sometimes at work, if a phone rings my heart skips a beat. Coworkers try to speak with me and I snap, 'Who gave you permission to speak?' I just want everyone to be quiet."

Like right now, the nursing staff, walking up and down the hallway, he wants to tell them to shut their damn mouths. Only he doesn't tell Dr. Towell this.

Dr. Towell says, "So you're back to working?"

"Yeah."

"Even after I wrote you off for six weeks?"

Growing irritated, Stanley says, "Yeah."

Dr. Towell rolls something around in his mind and says, "Have you been in an elevator since the accident?"

"No," Stanley says, "I use the stairs every day. I passed a petition around at work so people wouldn't use the damn elevator."

"Did it work?"

"No, it didn't work. These people I work with are so insensitive to my recovery. They're a bunch of lobbyists for the button-pushing generation. I really thought everything would be okay, so I went back to work. I thought I was bigger than all of this."

"Completely understandable," he says, "but these things take time. What you are experiencing is PTSD, post-traumatic stress disorder. A medical condition caused by witnessing a horrific event."

"Great," Stanley says, "I'm a freak of nonreproductive tissue."

"No," Towell says, chuckling, "you're having a rough time."

"Sure I am, it's not every day that a person dreams about a severed limb chasing them around their place of work."

"I'm gonna up your dosage on the Zoloft. And recommend a good psychiatrist. I'll contact him today, have him contact me after your first consultation, discuss what alternate medications he'd like to prescribe, if that's okay with you?"

What choice does he have, Stanley asks himself, and says, "Great, now I'm a science project for the medical community. I mean, you're upping my dosage, I've already got the upset stomach, dry mouth, indigestion, and agitation. Are you trying to make me better or worse?"

Stanley believes a person has to question these things or

else he'll end up toothless, sucking up Coronas in Tijuana with a guy named Valdez, no memory of how he got there.

"They're only temporary," Towell says.

"That's what you told me about the headaches on my last visit."

"You still having headaches?"

"No."

"Well, you may not experience any of the side effects. Also, try to get some exercise. It'll help reduce the stress."

Shaking Towell's hand and exiting into the hallway with the loud-speaking staff, all Stanley can think about is stabbing a pencil in someone's eye to reduce the stress.

Going back several months ago, Stanley watched his reflection split in half. The chrome doors parted, one atom segregated into two parts. A man was halfway through the open elevator doors when they started to close. He panicked and stepped backwards, his arm pinned between the doors as the elevator started going up. The man jerked at his arm, couldn't get it free. Stanley stood inside the elevator. The elevator moving up, up, up. Next thing Stanley knew, he had the man's arm in his grip, pushing, while his other hand pulled at the door, trying to open it, the man screaming.

No, he's yelling, "Do something." With his arm caught between the elevator doors. He's on the outside looking in.

Stanley, grasping the arm with one hand, begins pushing buttons with the other, and the man's pulling his arm, yelling, "You little prick, what are you gonna do?"

A bell is ringing, a signal for the emergency stop, only it doesn't stop. Nothing works.

Stanley screams, "I didn't invent the fuckin' elevator!"

The man gives Stanley the finger. Flipping him the bird. Stanley's pushing his arm, thinking, It's not doing any good.

"You son of a bitch," the man says. "LET GO." Something in Stanley changed in those moments. Something clicked off while something else clicked on. And Stanley thought, This man, he's an unappreciative knuckle sandwich. The wedge a person can't pick out of his or her ass. Stanley releases the man's arm completely, tries to pry the doors open with both hands, and through the crack of the doors, the man's face is a soaked candy apple and he's still floating Stanley the bird. The elevator's jerking as it inches up, up, up, and the more he pries the doors, the tighter they get. Kneeling down, he can see the man on his tiptoes. And the man is yelling, "You prick!"

The last thing Stanley remembered about that day, on the next floor up, in the elevator, aside from wanting to go home, was the open doors and a lot of red. The kind of red a person would find in a slaughterhouse after butchering a cow or a pig. And he thought someone at the Red Cross could have used it. All the red.

Everything Stanley thought about or looked at after that became fragmented. Turned upside down. Something came loose in his head. Everything was foreign.

Looking at the man on the gurney with his eyes shut, Stanley told him, "You gotta weigh out the benefits, the positives. Without the limb you weigh a little less. Free parking, a larger bathroom stall reserved for you in public places. Even a special license plate."

The man said nothing.

Stanley's wife always told him a person has to turn a

negative into a positive. But after that she wasn't around very much. She wasn't what you'd call a supportive partner.

It wasn't Stanley's fault. After an investigation into what went wrong, the state's elevator inspector discovered faulty wiring to the sensors that kept the doors from closing and the contacts that kept the elevator from going up when the doors were open.

Outside Stanley's house, the grass is a dark tripping hazard sticking to the rubber soles of his Adidas. Inside the house, all of Earleen's clothes are missing. Closets are bare. Her mirrored vanity empty of cosmetics. Walking behind a self-propelled Lawn-Boy mower, somehow Stanley's misplaced his memory. His wife, she didn't even leave a Post-it. That's normal. Common courtesy. Let a person, especially a spouse, know where you are going. How long you will be gone.

Walking behind the mower, more and more lights from the surrounding homes are being turned on. What Stanley refers to as Nosy Neighbors. He's trying to mow his lawn; he's engrossed in responsibility. Recovery. A doctor's recommendation, it's called exercise, maybe they should try it sometime instead of watching it.

Rounding the garage, to his left, he can see outlines moving behind the curtains of Brent's home. Brent Wallace and his wife, Vickie, are the neighbors a person drinks beer and cooks out with on the weekends. Always talking about their son, Stevie, who enjoys playing with purses and pretending he's a girl. They call it a phase.

Behind Stanley, the Connleys are peeking out of their double-pane windows. They have a child named Kip. He always misses the first step off their deck, falling face-first onto the ground. Then he cries like a wimp.

What they all have in common is they're nosy bastards. They're all in this together, trying to drive Stanley crazy. He thinks they should mind their own business. Or help find his wife. What he could do is call his mother-in-law. But that would be a bad idea considering she's six feet under. Then his father-in-law would really have an excuse to hate him. In-laws and their grudges.

Brent's standing on his back porch, one big silhouette with a bright light behind him. At least Stanley thinks its Brent. He's yelling something, but Stanley can't make out the words. Can't he see Stanley's busy? His voice can't propel a twenty-inch-cut mower.

Stanley wonders what Brent's thinking. He's got work to do. Problems to solve. A wife to find. And behind Brent come more neighbors in nightclothes, holding flashlights. Their lips moving and their faces crunched up in anger.

They probably want to borrow Stanley's new mower. Carl, he lives across the street. He's the reason Stanley bought a new mower. After Carl borrowed his old mower, he didn't check the oil and burned the mower up. Blew it up, actually. Then Carl borrowed the weed eater. Ran the choke full throttle. Sounded similar to Leatherface sawing up a corpse in *The Texas Chain Saw Massacre*. Caught it on fire. Smoked the entire neighborhood. Just because a person's deaf doesn't mean they're dumb. The entire neighborhood smelled the smoke. Someone even called the fire department. A week later Carl fell asleep smoking a cigarette and burned his back porch down.

Now if a person lives in this neighborhood they are

considered a "high risk" on their homeowner's insurance policy. That Carl, he's a son of a bitch.

To Stanley, Brent looks like an enormous firefly leading his swarm of other fireflies with their big Maglites, walking from their yards to Stanley's.

Stanley doesn't have time for small talk, his wife is missing and he has a yard to mow. Things to do. To figure out.

Brent steps away from the pack, starts shining his Maglite in Stanley's eyes. The mower is idling and Stanley thinks, He's wasting my time. The light must be a halogen, all Stanley can see is a silhouette. His outline.

"Hey," Stanley says, "if you want to help, follow me with the light so I can see better."

"What the hell are you doing?" Brent asks.

Stanley shakes his head, thinking, This Brent is one guy you do not want as your charades partner. And Stanley says, "Well, I'm not testing my allergies. What does it look like, I'm mowing my lawn."

"Stanley," Brent says, "it's two in the morning and people are trying to sleep."

"Oh, I see, now everybody else's life is more important than mine."

Distancing himself from Brent and the other neighbors, the mower still running, one step is no longer a step, it's a slip. A fall. With his foot under the mower what he experiences is one swipe of pain followed by a feeling of stupefaction. With the operator-presence control bar tied down so he doesn't have to hold it all the time and the drive-control lever in the downward position, the lawn mower proceeds forward. Mowing the lawn without Stanley. It's on autopilot.

Looking down at his foot, everything is blue, green, and

yellow spots surrounded by black mass. Brent, standing above him—at least he thinks it's Brent—blinding Stanley with the Maglite.

Stanley says, "Get that damn light out of my face."

His ass is wet with dew, he's blinking his eyes trying to see the severed pieces of his shoe. His toes cut, not off but close to it. His foot is wet and warm. Brent is touching Stanley's shoulder and he says, "Stay calm."

Stanley says, "I'm fine, just quit touching me."

Stanley can hear the mower in another yard. Mowing someone else's lawn. And to think he was nearly finished.

"Are you all right?" Brent asks.

Stanley tells him, "Aside from maybe losing my toes and not knowing where my wife is at, sure, I enjoy sitting here like a gimp. Spending quality time with my nosy neighbors."

Stanley thinks this is what having neighbors gets you. Sometimes you just want to poke out someone's eye with an ink pen. Not a Bic. But a Paper Mate FlexGrip, thick and comfortable. Stanley says, "Why don't you go wake Carl up and we can burn my house down, or better yet let him burn up my new mower."

The mower is becoming more and more distant. Motion lights are lighting yard after yard.

Looking down at Stanley, Brent says, "Stanley, Earleen left. She's gone. You don't have to find her. She's taking care of her father."

"What are you talking about?"

"Your father-in-law and the elevator," Brent says slowly. "They blame you for him losing his arm. You know this, Stanley."

Stanley wanted to pretend he was someone else. Pretend what had happened was one big accident. But in his state of mind, that wouldn't work. He had to accept that his wife wasn't on her way home and his father-in-law didn't love him like his own son. Instead Stanley looked up at Brent and the neighbors corralling around him and everything turned black. And he wondered, Will any of these nosy neighbors ever call an ambulance?

THE OLD
MECHANIC

Here was a time when the shell shock of war was ignored. What the repercussions of warfare did to a man's brain. The seeing, hearing, and participating. And like the war, the abusing of a woman was overlooked. People pretended it never happened. This was a time when till-death-do-us-part was an enforced rule of matrimony. When wives didn't leave their husbands. They obeyed them.

But when the Mechanic beat the woman, violation rattled the opposite room's walls. The woman's body bounced from wall to wall like a winning pinball. There were no electronic harmonies for a high score. Just her thick pleas of sorry with no pity in reply. Just savagery. And with the door closed to the eight-by-eight box of a bedroom, violation traveled through the Sheetrock walls, arrived and infected the living room. Where, on a couch worn down to comfortable seating, two girls' adolescent eyes stayed glued to the black-and-white television. A television that decorated a corner with Tom and Jerry. With their own cartoon addictions to violence, displayed for a child's entertainment. Their slamming of doors on each other's various body parts. Shattering of dishes over each other's skull. Wooden mallets matching the fist pounding on flesh in the opposite bedroom.

It was something the beautiful and bright wallpaper couldn't hide. All that ugly in the air. The girls knew that any attempt to defend the woman, their mother, would get them the same treatment. The rapture of ten knuckles divided by two fists.

Those thoughts took root through their innocent minds, became part of their daily living like inhaling air. They were the accepted norm of life.

Their eyes never blinked and their hands were never tempted to touch the coffee table before them, to dig into the glass bowl of the Mechanic's hard red unwrapped cinnamon candy in the center. It was an unannounced rule. Don't touch what belongs to the Mechanic.

On the television, Jerry slammed a wooden mallet down on Tom's head.

The bedroom door opened with the weeping pleas of their mother, and the Mechanic approached the coffee table, his body damp from the downpour of his abusive actions, stopped and scooped a handful of cinnamon from the dish. Filled his mouth. Shook his head, his laughter following his footsteps into another room.

In the kitchen a tin of beer popped. Then the savoring sound of lips to foam. The girls' eyes glued to the television, concealing their fears. Their mother still moaning. The Mechanic said, "Hope the two of you don't turn out like her. Irresponsible. Disrespectful." No reply. Not a word. Hiding their fear, the girls had their underage poker faces on.

"Two of you hear what I'm saying?"

Not a word, just their mother's weeping pain dying down in that box of a bedroom. Their tiny fists, images of squeezing them tight in their minds. Knuckles like peanut shells popping open. Those images hiding their fear.

The Mechanic yelled, "Two of you get married, supper is ready when your old man walks through that front door after busting his body down all day."

On the television, Tom choked Jerry.

With no reply, the Mechanic turned it up another notch. "Answer me. Quit acting like your irresponsible mother in the other room."

In unison, the girls glanced up at the Mechanic's face and, nodding, they said, "Yes, Daddy."

On the television Tom was squeezing Jerry's life to the limit. Then at the last minute Jerry spat in Tom's eyes. Tom dropped Jerry.

On the couch, the girls glanced at each other with identical thoughts in the black void of their eyes. Their inner jaws salivating and storing. Gauging their distance.

Grabbing another handful of cinnamon, the Mechanic went back into the bedroom. Slammed the door behind him.

Quick to take aim, from the girls' mouths to open air, two fountains of weak water pressure, taking turns, they spat and spat. Aiming into the dish and coating the candy, only stopping to mix their saliva into it. Every so often the Mechanic would take a break from the beating, grab a handful of candy. Their spit went unnoticed, and he'd return to the bedroom while they sat defenseless. But internally they laughed at the Mechanic's ingesting, his savoring and swallowing of their spit. But externally, nothing could drown out or stop the soundtrack of their mother's abuse, which sometimes kept them up until sunrise.

There were other times the Mechanic came home, evicted everyone from the house to the yard until dark. Bedtime. And even an evening when the girls' dog, Lucky, wouldn't stop his barking and the Mechanic shot him dead. The Mechanic's reasoning: he'd a bad day at work.

It took years and years before the mother built up the courage to ignore the understood rule of matrimony. Divorced the Mechanic. Got remarried, to a man she referred to as "crazier than a loon," but who adored her with respect, love. Not ten knuckles. And he let her sleep through the morning sunrise. Wake up to *The Price Is Right* while spooning Taster's Choice coffee into her mug of hot water without the bark of violence.

But the Mechanic wasn't out of the picture. He had visitation every other weekend with his two girls. One summer the Mechanic picked the girls up from summer school unannounced. Took them out west on a vacation to see the Grand Canyon. Mount Rushmore. Yellowstone Park. Unknown to their mother; she wasn't asked. All she could do was file a complaint with the local law enforcement and wait. For three weeks the girls wore the same clothes they'd gone to school in that day. It was a hostage vacation.

These were the stories the younger daughter, Sue, told her son, Frank. She referred to them as her early childhood memories. They were the stories she told Frank after seeing the Old Mechanic at the grocery, gas station, or bank. And Frank always questioned her. Why are we running away from him? Is he gonna attack us?

Pregnant, Sue had married out of high school. It wasn't long after Frank's birth when the calls started, then the letters from the Old Mechanic wanting to visit, to meet his grandson. She couldn't get the memories out of her mind, the hatred and fear she held against this man she viewed as a monster, not her father. Her husband, Will, couldn't fathom a boy not knowing his grandfather, let alone a daughter who detested her father. Will had lost his own father at an early age to cancer, grew up without that influence, wanted his son to have it. He just couldn't understand. And she told him if his father had made his mother spit blood every other day for years on end, he would understand. More words ensued along with back-and-forth arguments about life and the stress that it brought, bills, food, quality time, and how there never seemed to be enough of any of it, until neither Will nor Sue could hold it together. She didn't want Frank growing up in a home of raised voices and clashes of any kind. She filed for divorce after five years.

Sue focused on her son. Will had every other weekend.

Sue tried to raise Frank with a life devoid of conflict, tried to keep him away from the violence she'd known. Keeping it normal. With toys, a bicycle, and a swing set. It was a life that forbade contact with the Old Mechanic. After nine years had passed, punctuated with more unreturned phone calls, unacknowledged letters and cards from the Old Mechanic, Sue's sister, Mary, approached her. Their father had spoken with her about Sue and wanting to meet Frank. Mary told Sue she should give their father a chance because she had, and he'd changed. He was harmless now. Though he had never apologized for anything he'd done all those years ago, Mary thought Frank deserved to meet his grandfather. He was old enough to make his own judgment about the man.

After weeks of rationalizing, Sue told Frank, "Your grandfather wants to meet you. Take you on a little trip."

In Frank's mind, running away and joining the fair and living out of garbage cans didn't sound bad. Other than the stories and seeing him in town, the grandfather was present only in the Hallmark cards, on Christmas and birthdays, offering many Lincolns or a check made out from him to Frank.

Frank asked Sue, "Why do you call him the Old Mechanic instead of Dad? And why didn't you let me meet him before now?"

Sue told him, "He worked for the Army Corps of Engineers and later became a diesel mechanic who could do most anything mechanical. He was good with his hands. And I never let you 'cause I didn't want you around him after all I seen him do to your grandmother."

"What does he want to do to me, I mean with me?"

Frank imagined a road trip where the Old Mechanic would threaten him with those fists from the stories. Force Frank to gather up roadkill from the side of old country back roads. Hold him hostage until nightfall. Tie the dead, decaying animals from the trees of people the Old Mechanic holds a grudge against.

When the Old Mechanic had told Sue what he wanted to do with Frank, where he wanted to take him, she bit her tongue and let the fear pass. "He wants to take you to the Gun and Knife Show. Then out to dinner. Get to know you."

"And you agreed to this? Can't you come with us?"

Sue doesn't let on that it scared her at first and says, "Yes, Frank. He deserves a chance. And no, I'm not coming with you. For God's sake, you're fourteen. I'm thirty-two, it's high time I put the past in the past, let you meet your grandfather. He's an old man now. He's harmless. And it's not healthy to live like this."

Harmless? Frank thinks to himself. Angry, terrified, he plays through all of those horror stories. The beatings. The shooting of the dog. The summer kidnapping. Frank imagines the Old Mechanic taking him to some compound guarded by brick walls, razor wire, and booby traps. Inside he'll chain Frank to a wall in his bomb-shelter basement next to his punching bag that's stuffed with the men and women he has disposed of, with those hands flaying, carving, and grinding their bones into ash remains for whatever madness he found offensive.

Shaking Frank's hand, the Old Mechanic has a grip as strong as a vise. Frank believes the Old Mechanic could cave in another man's skull, crush his windpipe with one swipe.

The Old Mechanic, with his swollen belly of red, white, and black checkered flannel trimmed by two strips of red suspenders. Frank has seen him around town, but never up close. Age has settled upon his frame, sagging his skin like mucus. His hair is peppered with gray, matted down like Ward Cleaver's and hidden by a blue knit-cap reminiscent of what Nicholson wore in *One Flew Over the Cuckoo's Nest*. A book Frank's read and a movie he's watched with his father. Reinforcing Frank's imagination with the fear of loose-cannon lunacy. His face is pitted by liver spots. Old engravings of acne from his teenage years. The features remind Frank of some cross between an oversized whiskerless rat and ALF the sitcom alien puppet.

The Old Mechanic asks, "You ready?"

Frank just nods, says, "Sure."

The mother gives Frank a farewell peck on the cheek. Tells him to enjoy himself, eyes her father, at a loss for compassion or words, just memories. She tells him, "Be back by six p.m." Then stresses, "Don't be late."

Frank's blood thins and his heart pulses to an irregular rhythm in the front seat of the Old Mechanic's Dodge truck. The Old Mechanic beats the horn with one hand. Generously offers his displeasure at the navigation skills of the driver in front of him. Frank wonders again why his mother agreed to this. The Old Mechanic screams, "Drive like this in Tennessee or Texas and your ass'd be into the rail."

Not thinking, Frank blurts out, "This is Indiana. He's not driving in Tennessee or Texas."

The Old Mechanic glances at Frank with acidic eyes that corrode his sternum and he says, "See, Frank, you don't got no navigation skills. Can't follow these people poking on the road. They're only holding you back from your destination."

Frank frowns and says, "I'm fourteen, can't even drive yet."

The look in the Old Mechanic's eyes from Frank's comment, combined with the forward motion of his voice, the command and control, supports the fear in Frank's frame. Lets him know the Old Mechanic is feeling him out. And the gun show is a trial run.

At the gun show, tables are set up and spread out like an oversized school cafeteria. Vendors in black Hanes T-shirts with beer guts poking out over military green pants, selling new and used guns and knives. Some of what the Old Mechanic calls pot metal. Used junk. "But also some good deals," he tells Frank. "Just gotta know your hardware, keep your eyes open."

They walk between the tables. Up and down the aisles. The Old Mechanic appears at ease to Frank, happy. In his element. They stop at a table and the Old Mechanic picks up a gun. Frank closes his eyes, somehow fearing he'll load it. Begin a strain of elderly shootings. The Old Mechanic tells him, "See, this is what I'm talkin' about, it's a Beretta Modello, made in '34, used by the Italians before W. W. Two. A real antique."

Frank's at a loss for words as he watches the Old Mechanic place it back on the table without taking aim at anyone. They pass more tables. The Old Mechanic shakes his head, points to a table piled with guns and knives, tells Frank, "All that there is cheap knock-offs, used garbage they call antique firearms. More than likely they sat the shit out in the weather, let it rust, tried to make it look old. Not good for anything else."

Frank keeps his eyes forward. His mouth shut.

At another table the Old Mechanic picks up a pistol that reminds Frank of the one he's seen in a 007 movie, and the Old Mechanic asks, "Know what crisis this heifer was said to have caused?"

Frank offers, "A bank robbery?"

"No. This was believed to have been used to take out the archduke of Austria. Mr. Ferdinand. Initiated W. W. One. It's an FN Model 1910."

A vendor butts in, "Well, nobody knows that for certain, it's just—"

The Old Mechanic turns to the vendor, his face a bee-stung mask, says, "It's just none of your business. Can't you see I'm talking to my grandson?"

Frank's heart is running a gym class relay as the Old Mechanic throws the gun on the table. They walk off with the Old Mechanic grumbling, "Got no appreciation for men such as myself who fought for the civil liberties of that idiot and this country."

Frank's insides tighten as he visualizes the Old Mechanic wrapping his hands around the vendor's neck. Frank wants to hide beneath a table. Curl up in a ball. He knows how his mother and aunt felt being the Old Mechanic's audience every day.

Frank wants to leave but the Old Mechanic wants to buy Frank something. They stop at a table of knives. The Old Mechanic picks up a switchblade. Decides this is it. Not the one with a safety feature to keep the ejecting blade from puncturing someone or something. The Old Mechanic buys a NATO paratrooper switchblade with a surgical-razor-sharp blade. No safety. Just reinforced spring action. Enough force to plunge the blade through human skin.

He pays for it and Frank questions him about it, doesn't know if his mother will approve.

"Your mother? Frank, you're fourteen, what are you gonna do if you gotta use it on someone?"

All Frank can think as he puts it into his pocket is what his mother said: the Old Mechanic is harmless.

At a local Ponderosa Steakhouse, a waitress serves platters of an all-you-can-eat steak-and-shrimp. Everyone in the restaurant helps knives slice steaks on ceramic plates with blood and grease. Lips smack among muffled conversations surrounding Frank and the Old Mechanic.

Frank takes a slice of rib eye into his mouth, working his jaws and savoring the medium-rare juice as he swallows. Apparently the Old Mechanic's standard of medium-rare and what the grill man prepared are two separate things. The grill man doesn't know how to grill. The Old Mechanic locks eyes with Frank as his jaws work the meat and he says, "Shit's cold. Tough. Wouldn't feed this cut of cholesterol to a mangy hound."

Frank sees the rabid madness in his eyes as the nostrils in his pitted nose expand. He drops his fork and knife onto his plate. They bounce into everyone's earshot. Frank keeps his mouth closed. His jaws work the meat as he glances at all of the eyes that burn into the Old Mechanic. Hearing the clatter of silverware, the waitress returns.

"Everything all right, sir?"

The Old Mechanic says, "Where you find these cooks and cuts of cow, a janitorial service? It tastes like floor scrapings from the bottom of a slaughterhouse Dumpster. Had better C rations in a foreign trench. I brought my damn grandson here for a good steak. This is embarrassing."

Frank dabs a piece of crusted shrimp into the thick red sauce. Then his mouth. The waitress apologizes and says, "I'll get a manager." The Old Mechanic grabs his steak knife, holds it up. Frank watches those vise-grip hands. His throat draws tight as his innards swell. The waitress turns her back. The Old Mechanic pauses, then lays the knife back on the plate next to the rib eye, pushes it to the table's edge, and raises his voice.

"Hey?"

The waitress turns her attention back to their table and the Old Mechanic waves his hand, purses his lips, and tells her, "That won't be necessary." He goes quiet as if to consider something and asks, "Know who I am?"

The waitress offers a confused stare and says, "No, sir."

"I'm a veteran of W. W. Two. I didn't fight in a world war so incompetent slugs such as yourself could offer shit like this. Know what'd happen if I'd fought a war like this, like you grill and serve food here? We'd be speaking German or Japanese."

The waitress's eyes bubble up. Her body shivers.

"Have to excuse me, Frank, but the way people treat others in this country pisses me off. Tired of it."

His words go through Frank as he chews his last piece of shrimp. The Old Mechanic tells him, "Let's go."

In his Dodge truck, the Old Mechanic's either taking an alternate route to Frank's house or kidnapping him. Frank knows he's been planning this for years. This is it. He's taking Frank on an unannounced hostage vacation.

Frank grips his only defense. The switchblade in his pocket. The Old Mechanic tells him, "Going by my house, got something for you."

The compound. The Old Mechanic has picked out Frank's plot, where he'll push up daisies in an unmarked grave in his backyard. Frank's stomach churns with an expanding sickness of nerves and one too many shrimp. Churns with thoughts of all the things he's yet to do. Accomplish or encounter. Like sports. Prom. Booze. Girls and cleavage.

Tightening the grip on the knife in his pocket. Eyeing

the hands on the wheel. He could stab him in one of those strong voice-box-breaking hands. The Old Mechanic asked, what if he had to use it on someone. Is this what he meant? But that could cause a wreck. Frank could die. He doesn't wanna die. The Old Mechanic slows the truck down. Turns down a gravel road. Frank's starting to shake, glancing at the Old Mechanic, who navigates the wheel to a stop. There's no brick wall or razor wire. No compound. Just an old graying cabin with a tin roof on a dead-end road. The Old Mechanic tells Frank, "This is it."

His hand still holding the switchblade in his pocket, Frank sits on a musty brown corduroy couch, his nerves rattled by the unknown of the house his mother grew up in. He takes in the scenes of timelines past. Old yellowing newspapers stacked on a worn blue and rarely vacuumed carpet. The log walls are lined by black-framed graying photos of soldiers smiling. Giving the thumbs-up. There are portraits of Frank's mother and aunt as kids with gapped buckteeth. Frank watches the Old Mechanic come from the narrow shotgun hallway out of what he's guessing is a bedroom. He's holding an Army green rectangular metal box. The Old Mechanic sinks into the couch beside Frank. Pulls his knit cap off. Frank's heart pounds red lines as he keeps a tight grip on the switchblade, wondering what's in the box.

The Old Mechanic clears his throat, says, "Guess you know I served in W. W. Two?" Fearing what's in the box, what's gonna happen, Frank tells him, "No, mother never talked about you serving in no war, just the other."

Giving Frank an odd-eyed glance, he says, "The other?"

Frank glances at those hands and says, "The beatings."

The Old Mechanic shakes his head. Runs his dry eighty-grit tongue over his lips.

"Times change just like people, that's my reasoning for bringing you here."

Staring at the green box, Frank tells himself he's gonna stab those hands until they're no longer functional if he lays a finger on him.

And the Old Mechanic says, "War'd been hell for me, Frank. Things I did and seen. Coming home, I didn't know how to talk about it. Didn't know how to behave."

Frank's grip is sweating on the knife in his pocket and the Old Mechanic says, "Stored it my head. All those images boiled my temperament into a violence I couldn't contain toward other people. I became a boozer and a beater with a short fuse. It felt good to smash someone." Frank imagines those chicken-skin hands around his neck, and the Old Mechanic says, "I can only imagine what your mother, your aunt, your grandmother have told you about me. Things I done to them."

Frank's insides are an unanswered voice in a deep black well. His thumb rubs on the button, ready to eject the blade. He wants out of here. Away from this disturbed old mechanic opening a metal box. He could stab the old man and run off, but he doesn't know where he is. What if he just injures him and the old man chases him down? It will only be worse.

As he reaches into the box, the grooves of the Old Mechanic's acne-scarred face draw tight and he grits his coffee-stained teeth. He's obviously planning something. Tells Frank, "Maybe someday you can understand all that I've done, bad and good."

Frank's imagination tells him there's probably a gun in that box. Handcuffs. Rags and rope. It's his little torture kit. Frank wants to pull the knife from his pocket. Wants to eject the blade, wants to demand, "Don't go getting all crazy on me. I already know things you done, just take me home!" But he sees his little knife isn't going to help him now.

The Old Mechanic pulls the long black steel blade of a bayonet from the box and says, "Hold on." It's too late.

Frank takes in the dark stains that he guesses are blood from everyone who has ever crossed the man and says, "Why, so you can stab me with that machete?"

The Old Mechanic shakes his head, chuckles, and says, "I ain't gonna stab you. And this ain't no machete. It's a bayonet. Belonged to Howard Case. Old boy I served with from Kentucky. Big as a barn. Pale as cream from the top of fresh-squeezed cow's milk."

Franks says, "You stole it?"

The Old Mechanic inhales deeply and exhales slowly. "No, Case and I was dropped out on a beach in Okinawa with other soldiers. Expected all hell to rain down. But the hell didn't come until farther inland." Lowering the bayonet, he pauses and says, "Was running for position, Case and me, the earth was smoke-holed explosions. Had a wooden crate of grenades strapped down on my back. Case was next to me, dodging swarms of lead. The earth opened up. Didn't know enemy fire from our own. We hit the earth for cover. A round traveled through the crate. Missed every grenade. Come out the other side. Took Case's face with it. I grabbed his rifle. Didn't realize it until later. Seen his initials carved into the rifle's wooden stock." The Old Mechanic lifts the bayonet. Hands it to Frank, says, "It's yours if you want it."

Frank releases the switchblade in his pocket, pulls his hand free, and takes the bayonet. Feels the cold solid weight in his one hand while the finger of the other runs over the stains.

The Old Mechanic pulls something else from the box. A triangular piece of red cloth with a blue stripe down its center and a five-pointed tarnished brass star hanging from the cloth. Frank squints his eyes. "What's that?"

The Old Mechanic's lips tighten and his face draws tight with seriousness and he says, "Bronze Star. Army give it to me for fighting the Japanese in Okinawa. For killing men."

Frank looks at the Old Mechanic's scarred mitts and is reminded of the stories that surround them. "This your excuse for what you did to my grandmother?" The Old Mechanic lays the Bronze Star back in the box. "Look, I don't got to justify anything I done, not to you, not to anyone. I got no excuses. Just what's in this box. Wanted you to see and know who I was and how I earned these before I died."

A bead of moisture travels down the Old Mechanic's acne-scarred face. A warmth begins to build from within Frank.

The Old Mechanic points to the pictures on the wall.

"All I can say is I took my anger and resentment for life out on your grandmother. It wasn't right. She suffered until she could suffer no more. I's unable to adjust from what I'd seen and done. 'Cause once a man takes another man's life, it's the guilt of memory that haunts him and he will forever live in the shadow of the dead."

The Old Mechanic bends his neck. Lowers his face into those hands Frank fears.

All that forward motion, that command and control, in the Old Mechanic's voice is gone. Harmless.

Frank is torn between not knowing the Old Mechanic and wanting to know him. He places the stories he's grown up with in the back of his mind, the cinnamon candy and Tom and Jerry, the dead dog, and remembers what his mother told him: the Old Mechanic deserves a chance.

Frank stands up and faces the Old Mechanic, places a hand on his shoulder, knowing the Old Mechanic could just be tricking him. He's not letting go of this bayonet. But he also wants to know. "Really, you really served in a real war, in World War Two? You really killed people?"

ROUGH
COMPANY

The August sun boiled through the Illinois farmhouse's tin roof. An argument over an insurance scam festered into full-blown rage. Cooley, a mulatto-skinned Indian, backhanded Connie's thin ivory face across the kitchen table, where her son, Pine Box, sat eating a plate of mashed eggs. Connie pulled Pine Box's fork from his grip. Came off the table. Dug the fork deep into Cooley's jugular.

Cooley pawed at the fork with red erupting like fresh-struck oil from the earth as his heart raced and he gritted out, "You bitch!"

Connie stormed from the kitchen, went down the hallway, grabbed a double-barrel .12-gauge from the bedroom. Back in the kitchen, she stood hefting the shotgun at Cooley's head of Crazy Horse locks pigtailing down his bearlike shoulders.

Her hick tone ordered, "Pine Box, get us a Falls City from the fridge. Wait outside for Mama."

Pine Box opened the fridge, grabbed two cans, crossed the kitchen. The boot-scuffed screen door bounced against the jamb behind him. Followed by both barrels exploding and the Indian who had stitched Pine Box's mind with daily fists parted across the linoleum.

Connie took Pine Box and ran off with Cooley eight years ago from Indiana to Illinois after her father tried to drown Pine Box, believed he was a bastard child. Connie'd been raised to recognize attention and abuse as equal hands drawn from the same deck. What mattered to Connie was how the hand was played. Her boyfriend Cooley had played the one hand too many times.

Eight-year-old Pine Box sat with cheeks and fingernails plastered by dirt. Tire tracks of three-week-old chocolate milk and egg ringwormed around his lips. His lungs tasted a Pall Mall and his tongue shared a Falls City with his mother beneath an old hickory tree.

He asked Connie, "What we do now, Mama?"

Connie pushed her golden locks, with muffler-burned roots from a dime-store dye job, from her face, belched. "Now we pack up, make the two-hour haul over to Indiana, hook up with your uncle Lazarus, do that insurance scam with no Indian to drink up our cut."

Tires flung gravel, leaving Pine Box at a dead-end turnoff encircled by thick oaks down in the southeast woods of Kentucky. He stood watching Connie and Lazarus disappear into the purple neon morning, remembering the unlocked windows he'd climbed through to steal jewelry. Working-class cash tucked between mattresses. Coffee cans of the same hidden in drawers. Freezers. Fridges. He knew all the hiding spots where Cooley and Connie had taught him to look. But he'd never helped to vandalize a car for insurance money before.

His uncle Lazarus explained, "Some people believe sweating their lives away in a factory is making a living. That dream died when Reagan became president couple years back. Scamming. Swindling. Stealing. It's the only life your uncle Lazarus and mama know. And it's all you'll ever know, little man."

Nicotine-stained fingers swung steel. On the left. Then the right. Shattering the front lights on the nipple-pink '82 Cadillac with a sugarcoated top. Lazarus had driven to Hazard, Kentucky, a three-and-a-half-hour drive from New Amsterdam, Indiana, where he sometimes laid his head. He'd picked out the area because of its rural setting. Nothing but hills and people separated by miles and miles. Plus he didn't have any acquaintances down this way. Nothing to connect him to suspicion when he reported the car stolen.

Lazarus had parked the Cadillac at this dead end surrounded by green-wooded mountainous lumps with houses unseen. Connie followed. Swapped Pine Box for Lazarus. Now he had five minutes until Lazarus and Connie came back in the Dodge Duster. They sat at the end of the road watching for cars, just in case someone came by. Lazarus had stressed to Pine Box that the Caddy had to be totaled, turned into junkyard scrap.

Pine Box's boots climbed the mirrored bumper. He thundered his heels up and down on the hood. Six swings from the crowbar and the windshield was cracked ice. His boots trailed up to the sugarcoated top, doing the same heel-dent dance that he did on the hood. He slid down the back window. Over the trunk to the gravel. His heart flicked in his chicken-wing chest. He heaved the steel, shattered each taillight. Lifted the snake-tongued end above his head. Battered the trunk. Walked to the driver's side, opened the door. Laid the steel across the white leather seat. Sweat burned his muddy-water eyes as he offered up a tiny Buck knife from his pocket. Thumbed open the blade and murdered the seat. Made it bleed foam.

From under the seat he pulled the book of matches and rubbing alcohol left by Lazarus. Bathed the interior until it made a wino smell clean in comparison. He grabbed the steel, cradled it in his armpit. Held the book of matches open. Felt a clawhammer hand dig into his jerky-tinted locks, skip him backwards across the gravel like flat flint across a pond's surface. Steel clanked. Pine Box's palms and knees bit gravel.

Tears bubbled up and turned into pissed off. Pine Box stood, taking in the old man with gray corn huskers hair. A tobacco-stained Hanes beneath bibbed overalls spitting black sludge.

"Think you're doin' on my property, you little son of a bitch?"

The old man glanced up the gravel road, listening to the Duster tear through the early morning air.

"Who in the shit?"

Pine Box's hands stung with the violence he'd watched Connie and Cooley perform on each other like Saturday-morning cartoons. He gripped and swung the steel into the old man's shin. Bone chipped into particles beneath denim. Dropped the old man to his knees. His vision ruptured with broken vessels. He spat. "Little shit! Know who you're fuckin' with?"

The old man backhanded Pine Box to the gravel. Pine Box hollered, "Dammit!"

Cooley had busted him until he spat and pissed red, making it hard to walk, talk, eat, or sleep. Pine Box swallowed the bitterness, eyed his target through watery sight. Stood up. Indented the old man's flesh with a Hank Aaron swing. Rolled him backwards onto the gravel with both hands gripping his face and moaning.

Tears connected dirt dots across Pine Box's cheeks like freckles on a redhead. Mucus seeped from his nose as he grabbed the book of matches from the gravel. Connie stomped the Duster's brakes. Pine Box pressed a flame from the match. Lit and tossed the pack into the Cadillac's front seat, which ignited like the hell Baptists preached every Sunday morning.

Lazarus opened the passenger's side door and hollered, "Shit, boy, get in here!"

Pine Box limped to the Duster, sucking snot and spitting blood. Lazarus pulled him in and heaved the door shut. The old man made it to his feet with liver-spotted features coated by blood, his jaw gaping and unmoving, his throat gargling incoherent tones. His hands met the Duster's fender on the passenger's side. Connie stomped the gas, made the old man disappear. Lazarus yelled, "Stop so I can finish him."

"Ain't no time," Connie told Lazarus as she cut the wheel back to the main road while Pine Box burrowed his tears into her lap. "We got a three-hour drive back to Indiana, dump Pine Box and me back at your place. Get him patched up pretty as a Methodist boy in Sunday school." She drove with one hand on the wheel, the other caressing Pine Box's greasy locks. Out the driver's window trees and fenced pasture combined into a blur.

She cut the wheel out onto the chewed pavement. The rear tires barked. Black smoke bolted up like a violent summer storm from the oak trees at the dead-end turnaround.

An explosion swarmed the early morning air. The surrounding pasture and pavement rumbled, jarring the rear fender of the Dodge Duster. Connie kept the gas pedal floored. Rubbing the mucus-red mixture from Pine Box's busted nose and warped lips, feeling the same pain she'd known since having sight of this hell that everyone called living.

Before the uneven textures of his hand rattled the screen door he smelled the memory of charred bones on foreign soil. Gripped his nickel-plated .38 snub-nose from his waist. Thumbed the hammer back and opened the door.

Decomposed features spoiled the air inside the farmhouse's kitchen, similar to the Commie skin he'd whittled, pliered, and burned in the jungles overseas.

Green flies hummed in the humidity while maggots burrowed and swam within particles of marrow and black-cherry blood that sketched across the linoleum.

Shell shot had peppered the rusted fridge and yellowed-wallpaper walls. But what stood out at first glance was the fork rooted in the neck. Hands mortared around it as if the male had planted a tiny pole for a surrender flag.

Kurt's brows pushed wrinkles into his forehead. His bottom lip puckered into his top and in a deep gravel tone he muttered, "Twisted bitch."

He wore a beaded belt, bracelets constructed from animal hide braided around each soup-can wrist. His skin was tattooed by shrapnel fragments from twelve months of recon jungle heat. The firefights that created what he was to this day. Something hollow.

He thumbed the hammer of his nickel-plated .38. Slid it into his waistband. He knew the female and her son were gone. Just like he knew what she and the male who was scattered across the vinyl had enjoyed.

Stepping over the male, Kurt admired the skull; misshapen like a cantaloupe attached to a neck and shoulders with its fruit busted and etched into crusty decay.

Kurt had kept company with their type since he could remember setting his bare feet in every hole-in-the-wall shack, trailer, backroom bar, or barn-lot cockfight. Seeing a male who abused a female and the female who craved it. Both types twisted his intestines, brought back memories of his mother, blue flame from a gas stove heating a paring knife. Taking turns singeing her privates, then his. Mixing with Mama, she'd laugh. Scarred is what he called it, shaking the memory from his head. It sickened him, imagining what the boy had already seen and done.

Kurt had been assigned to find the female and her son by the man they'd left for dead. Mr. Hayden Attwood, who owned a farm way down in Hazard, Kentucky. But who now lay in a hospital bed with second-degree burns from being close to the car when it caught fire and exploded. His jaw wired shut. Ribs fractured and with a splintered left shin. Pissing red through a clear tube. Unable to slur a sentence, he wrote down for the Hazard County deputy sheriff and detective what he remembered. Nothing.

The deputy sheriff told Mr. Attwood the charred license plate they'd found had been traced back to a Mr. Lazarus Dodson, who stayed up north in Indiana. He had no permanent address or employment. He was a gambler, pool shark. Had been drinking late one night at bar in Corydon. Came out to find his vehicle gone. Reported the car stolen. But Mr. Attwood wasn't a big fan of the law. He wanted the boy who beat him and the silhouette of the woman that ran him over to bleed, and he had his own justice for the maladjusted lawbreakers who crossed him. That was Bonfire Kurt, who'd been working for Mr. Attwood since his discharge from the U.S. Marines twelve years ago, back in '72.

Mr. Attwood had written down the plate number of the Duster that he'd tattooed into the hard marrow of his mind after being clipped by it. Left for buzzards to circle while his body baked by the exploding Cadillac.

He gave the plate number to Kurt, who believed Lazarus was connected to the woman and the child. Attwood wanted Kurt to focus on the kid and the female driver. But Kurt went to Lazarus first. Wanted to see his routine. See if the woman and boy showed up. He found Lazarus at a bar in Indiana. Watched him drink and shoot pool, then shack up in a flophouse at night. The Duster with the woman and the kid never showed. But the cops did. A plainclothes was keeping tabs right along with Kurt, drinking coffee and eating donuts.

Kurt let the heat simmer, used his other connections for finding people who didn't want to be found. The Duster's plate number yielded Connie and her son, Willie Voyles, shacked up at an address two hours away from Lazarus along the Illinois-Indiana line with some Jimmy Joe Cooley. Part-time thief and swindler. Full-time drunk. Kurt formed a scenario. Connie and Cooley had taken the Cadillac for Lazarus. Connie followed in the Duster so Cooley could dump it. Willie vandalized it. Then she and Cooley came back for Willie. Lazarus reports the car stolen. Police find it torched in Kentucky. When the insurance check shows up in the mail Lazarus pays them for the job.

What had happened in the farmhouse took place days before the '82 Cadillac had been stolen and ignited. Cooley's frame was bone-stiff with at least a week into rot. Poor son of a bitch had nothing to do with the Caddy scam.

Wanting to place features to the hunted, he followed the hallway's flea-infested carpet to a sheet that doubled as a bedroom door. Inside, a king-size mattress furnished the far left corner. Bullet holes and rape stains intact. A single wadded quilt lay in its center. No pillows. The air was mold and mildew. A few flies had taken up residence on a dented and scuffed file cabinet that was used for a dresser. Shirts, jeans, socks, and boxers hung out of the open drawers. No pictures on the smoke-damaged walls. Just a few fist-size holes. He opened a closet door. Found a wilted, freezer-taped cardboard box labeled "Family Photos." Removed the lid. Leafed through scattered black-and-white pics of men and women, some young, some old, until he found a color Polaroid with "Connie and Willie 1980" chicken-scratched along the bottom. The female was white-trash erotic. Dirty peroxide locks. A remorseless marrow-white complexion. Eyes so bottomless they were carved out by a god that substituted pleasure in the form of pain.

The boy had kippered locks. Eyes gouged into two puddles. His pigment corpse-pale. A grin pasted on for a smile. His mother in male form.

He slid the photo into his shirt pocket, remembering his own mother, her clammy hand against his cheek, heated breath in his ear, the scent of garlic boiled in hops. Kurt shook his head, feeling a butcher cleave his spine down to his Achilles' heel, and he said, "Know your kind all too well."

Moisture heated the back of his neck. Dripped from his brow. He pushed the sheet from the entrance. Followed the hallway carpet back to the kitchen. Stepped over Cooley, out the screen door. The mid-morning heat stole his breath as his hands tremored. He pulled a flask from his back pocket. Twisted the cap, took a hard slug of Wild Turkey that ignited his insides.

Men of his state had watched the world bleed its own too many times to feel pity. He'd seen half-strung eyes, beaten faces, and limbs removed. Enough pain to make anyone believe in hell. This Connie, what she'd done to Cooley reaffirmed that hell's existence. Reminded him too much of what his own mother had been capable of.

Sliding the flask back into his pocket he walked toward his orange International Scout, knowing he needed names. Addresses. To go back and wait. Watch Lazarus. To find where Connie and Willie could have gone, catch them all together. Of course, people this malevolent didn't keep close company for long.

From the distance, a salvage-yard-ready Pinto bounced down the dirt drive, pulled to a stop. Stepping from the Pinto was a female in cutoffs that used to be white, with her ass cheeks peeking out, blowing kisses as she turned to close the car door. She'd a cinnamon-striped tube top that held the shapes of two ripened tomatoes ready to be handpicked. Her waving locks matched the spots on her face, the color of rust, while her leech lips smacked the sugar of the Bazooka Joe bubble gum. She swayed barefooted toward Kurt, speaking in an unsure tongue. "Connie around?"

Making a deviant blush, Kurt's eyes trip-wired her with "No. Wouldn't know where she and Willie might be, would you?"

"Who are you?"

"An acquaintance."

"I ain't heard from her in better than two weeks. Thought I'd come by. Make sure that drunk hadn't beat her black as a milk snake again."

Her river-green eyes glanced down to his crotch. Moved up to the .38. Her eyes got confused as she met his.

Before the female could exhale, Bonfire had a fist full of her rusted locks twisted in one hand. The thumb of his other clicked the hammer of the .38, the barrel bruising her cheek.

"Didn't catch your name, sugar."

"B-B-B-Barbra Jean."

He could smell the trash she'd been burning in a steel drum wafting from her body, topped off with a hint of panic.

"Well, Barbra Jean, I need names of any acquaintances of Connie. Someplace she and Willie might hole up."

"Only person Connie ever spoke of was her older step-brother."

"Does he got a name?"

"Lazarus."

After removing the cloth wrapped around Pine Box's palms, anger flared from Lazarus's lips.

"So, little man, was that spent-liver Indian the one who used your palms for ashtrays?"

A single cigarette dangled from the corner of Lazarus's mouth. Smoke twined into the bacon-grease air of the trailer. He'd been lying low in town, waiting until the heat was off his back. They'd been eye-fucking him for a few weeks. Connie and Willie stayed at the trailer he rented from Buck

Shields on a five-acre plot out in nowhere land. No one knew about it.

Pine Box sat at the Formica table taking in the oozing pink of his palm. With tiny marble-size indentions scattered about it. A cornmeal crust infected the corners of his eyes, which were dirty streams identical to those of his uncle, who slammed his fist on the kitchen table's cracked surface.

"You gonna answer me or play Anne Frank all damn day?"

"Anne who?"

"Dammit, Pine Box, answer me?"

The boy bit his lip and sighed. Said, "Ever time Cooley got to drinkin' and Mama was out earnin' her way he'd get some kinda yellow-jacket meanness in him. Wanna play chicken. I wasn't scared. I played."

From the kitchen's gas stove Connie stood braless in a worn wifebeater and Kentucky blue nylon shorts, saying, "Well, that Indian's ten kinds of stink now, sugar." Stubbing his cigarette out, Lazarus shook his head of shoe-polish-slick locks. Rubbed his chin, wanting to be a part of Pine Box's life before it was too late. Living hours away, Connie and Cooley hadn't been giving the boy any history. Didn't even know who Anne Frank was. Probably didn't know his namesake. And Lazarus asked, "Connie ever tell you how your name came about?"

Behind Lazarus, Connie's hand quivered. She stabbed crisp strips of bacon from the cast-iron skillet to a paper plate. Remembered how her stepdaddy couldn't keep his hands off her. Made her stepbrothers move out into the barn when her Claymation features thinned out into a shapely woman. She never wanted Pine Box to know anything of her past. How he was conceived. Almost killed and named.

Anger charred her face and words combusted from her lips. "Lazarus, shut your damn mouth!"

Lazarus remembered his daddy. The man who'd offered a lot of love in the form of pain. A year ago he'd passed. Liver cancer. Left his insurance policy to Lazarus. He used some of the money to purchase the nipple-pink Cadillac. What was left he gambled away. He hated that bastard. Growing up out in that barn, he felt a lot of rage for him. That rage returned when he'd seen Pine Box weeks ago. He held Connie responsible. Feeling as though he were being cheated, letting some half-breed raise Willie.

"Done about fucked us on the car job. Should have let me out, made sure that man was dead."

"That man was redder than canned tomatoes. Hazard County police told you he can't remember shit. Laid up in a hospital. All we's waiting on is the insurance check. Besides, you the one who went and parked the car on his property."

Lazarus's hands dampened. The road where they'd parked the car looked like a place people went to get their fuck on, nothing for miles. How was he supposed to know that Attwood was some wealthy landowner? Shit, he wasn't from Hazard, Kentucky. He was from New Amsterdam, Indiana. Three hours away.

He seared a stare at Connie, thought of squeezing her complexion from bone-pale to the same shade of red that pumped through her black heart. Pay her back triple for what she'd let that Indian do to Pine Box. Then a bullfrog belch pushed from Pine Box's mouth.

"Where my name come from, Uncle Lazarus?"

Fuck her, he thought. This was his kid too. It was time the boy knew about his history.

"Your granddaddy Dodson said you came not out of

love but out of sickness. When you was born he fetched your wrinkled ass up. Put you in a burlap sack. Took off down the road in his beat-to-shit Ford."

Unsteady, not wanting Pine Box to hear the story, Connie flipped the blue-orange gas flame off. Yelled, "Dammit, Lazarus, shut your friggin' mouth!"

"His name has got meaning. It's his birthright to know." Glancing at Pine Box, he continued, "Connie, she took off after your granddaddy. Running barefoot down the gravel drive. Followed him all the way down to the creek. Now picture that burlap sack you was in being tossed from the Ford as it crossed a one-lane bridge. Smacking against the current of the creek. The weeping whine of you, the just-born child getting his first swimming lesson. Connie waded in. Thinking she'd have to build a pine box to bury you in. Pulled you from that sack. You coughed creek water and cried. That's the story Connie always told. How you wasn't born. You was salvaged. And she named you Pine Box Willie: the just-born burlap baby."

Remembering that day, how she'd cradled him while telling the tale to others in the town at the Silver Dollar Tavern. Getting hitched on whiskey shots, pain jarred and split her insides. Hardened her grip around the cast-iron skillet's handle. To pick up. Bust over Lazarus's skull.

Then the trailer's door burst open.

Lazarus stood up hollering into the outdoor light, which created a silhouetted shape in the doorway. "Who the—"

The silhouette interrupted with "Lazarus?"

"Yeah?"

"Compliments of Mr. Attwood."

Orange gunfire opened the sticky trailer air. Parted

Lazarus's right knee, then his left, like two eggs against pavement. Lazarus dropped backwards, screaming. Pinned the table down on Pine Box's legs. Connie screamed, came at the silhouette with the skillet of popping grease. Her nose met the butt of the .38. Her eyes stung with liquid. Blood creased her lips and her knees punched the floor. The skillet dropped. Bacon grease splattered. The man smiled. Aimed the nickel-plated .38 at Connie's face.

"You're rough company, girl."

"Who the hell are you?"

"Bonfire Kurt. Work for Mr. Attwood. Man's property you parked that Cadillac on. Vandalized. Man you left for dead."

Pine Box clinched his eyes. Squirmed and pushed to get from under the table that Lazarus deadweighted down, bleeding like a bastard.

"Picked the most vindictive man in all of Hazard, Kentucky. Way I figured, Lazarus and you dumped the Cadillac. Willie destroyed it. Lazarus reported it stolen. Now you and he expect to split the insurance."

Losing feeling to cold, Lazarus screamed, "Fuck you!"

Kurt glanced over his shoulder, smirked, said, "No, fuck you!"

Connie asked, "How you know who we are?"

"A personal contact, little recon, and some Barbra Jean."

"Barbra . . . ? What'd you do to her?"

"Not near what you did to Mr. Cooley. I paid you a visit over in Illinois. She showed up. Gave me some answers."

Connie spat. "You son of a bitch!"

Five fingers clasped into Connie's hair. Pulled her to her feet while the .38's heated barrel singed her temple. She twisted her neck into his forearm. Dug her teeth into his shrapnel skin. Took a blood sample. He yelled. His trigger finger twitched. Gunfire quartered skin and bone across the trailer's kitchen. His knees buckled with her weight. He lowered the mess that was once her to the kitchen's floor.

Willie stood behind Bonfire with waterlogged eyes looking down at the motionless red mess.

"Mama?"

Bonfire bent his knees to standing. Turned to Willie, whose taffy-pink palm reached for Bonfire's hand that held the .38, pressed his forehead into the heated barrel. His clouded eyes dug through Bonfire.

"I ain't scared."

Blood pumped from the chewed opening of Bonfire's forearm, coating the pistol as he lowered it. He looked at Willie, thought of the man who took him from his mother.

"No you ain't, boy, no you ain't."

Through fogged vision, Lazarus watched Bonfire's empty hand open, palm up. Offering Willie another choice.

A COON HUNTER'S NOIR

J. W. Duke was choking down his fifth cup of kettle coffee, nursing a hangover, when his wife, Margaret, came through the kitchen door, screaming as if her skin had been pressed through a cheese grater. "J.W.? J.W.?"

His head was swelled up with a fever of pain from the bottle of Old Grand-Dad he'd sucked down the night before. He wrinkled one eye small, viewed her through the one opened wide. "Woman, what the hell are you hollering about?"

Tense, she tells him, "It's Blondie, she's—"

J.W. cut her off. "She's what?"

He hadn't seen her this keyed up since she got the bad news from her doctor about not being able to bring a child into the world. She fired her fury off. "J.W., she's gone!"

People need to understand the severity of the situation. Blondie was a purebred mountain cur. A dog some use to hunt and track bear out west. Being a coon hunter, J.W. had an idea that if a cur could hunt bear out west, why not train it to hunt coons in southern Indiana? Raccoons. See, in southern Indiana coon hunting is as prosperous as Sunday hymns to a Baptist. The meat from a large coon could feed a man a few times and a single hide would bring twenty-five to thirty dollars. To J. W. Duke coon hunting was the damn gospel.

J.W. created a champion bloodline. A top-notch coonhound. Made all those blueticks, redbones, and treeing Walkers look like some Mississippi mutts.

He took a nice chunk of his monthly disability pension from the U.S. Marine Corps for being half deaf in one ear, for being too close in proximity to someone trespassing over a land mine in a rice field back in '68. That was eight years ago. Now he was twenty-eight, had invested that chunk of money into this hound.

J.W. and his hunting buddy, Combs, a man living off an inheritance, drove all the way to Colorado. J.W. had pick of the litter. Paid the breeder cash. Brought the golden cur pup home. He raised her as though she were from his own flesh, like teaching a child to speak, to use their limbs to walk and nourish themselves. He taught Blondie to strike the right scent, tree the correct animal.

He trained her just like his daddy taught him. His daddy was the connoisseur for coon hunting before his choice of permanence. A .38 to the rear of his neck. He'd gotten the depression bug after J.W. left for the Vietnam War and his mother became eaten up with the cancer.

Daddy Duke knew a canine's family bloodline. Which bitch was to be bred with which stud to produce the best hound for hunting. J.W. became the only certified trainer and breeder of mountain curs all through southern Indiana, Kentucky, and Tennessee.

And when J.W. returned home from the war, he met and married Margaret. Soon after, she wanted a child. They had tried and tried until they couldn't stand the sight of each other. Her insides wouldn't take what he was offering. The doctor called it a jigsaw puzzle with too many pieces that didn't mesh.

She'd cursed God for how he'd made her. Told J.W. she'd do anything to change how her insides were. Margaret had become so eaten up with it that J.W. couldn't mention it without her tearing up.

But Margaret warmed up to Blondie like a combine picking corn. One was invented for the purpose of cultivating the other. She took to those big brown eyes and that short velvet coat the color of a cold lager beer. Blondie became their baby girl. Margaret helped J.W. train her. She bathed and brushed Blondie from the pup stages into the adult stages. Took her on her morning walks. Late-evening fetching trials of a ball with a coon hide hidden inside. And even took her into town when running errands, the truck window down, Blondie's head taking in the passing wind with ears flopping like a flag. She taught her the commands: Stay. Sic it. Get 'im, girl. And on those zero nights of winter Margaret brought Blondie into the house, left her to rest at the foot of the bed or next to the wood heat of the Buck Stove.

They took her to coon-hunting contests. Never shy, Margaret mingled with other hunters who knew J.W. and his daddy. A lot of hunters came by the house with good intentions, wanting to breed a hound with their Blondie or wanting J.W. to train one of theirs. They'd pay top dollar. But his daddy taught him not to go training just any man's hound.

Now J.W. is out the door, Margaret following behind, asking, "Where the hell you going?"

He tells her, "To the barn to investigate the situation."

And distraught, she's asking, "What about going to town, getting Mac?"

J.W. cuts her off. "He'll be around sometime this morning, supposed to go fishin' on up over the damn hill with him and Duncan."

"You never mentioned anything 'bout it to me."

"Woman, they's plenty I don't mention to you, and for damn good reason."

Up by the barn, J.W. examines Blondie's run. A circle of gravel J.W. laid that looked like a small horse track so she could trot. Keep the cushions of her paws tough. Cut down on the mud. In the center of the run the soil is damp from a late-night rain shower. Her collage of paw prints leads all around her doghouse, full of fresh cedar chips, to help to keep fleas and ticks at bay. Her chains are unbroken. No dog collar, meaning she's been unleashed by someone.

And J.W. shouts, "Shit!" Telling himself it was only a matter of time before they got her, because he knows some shady son of a bitch has been stealing folk's top-of-the-bloodline hounds for months. And from southern Indiana all through Kentucky and Tennessee this thief will reap top dollar from the right proprietor. All a man's got to do is glance through the ads in the back of a *Full Cry* or *American Cooner*. Find a buyer. That's why J.W. hated to train or breed hounds for just any man. Greed.

As he kneels down, his lip starts twitching, eyes an acidic overcast. J.W. put a lot of time and money into that hound. A ten-pound bag of Ol' Roy or Alpo dog food doesn't come cheap week after week. Let alone catching a coon, trying not to get one of his limbs ripped off. They get kind of pissed when you catch them, take them out of their habitat, put them in a steel-mesh roll cage, similar to a hamster's wheel only it's a cage, so the dog can sniff the coon. Get familiar with its scent. While the coon runs, it rolls the cage. The dog chases it around. That shit takes time. Coming home from the war to a dead daddy, all J.W. had was what his daddy taught him, how to train a hound.

Scaling the terrain of Blondie's run. Surveying the situation. Any overlooked details of sunken paw prints. Prints leading away in another direction. Nothing. Just a lot of loose gravel.

Then, an imprint on the outer edge of the run. Still kneeling down. Lip twitch doubling on the nerves. J.W. knows imprints. Tracked many animals as a young man with a hound at his side. Carried the skill overseas to the war. Foreign soil. Jungle trails of Vietnam. A recon tunnel rat. J.W. and a shepherd hound tagged as Merck One-Eight, distinguishing boots from sandals. Learned mud was mud regardless of continent. It became his specialty. Two of them tracking the Vietcong to their underground supply tunnels in Cu Chi. Smoking their Commie asses out.

Standing off to the side, Margaret asks, "What is it, J.W.?"

On the inner edge of the run there's another imprint. Imprints don't lie. It's not his or hers and it ain't canine. Ignoring Margaret, J.W. inhales slowly and deeply. He takes in the details. Boot, size twelve. Not ours. Overpriced Red Wing. No comfort. No support. He knows it and knows it well. Those details make the bad boil over. And all that bad in there from the war doesn't simmer down. It's like a strong case of chicken pox or poison ivy, has to run its course.

Something clicks in his brain.

And the worry in Margaret's voice insisting, "J.W., I ain't asking you again, the hell is it?"

Taking a Lucky Strike from his black-and-brown-checkered flannel's breast pocket to his anger-twitched lip. His thumbnail to an Ohio Blue Tip. A match that strikes a flame on any surface. J.W. firing up the unfiltered smoke into his lungs and saying, "Woman, we got ourselves one greedy stain of a shit heel."

Going into the white-brick milk house that's attached to the ocean-blue barn, about the size of a spare bedroom, glancing at the shovels, axes, mulls, sledgehammers, corn knives, and machetes. J.W. doesn't want to chop the man's ass up like cornmeal. Just facilitate consequences for actions, payback for thieving his hound. Grabbing a can of leaded fuel, the fox traps, the type of trap that if a man were to step in, he'd never walk a straight line again. Let alone limp one. He'd attain to be a stutter-stepping son of a bitch for stealing a man's dog.

Putting everything in the rusted rear of his orange International Harvester Scout. Going into the house. Straight to his bedroom closet. Pulling his chipped military green metal box down off the top shelf. Opening it, taking out his Springfield Armory .45-caliber Colt. The same model he used overseas to decide a man's permanence. Has a recoil that can dislocate a common man's shoulder.

Pulling the slide, shelling a piece of brass filled with gunpowder and lead into the chamber, Margaret coming into the room and telling him, "Quit acting the fool. Just go find Mac, let him handle this."

Pushing the .45 down the back of his worn-for-hardwork dungarees, looking into her face. She's calm as a clear blue sky. But not J.W.; when he's hopped up this high on hate, any pleas from the opposition are like the Vietnam jungles. Foreign. Telling Margaret, "Done told you he'd be here this morning to fish. 'Sides, the only fool will be the man I'm paying an unexpected visit to."

Margaret looking on, fed up. "Guess all that orange you ate over there done fried that brain of yours to plumb crazy."

Outside, J.W. is placing his .45 in the Scout's glove box when Marty MacCullum pulls up. Locks up the brakes of his cruiser, throwing gravel from the driveway.

His laugh insane and high-pitched, he sounds like an untamed rodent shrieking from a large leather sack. Mac greets him, "Where the hell you going so damn early? Thought you, me, and Duncan's goin' fishin'?"

J.W.'s lip twitches with a distaste for wasted words and he tells him, "Something personal's come up."

Marty, everyone calls him Mac for short, is Mauckport's town marshal. Not a town clown or county mountie. An odd man who keeps odd hours, with a twisted sense of humor and a taste for the brew. He's older but like J.W. he's got a dark section of mind that others have no business trespassing on.

He and J.W. use the three hundred acres of private property that J.W.'s daddy left him in his will after making a mess of his mental state. They hunt and toss back brews, shoot the shit while treeing coons into the midnight hour at least once a week, and they fish on down along the Ohio River every so often because a good portion of J.W.'s property borders it.

With wild eyes hidden behind mirrored specs, pushed tight over his scarred pits of a cracked-clay face, spitting some Red Man chew, Mac throws back a tin-can swallow of Pabst Blue Ribbon. Savors it with the filthy sound effects of a lip-pounding pucker and asks, "Anything I can help with, J.W.?"

J.W. tells him, "Like I said, it's personal."

Mac says, "Well then, want one for the road? It's last one and ice-sickle cold."

J.W.'s mind is boiling and he starts to mention Blondie, but it's got to be his way and he says, "Better not."

While J.W. fires up the Scout, Mac throws back another swallow and laughs, passes on that shady sense of humor and says, "You ain't gone cold turkey on the brew during morning hours, have you, J.W.? Having them withdrawals? Corner your lips about to jab your eyeball out of its socket."

Closing his eyes, J.W. shakes his head. His brain rattles in his eardrum like loose buckshot. This conversation's holding him up. Blondie could be headed to another state by now.

Mac throws back another swallow. Savoring that tin-can taste, Mac says, "You're going mute on me, J.W. If this 'something' got you all worked up, maybe I should come along. Help out a friend."

J.W. comes clean, tells Mac, "I might've found the person been stealing the hounds, but if I'm wrong there's no sense in you coming along, making a scene."

Mac mashes the tin. Tosses it onto the floorboard of his cruiser. Pops his last Pabst open, glances toward the barn, looks back at J.W., and says, "Well, I be damn, no wonder you's all worked up. You trained many of them dogs that got stole. A man might look the other way so a friend could have a debriefing with the thief. Guess I best radio Duncan, see when he's comin' down to fish. Says he's gonna meet us in his boat."

J.W. tells Mac, "Appreciate it." And he offers, "There's two cases of Pabst in the house's fridge. Help yourself."

Laughing, Mac continues, "Here I thought you'd gone retard on me, son, that eye flaring up. See you in a bit."

J.W. puts the Scout into drive. His lip twitching into his eye, he glances at Mac, nods. Stamps the gas. Pelts Mac's cruiser with loose gravel.

Everything a man survives in life is a lesson. Some lessons are taken, others are given. What J.W. learned from the war carries over to everyday life. Men lie. Men die. And one thing J. W. Duke can't tolerate is lies. Trying to swallow why this leech of a man would go cross on him, reasoning says he's been living off that family money too long. An inheritance from his deceased doctor daddy. He's a few years older than J.W. but never had to work a day in his life. Inherited everything he's got. And what he's gotten is greedy from never having to work for anything. Thinks he's entitled. Decided to steal J.W.'s hound and prosper from it.

Parking the Scout. Getting out. Tucking the .45 down the back of his dungarees, grabbing the can of fuel. Slinging the traps over his shoulder.

He should have paid more attention to all the times he went coon hunting with Combs. Always using J.W.'s hound. Driving his truck. Drinking his Pabst Blue Ribbon. Son of a bitch never packed his own lunch, always shared his bologna sandwich with the freeloading prick. Combs would laugh, call it a poor man's steak sandwich, while they listened to the bawl of the hound striking the trail. Then the echo through the valley of trees when the dog treed the coon. Then came the long walk through the woods, up and down the gullies and hills, deciphering the direction of the barking. Lugging a .22 rifle, battery clipped on his side to power the hunting light attached to his head like a caver's. Most hunters hoped their dog had struck the right trail, hadn't run a squirrel or possum up a tree. Those types of hunters didn't know the old ways to break a hound like J.W.'s daddy had taught him.

Sometimes J.W. climbed the tree once he spotted the coon's eyes reflecting the light while it hunkered up in the limbs. He'd knock the coon to the ground, let his hound battle the hiss and claw of it, get a good taste of battle before he killed it. Other times he'd shoot it from the tree. J.W. preferred both ways to keep his hound in check.

The more J.W. went over it in his head, he realized every time Combs and he went hunting, Combs would be breaking him down, wanting to get him into a partnership. A deal that involved breeding Blondie with one of his hounds. Talking about how big a wad of dough the two of them could make off her bloodline with the pups, six to eight hundred dollars a dog. Even pressuring Margaret to sway him. Filling her head full of false beliefs about getting rich from J.W.'s knowledge.

Telling her about his connection with a doctor, a specialist who had a second opinion about her insides. How extra cash could pay for surgery to fix her damage. The whole time J.W.'s telling both of them *no*.

Now J.W. surveys the surrounding hickory trees with leaves veined and green shading the rectangular sandstones of Combs's home, the ferns that decorate the perimeters of attack like plants in a jungle. J.W. walking up next to Combs's black Chevy Bronco. Inside, a bag is packed, flashlights and power packs attached to spotlights, the rubber floor covered with mud. Bastard never offered to drive when the two of them hunted. But he can drive to J.W.'s home. Filch J.W.'s hound while he's passed out drunk. Pack up his Blondie. J.W. knows what Combs is planning to do. Thinks he'll breed Blondie with different hounds for quick cash from state to state, charge a lot of money and a cut on the pups.

Up the creek-rock pathway, smears of mud draw J.W.'s eyes up the steps of the planed cedar porch, where dried gourds hang orange and yellow. Up by the front door an old cola machine sits red, white, and rusted with a cracked glass side door. Down beside it lie muddy boots. Red Wing. Size twelve.

Up next to the side of the house, kneeling below the dining room window. Lip twitching into his eye.

Back pushed against Combs's home, J.W. turns and peeks in, seeing Combs's location, but no sign of Blondie. His heart's pounding with the influx of enmity. The bastard's seated at a table littered with newspapers and magazines. Calm as a crustacean. That harelip smirk he postures as a stupid smile. Having his last breakfast. Shoveling chunks of egg into his mouth. Yolk cobwebbing down his thorny beard of a chin.

Kneeling back down, J.W. shakes his head, thinking Blondie was the only thing he had left from his dead daddy and Combs went and stole all that time and knowledge.

J.W. removes the cap from the can of gas, staying low to the ground and walking backwards, saturating the perimeter of the home. Leaving space between fuel and sandstone. Enough to get his attention. Giving a gap. To get this Vietcong out of his hole, he's gotta give him some heat.

He takes a front-row seat to confrontation, standing in

front of Combs's home, on his creek-rock path. Empty can of leaded fuel on the ground. Fox traps in front of him. Open. Ready to bite.

Flint to flame. J.W. inhales his Lucky Strike. Lets it dangle from his lip, .45 Colt in hand. Safety in the unsafe setting. Taking a last deep lung-gagging draw, he tells himself, This is for my daddy, then he gives the Lucky Strike a middle-finger-to-thumb flick through the air to the fuel-soaked ground. The trail leading around Combs's stone shelter. Lighting up in arcs all the way around the home.

Combs busts out of his front door, denim pants half buttoned and cream-colored belly hanging. Holding a single-barrel shotgun. His energy's a big blast of napalm. Buckles down the steps of his porch barefooted. Mouth packed with food. Hollering, "Crazy son of a bitch, you done lost your mind?" Food particles rain like confetti with his words. He raises his shotgun and his eyes meet J.W.'s.

Those huts. The way a Commie would come out screaming some foreign-tongued mojo. Never did a damn bit of good. Combs has no sense as he shuffles toward J.W. dumbfounded, left foot first into the center of a fox trap. Like a heavy book smacking a hardwood floor just right. Loud. Would send a shiver of numbness up a person's back. J.W. watches the metal break denim, puncture flesh, dig into bone. Blood bleeds through. Combs is screaming like a boar hog being castrated. Drops the shotgun.

J.W. aims the .45 at Combs. The arc of fuel-induced flames is dying down. Smoldering. J.W. spits, "Planning a trip with my damn hound? Maybe breed her for profit?"

Combs's eyes water down his thorn-stubbled cheeks and he cries, "You dumb son of a bitch."

Ready to give a cold steel alignment to his speech, refresh Combs's tone, put a bit of truth back onto his tongue, J.W. says, "Last chance, Combs, where's Blondie?"

Whining like a pup being weaned from its mama's tit, he says, "I ain't got your damn dog!"

When J.W. asked why Combs did what he did, Combs said, "Money." Combs had blown all of his daddy's inheritance. He started filching top-bred coonhounds for a guaranteed fifty-fifty split.

Seeing Blondie missing, J.W. was supposed to have gone into town to find Mac. Of course, Mac hides out and binges a lot of booze on Saturdays, and J.W. would never have found him; everyone would have been long gone by the time they got back. The only problem was Mac and he had fishing plans.

Combs thought he had time for one last meal before skipping town. He more or less did.

Now, J.W. is back home. Out of the truck, .45 in hand, going into the house. Bloody footprints have redecorated the kitchen. A slaughtered steer.

He follows the trail of blood up behind the barn to Mac's cruiser. All around the trunk. The surrounding perimeter. Traces of red. Last option: go to the woods, up the hill, down to the Ohio River.

He reaches the bottom of the hill. Winded. Mental state moving a mile a minute. One part focused, one part pain. Anger pelts his insides. Trying to hold it together, hoping he's not too late, glancing at the cabin his daddy built for fishing, camping out. To get away.

His heart's trying to find a way out of his chest. Foot to

the cabin door. Bursting it open, .45 raised. Stepping inside. Glancing down, a wave of relief.

There she is laid out, those soft brown eyes weak, weeping to a muffled whine. She's still doped up, barely raising her head to acknowledge J.W., her salvation. Then he recognizes the hammer pull in the rear of his skull. Six rounds of a .357 Smith & Wesson. Mac's handgun. Followed by the words of a two-timing female. "Don't make me open your thought process just yet, J.W. Drop the gun."

J.W. drops the .45.

Her words are piercing and to the point. "Didn't see it coming, did you?"

All these years and she breaks their vows and he says, "How the shit could you do this?"

"Easy money. Combs tried to persuade you. You wouldn't give an inch. So we devised a partnership with a guy goes by the name Puerto Rican Pete. Deals in dogs for dogfighting. Does it by boat on the Ohio for the Evans family, they been doin' it for generations."

Not sold for hunting, sold for fighting.

The pressure in J.W.'s chest is a pitchfork stabbing a bale of hay. His mind still catching up, he says, "Made it easy seeing as how our property borders the Ohio River."

Margaret tells him, "This morning figured you'd go to town and search for Mac, I'd be long gone 'fore you got back."

How could this female help train and care for Blondie, then just throw it all away? J.W. wonders how long he'd been living a lie. And Margaret says, "'Course, between you finding a boot print and Mac coming by, I had no way of warning Combs 'cause J.W. has no need for a phone."

J.W. tries slinging some dirt her way and says, "Too bad about Combs, he had a hard time explaining all the details with his foot caught in a fox trap."

With no compassion, she laughs. "Poor Combs."

Remembering the mess Margaret left in the house, J.W. tenses up, remembers the last words his friend said, "See you in a bit." He asks, "What about Mac?"

She says, "Son of a bitch come in the house for some beer, I'm bringing Blondie from the basement into the kitchen. Tell him she's sick. He has his head in the fridge, grabbing a few of your Pabst. I grabbed a butcher knife. Gave it to him quick."

J.W.'s mind is quivering with loss, betrayal, and anger as he musters, "All this for some cash?"

She tells him, "More than money, for that doctor Combs told us about that could fix my jigsaw-puzzle insides, one you said we couldn't afford. Selling hounds done paid him in full. Sorry, J.W., your simple ways of living went stale."

She laughs again, tells him to turn around. "Wanna see how proud you are when I shoot you in your face."

Before turning around, J.W. smiles at Blondie. She's all laid out on the floor, all that time using what his daddy taught him, all that knowledge waiting to be sold for a profit, his heartbeat matching the pounding of blood in his brain from hearing all the facts from his deceptive wife's lips. He turns around. Face-to-face. She says, "Goodbye." He closes his eyes. Grits his teeth. Balls his fists. Wants to react. To take all of his confused hurt and loss, use it against her when his ears go deaf. His face goes warm. But his knees don't give.

.

Mac radioed Duncan. Gave him the heads-up before going to J.W.'s house, told him he was on his way to the cabin for some drinking and fishing. Duncan packed a handgun off duty, and seeing Margaret had put pressure between J.W.'s eyes with a .357, there was no time for second thoughts. Duncan aimed and pulled the trigger, made J.W. a widower.

J.W. got three to five in the Indiana State Prison for attempted murder. His residence, a six-by-six man-made concrete box with bunk beds. Steel bars. He'd get three squares a day. Plenty of time to lift weights, read books, get free tattoos and enough male bonding to make a man sick. Duncan promised to take care of Blondie. Keep all that knowledge his daddy gave him safe.

AMPHETAMINE
TWITCH

Alejandro's knuckles sprayed backdoor glass across kitchen tile. His fingers twisted red on the doorknob and dead bolt. He maneuvered through the kitchen and down a dark hallway of family-framed walls with his scabbed skin and hair salved over his head in all directions. Stepped into a bedroom where a silhouette sat up from a bed. Alejandro's breath was suffocated by the sudden movement like a large quilt smothering a fire.

A voice yawned, "You're home early."

Tasting fear, Alejandro panicked, pointed the 9 mm. His chewed and blackened finger pulled the trigger once. Twice. Shadows fragmented upon the bedroom walls. The silhouette thudded onto the carpet.

Footsteps drummed like soldiers marching down the hallway behind Alejandro. He turned with the gun raised, his free hand digging into his neck, scratching for a fix. He leveled the 9 mm on the small outline that screamed, "Mom!" Alejandro gritted his teeth and said, "Should not be here." Warmed the child's insides. Silenced his screams.

Amphetamine hunger pained through Alejandro's brain as he pushed the pistol down the front of the jeans that hung on him like a used painter's cloth, rifled through the dresser drawers. Socks. Bras. Panties. Nothing of worth. He screamed, "No, no, no!"

In the closet he found a Beretta .380, stuffed it down the back of his pants. On a chair in the corner he found a purse. Dumped it out onto the carpet. Saw the wallet, kneeled down, opened it. Found a wad of bills. Pay dirt.

He exited the bedroom to the hallway. Cleared the child whose lungs heaved. Alejandro diminished like a dream.

Detective Mitchell's charred hair matched the bags beneath his vision of flesh gift-wrapping bone. His black tie hung loose from the open neck of the white button-up. The bottle of Jim Beam met his lips. Eroded his guilt.

"Should've stayed home that night," he mumbled. He'd been catfishing in the late hours of morning down on the Blue River, checking the plastic fishing jugs he'd hidden down in the deeper honey holes, when he heard the crunch of gravel and limbs. Saw the lights firing up the bank and surrounding trees. A truck engine stopped. A door slammed an echo down off the water. And then that familiar voice yelled, "Mitchell?"

Getting out of the water, tugging on the rope attached to his johnboat. Even without a flashlight the full moon highlighted Sergeant Moon's complexion while his words hollowed Mitchell's being with the news.

Wife. Son. Shot by a burglar. DOA.

Though he policed a small town, Mitchell had seen a lot in fifteen years of service. Bodies floating in the Blue River. Domestic disputes where beer-breathed men gave purple abrasions, cracked marrow, and lipstick-red welts to a woman's flesh with their fists. Cars wrapped around trees where bodies were removed with no pulse. And in the past few years everything had become tense. Meth had scourged the land. Made working-class folk less human. More criminal. He'd even busted a member of the Mara Salvatrucha, which nearly cost him his rank for going behind law enforcement's back, doing his own intel without written consent from the higher-ups.

But at the county hospital, seeing his son laid out like meat in a walk-in freezer, cold innocence removed of character, changed him. Then his wife. His crutch after a homicide, the person who recorded his every word when he spoke of the unsolved thieving or killing of the innocent. She never offered judgment, only listened, gave him space when he needed it most. Now she was gone.

Mitchell shook his head, taking in the hallway of his home. Two bullets opened the drywall where his son found his end. Dried innards smeared from wall to floor. Mitchell knew State Police Forensics had collected a mess of blood evidence. Ballistics would take a few weeks.

Entering the bedroom, Mitchell swigged the bottle of bourbon, saw the clothes hanging from dresser drawers. Looked at where his wife had dropped from the bed, soiled the carpet. Forensics would never find who had done this.

Glancing into the open closet, he noticed the empty shelf, and it came as quick as losing his family. His backup gun was missing.

Alejandro was on all fours, mistaking carpet lint for crystal. Around him, bony-framed men whose faces reeked of malnourishment slept in sleeping bags on the body-soured carpet and matching couch.

Scuff marks and fist- and foot-sized holes decorated the walls of the shack like second-grade graffiti.

Alejandro placed a piece of lint over the pin-needle holes on top of the aluminum can he held between middle finger and thumb. His other hand flicked a flame. His mouth huffed on the opening but got nothing.

His hair was the shade of creosote, melding to his pot-holed face and bored-out eyes. He'd chewed the skin from his lips, creating miniature puddles of blood. Fingernails tracked up and down his arms, which had become like his lips. Sleeping was twitching until his crave jerked his orbs open, raising him from rest in a sweat-bathed shower of self.

He'd been holed up for a week with a new crop of illegals in the one-bedroom shack. Men with frayed ends and raisin features plastered like the dead on a battlefield across the room. He'd tried sleeping in the day. Smoked his meth while others slept at night. Now the meth was gone, just like the money from the last robbery, of the woman and child he'd shot, though that didn't seem real. The only thing that felt real was firing the chemical and letting that jolt of electricity smoke his mind as he chased that feeling from the first time.

On the couch Alejandro's hands patted through a man's pockets in search of money. The man blinked his bug-eyed whites awake with horror. He covered Alejandro's left eye with five knuckles. Falling backwards on the carpet, Alejandro pulled the 9 mm from his waist. Pointed it at the man, whose eyes sparked white. Two shots opened his chest.

The gunfire pierced the surrounding ears and pulled

their eyes open. Alejandro didn't quit pulling the trigger until the gun was empty.

It was a long shot, but Mitchell tossed the piece of paper on the counter of Joe's Pawnshop.

Dressed in a hole-worn Drive-By Truckers T-shirt, Joe blinked his razor-thin eyes and twisted the gnarly hairs of his ungroomed collie beard between index finger and thumb. Mitchell's bourbon breath irritated Joe's face, reminded him of paint-thinner fumes as he picked up the paper.

"Serial numbers?"

"For a .380—"

Joe shook his opal skull, the shaggy braids that went from chin to chest. Cut Mitchell off. "Beretta. Polymer grip. Matte black. Seven rounds plus one in the chamber. I got the fiddle. You got the banjo. We can stomp down some sweet tunes."

It was no longer a long shot.

"Who pawned the son of a bitch?"

Joe glanced up about the wall as though he'd hidden the answer behind a radio or tennis racket and said, "Don't 'member his name."

Mitchell laid his detective's badge on the counter.

"White? Black? Asian—"

"Mexican guy with a tweaker. Mexican was clean-cut. Runs that authentic restaurant up the hill. Usually there from daylight to dark. Got a kick-ass lunch special. Dollar beers and Margaritas on Thursday nights. Never seen the tweaker before."

"Where's the gun?"

Joe turned away. Unlocked a metal cabinet behind him.

"Shit fire, should've said you's a cop, I got it right here."

"What about footage?"

"No smut tapes here, Officer."

Mitchell wanted a make on the Mexican. Pointed up in the corner behind the counter.

"Surveillance footage of the guy who sold the gun."

Laying the gun on the counter, Joe answered in a confused voice, "Yeah, sure. But I done told you it was the Mexican guy from on the hill."

"I need a positive ID."

Mitchell picked up the gun. Matched the serial numbers.

"I'm taking the gun for evidence. Now, show me the footage of the Mexican. I'll need it and today's footage to take with me."

"Take with you?"

"Yeah, I was never here so we never had this conversation. These last few minutes have been one big fuckin' blur, got it?"

Alejandro pulled into the small town's pay-by-the-week flop, slop, and drop motel. He stepped from the idling Buick. His complexion was greasy dishwater with eyes floating in fire. His head twitched, shoulders jerked, while his hand went from etching open old wounds to fisting a door dotted by body fluids.

A chain rattled. A lock clicked. The door cracked open with the television bouncing light and conversation. The smell of hot chemicals boiling in rubbing alcohol wafted behind a single brown eye spiked with blood. The other eye was missing.

"How much crystal you need?"

The white chalked-up corners of Alejandro's broken English said, "Another hundred dollar worth."

The door closed. Alejandro's hands balled into his sweatshirt pockets. He glanced down the concrete walk. Darkness hummed. Window curtains of connecting rooms parted in the corners. Eyes and noses smudged glass, breathing fogged it, making Alejandro's palms damp.

The door opened back up, a bit wider than before. One hand held a small brown paper sack. Another hand reached out, open palm, wiggling four fingers minus a thumb. And the raspy chain-smoking voice said, "Cash."

Alejandro slid his right foot between jamb and door. Pulled the 9 mm from his sweatshirt pocket. Pointed it at the single brown eye. The first shot added more decorations to the door. The body dropped backwards. Alejandro stepped on it. Entered the flop-drop meth factory. A shadow fought movement from the bed. The second and third shots deformed the shadow, let it keep the bed weighted down.

Alejandro flipped the light switch on the wall. Plastic sandwich bags full of ice crystal covered a metal table next to the bed, beside wrinkled empty sacks. Sweating for a fix, he slid the 9 mm into his waist. Removed his hooded sweatshirt and piled the bags into the body of it. Picked the pockets of the ones he'd paid with bullets. Threw their crumpled bills in with the bags. Tied the sweatshirt into a ball. Picked it up. Ran out to the Buick, already imagining the crystalline chunks ricocheting behind his eyes as the car turned out onto Highway 62.

Headlights flared off the yellow-and-green concrete building's glass windows. A car door drummed in the parking lot. The brass bell rang above the entrance door, which Gaspar had forgotten to lock. He looked up from cashing out the restaurant's register and a gloved hand introduced his forehead to the butt of a .45-caliber SIG SAUER. His knees went liquid. His mind fogged in and out, feeling the twist of arms behind his back. The clamp and click of metal around his wrists.

Red warmed the parted flesh above Gaspar's blinking eyes. Metal burrowed into the back of his neck, his face pressed into the still-warm surface of the grill in the kitchen. A handgun filled his view.

Mitchell's gloved hand tightened around the pistol. "I'll ask you one time. You and some tweaker sold the gun you're looking at to the pawnshop down the hill. Where'd you get the gun?"

Gaspar took a deep breath. Pondered the blood relation to the man he'd smuggled to America.

"I'm businessman. Come to America to run business."

"Sure, the American fuckin' dream."

Mitchell reached to his left, twisted the knob below the gas burner to high. A blue-orange flame hissed. He slid the Sig down his pants. Clamped both hands into Gaspar's black wad of grease. Slowly pressed his face toward the hiss.

Like a dog that didn't want to lead, Gaspar's head tried to fight Mitchell's grip. Begged.

"No! No! Please!"

"The gun. Where'd you get it?"

With no answer, the orange hiss heated Mitchell's hand. Warmed his forearm. Gaspar's brown skin curled black like melted plastic. Tears fell and sputtered off the blue heat rimming the orange. Mitchell thought about his wife and son. Pushed Gaspar until he thought his leather gloves would ignite.

"My brother! My brother!"

He pulled and turned Gaspar around. Mucus spread like poison ivy from nose to mouth. Tears ticked over the gooey gum-colored boil pushing from the black burn on Gaspar's cheek. Fear flowed hot down his leg. Puddled onto the floor. Mitchell grabbed the stolen gun.

"This gun you sold, stolen from my house. Your brother, where the fuck is he?"

In the shack, fluorescent lights hugged the loaded needle trespassing in Alejandro's vein. No smoking tonight. He'd more than enough to shoot for days. His thumb pushed the plunger. Endorphins swam and multiplied in his brain. Eyes darted with black pupils hiding the hazel as he pulled the needle from his arm. His tongue ran over eroding teeth and said, "You guys need try. Some good shit."

He waited for a reply from the bodies that lay scattered and stiff against the walls, dressed with matching bullet holes, scented with the waft of bladders gone slack.

Some had heads resting on shoulders. Others bent forward, chin into chest. Mouths trapped in a permanent yawn with lips changing to the shade of fruit juice.

He placed the needle in a glass of water clouded by crystal. On the coffee table, where Ziplocs stuffed with jagged chunks of amphetamine lay like homemade Halloween treats. He loaded another fix as the front door opened. Gaspar limped onto the carpet, his arms behind his back. Blood and bruises disguised his appearance.

Alejandro barked, "Gaspar!"

Mitchell's heel stomped the bend behind Gaspar's knee. "Heel, shit bag!"

Enraged, Alejandro jumped up deuce-eyed. Stormed Mitchell with the loaded needle in hand.

Mitchell raised his .45, squeezed the trigger, cubed meat from Alejandro's chest.

On a full-blown meth rush Alejandro gritted his stalactite teeth, smothered Mitchell into a wall. Grabbed for the gun with his free hand. Stabbed the needle into Mitchell's jugular with his other. "Fuck!" Mitchell hollered. Alejandro thumbed the plunger. Liquid roared a surge of strength through Mitchell's veins. He pushed the .45 toward Alejandro, the barrel over his foot. Squeezed the trigger. Separated the toes of Alejandro's foot. Alejandro fell backwards. Mitchell leveled the .45, felt the rush of amphetamines ignite his bloodstream, took in the blanched eyes and finger carvings that shaped Alejandro's face, then he removed it. Pulled the needle from his neck. Turned and lowered the .45 on Gaspar, who lay screaming on the floor like the amphetamine twitch behind Mitchell's dilating eyes.

He glanced at the dead in the room, their frames beginning to bloat, the smell full-on rot bordering on decay. Pointing the pistol at Gaspar, who was filling Mitchell's ears with everything but English, Mitchell shook his head, said, "No."

Sacks of crystal lay across the coffee table, a needle loaded with the water matrix of an amphetamine rush. Mitchell pulled the needle from the table, smiled, and said to Gaspar, "Yeah, this'll fix your illegal smugglin' ass."

In his car, Mitchell's face calmed, the amphetamines bringing a peace within his mind, a high unlike booze, and his life felt almost calm in the tsunami rush. His ache of loss had been quarantined, for a bit. Gaspar's screams lined his brain, barking as Mitchell had driven the needle into his arm, emptied it into his vein. Refilled it and emptied it again, until Gaspar's eyes were bright white gumballs in his sockets. Mitchell shifted his vehicle into drive, glanced at the bags filled with what looked like broken glass on the seat beside him, knowing he could chase this stiffening jolt of endorphins for a couple days and forget who he was, but never what he'd lost.

OLD TESTAMENT WISDOM

If men strive, and hurt a woman with child, so that her fruit depart from her, and yet no mischief follow: he shall be surely punished, according as the woman's husband will lay upon him; and he shall pay as the judges determine.

And if any mischief follow, then thou shalt give life for life,

Eye for eye, tooth for tooth, hand for hand, foot for foot,

Burning for burning, wound for wound, stripe for stripe.

—Exodus 21:22–25

In ten years bruises would heal externally. Not internally. Knuckles would flatten from not wearing hand wraps or bag gloves. Scabs would become scars from beating the same green army bag that a man hung from a dusty basement rafter for the girl. But now the girl sat within the darkness, glancing out the bug-spattered windshield at the rusted tin building across the road. While those same knuckles double-checked the bullet-filled clip of the .45-caliber Colt.

The man who'd hung the green army bag was the one who'd raised her. Taught her how to twist punches into the bag with her hips at an early age. Taught her how to sight, load, and shoot a gun. The man taught her about Old Testament wisdom. It was something that the outline seated next to her in the darkness had never been accepted into before that week in late September. That was when the man who'd raised her had his flesh go from sun-beaten leather to a melted one-gallon plastic milk container. After his wounds healed and he was released from the hospital, he had time to serve.

Her family lost everything. They moved in with her great-uncle. But during that week, men were beaten and disfigured while others lost their lives. And this is how it all started. Ten years ago with a touch.

Jacque's heart pumped blood black like a dead opossum bloated by the sun on back-road pavement when Abby rolled up her sleeves. Bruises fingerprinted the buttermilk flesh of her arms.

His flat-knuckled fist vibrated the table. His eyes were a Case XX carving into Abby's.

"Who did this?"

Abby's upper lip quivered as she sat with the memory of hands marring her skin. Of panting breath scented like hog manure warming the side of her neck. Lips pleading, "STOP!" She sat with that memory ingrained behind her moss-green eyes as they bubbled with the fear that it was her fault. Chewed fingernails pushed her fudge-colored locks over her ear and she said, "Hersey did it. I'm sorry, Grandpa Bocart. He said it was a game. I didn't mean to—"

Anna May grasped Abby's shoulders from behind as Jacque bent forward, holding Abby's hands within the grit of his trembling lifeline.

"You got nothing to be sorry for."

Jacque inhaled the secondhand smoke from his daughter Avis's coffin nail. His mind exploded with buckshot, imagining Abby's stolen innocence. Avis sat at the kitchen table, rolling her fogged-over eyes within the oval shapes of running mascara as if to say "the hell you looking at?"

Reminded of how many times he'd warned Avis about taking Abby around to Medford Malone's salvage yard, Jacque released Abby's cotton hands. Stood and turned to Avis. No words. Just his flat-knuckled fist planted into her remorseless features, knocking her against the wall. She exploded, "Son of a bitch!"

Jacque scalded back, "That's for taking my granddaughter around that crankhead and his deviant son while you get blasted on that shit!"

He knelt back down to Abby, knowing he had to ask what he didn't want to know. Anna May felt Abby shaking from what she'd just witnessed and told her, "It's okay, Abby, Grandpa's just angry at who did this."

Jacque's gray slits burned an unrecognized fear through Abby, charcoaled her insides as he gritted his teeth. "What did he do to you?"

Hersey didn't hear the black-primered no-muffler Chevy S10 roar into the gravel lot. He just sat at the Leavenworth Tavern. Lean and wired like an electric fence. Poe the bartender served him another Jack and Coke. Johnny Cash blared from the jukebox with "Folsom Prison Blues." Hersey had his back to the entrance. Karl Bean sat scented like a peeled onion on one side of him, sprinkling salt into a Falls City beer. Bubble-lipped Ty Wilkerson sat on the other, sipping an Old Style. And like everyone else in the Leavenworth Tavern, they were two simple names associated with the wisdom of the land; they knew when to mind their own.

Stale cigarette smoke accompanied Jacque as he walked through the entrance to the bar, stepped to the stool where his left hand gripped Hersey's right shoulder. Jacque offered no words. Just four fingers digging into lean tissue. His thumb guiding the turning around. His unflinching gray eyes burrowing into Hersey, who was all piss and vinegar, spouting, "Who the hell—"

Ty and Karl grabbed their beers. Swiveled their stools. Work boots met the scuffed hardwood floor and they separated like cockroaches, smelling the onslaught that was about to paint the bar's interior.

Jacque's right hand slapped Hersey's lips into his yellow teeth, drawing first blood down his peach-pitted chin. Ty stood a few stools down, watching and chugging his Old Style with his right work boot tapping to the strum of Johnny Cash's voice. Bobbing his head. Watching Hersey's features part from Jacque's flow of violence. Jacque drove his left fist down onto Hersey's nose, dissipating the cartilage. Then pounded Hersey's left eye into an olive-textured slit. Hersey grunted. Pleaded with pain. Jacque spun him around on his stool to face the bar. Dug both hands into the rear of Hersey's oil-thick tresses. Ricocheted his face off the sticky stains and cigarette burns.

Karl stood at the other end of the bar in his work-worn bibs, grinding his bare gums. Watched Jacque Bocart exit the Leavenworth Tavern the same way he'd entered: without a word. Karl walked over to where Hersey lay whimpering. The ruby fluid of his insides dripped from the bar. Decorated the hardwood. His face blistered with abrasions. His teeth were a shattered windshield, scattered about his mouth in red-white shards. Karl shook his head. Behind the bar Poe talked on the phone to an operator about needing an ambulance. Ty walked over and said, "God almighty," then chugged his Old Style. Karl said, "I didn't see anything, did you?"

And Ty replied, "Not a damn thing."

Jacque came through the kitchen door and onto the porch when he heard the cruiser's engine humming to a halt. Behind him in the house, Anna May, Abby, and Avis sat at the kitchen table eating a late supper. Jacque stood with his tight salt-and-pepper stubble and leathery face hidden beneath the shadow of his worn John Deere cap, watching the outline step from the cruiser.

Billy Hines, the town marshal, dabbed his forehead with a sour-scented hanky and said, "Evening, Jacque."

"Evening, Billy."

"Hate to show up unannounced, but Medford Malone's boy Hersey got hisself beat into stewed meat earlier today at the tavern. Seen you cruising out of town about the time I got the call. Thought I'd stop by. See if you seen anything?"

"Just a gas pump. Needed gas in the truck."

"So you didn't stop at the tavern?"

"Can't say that I did. Why? Don't you got no witnesses?"

"Funny you'd ask that, 'cause Poe, Karl, nor Ty seen a thing even though Poe called it in while the others sat feeding their livers. Last thing Hersey remembers was sipping his Jack and Coke. Least that's what I think he stuttered."

Jacque laughed to himself, knowing that regardless of who had been in the tavern when he touched Hersey they'd not breathe a word to Hines. They kept their mouths shut when a conflict occurred between families. Let them settle it with scorn.

"Maybe he touched someone so they touched him back."

"You mean an eye for an eye. Tooth for a tooth."

"Old Testament wisdom."

"Why you say that, Jacque?"

"I know how young men are at that age. Do things without any regard to backlash. We were young once. Ignored the doctrines of existence."

Marshal Hines leaned back against his cruiser's hood and fished a coffin nail from his shirt pocket. Flicked a flame and puckered a thick breath of smoke. Blew it from his nose, knowing Jacque was hiding something. He had kept a stone face when Hines told him what had happened. Didn't even try to act surprised. Hines said, "We was damn good friends, Jacque."

"Until you decided to become Johnny Law."

"It's just a job. And right now that job is finding out who did this to Hersey and why, before Medford does. 'Cause Medford is a copperhead with his tail tied to a stake right now. Unable to escape; pissed off. If you know something, I suggest you cough it up."

Before going back into the house, Jacque told Hines with a smirk, "I hear anything on the party line or otherwise, I know how to get in touch."

Rusted ringer washers. Gas stoves. Dry rotted tires and busted television sets decorated the flat rock hollows. The country yards of rusted trailers and broken-down farmhouses with abandoned red clay tractors. Vehicles on cinder blocks. It was the poor man's fairy tale of rural survival. Hines could smell the survival's waste like the sweat that his pores excreted as he sped down the valley road.

He'd been born and raised here. Knew Jacque was a farmer with blood relations to the Hill Clan. That Medford ran a junkyard-salvage and held court with the Evans family. He knew each man wasn't to be crossed. He'd run with each of them. They'd once accepted him as their own, until he became an officer who would not be bribed. Then town marshal. They'd considered him an outsider for nearly eighteen years. He knew the small population of families within Leavenworth were so tight with one another that when one of them pissed, another's eyes blinked.

They had their own wisdom when dealing with one another that excluded the law he was paid to enforce. He knew something had gone cross with Jacque and Medford. But with no one talking, all he could do was wait for that wisdom to rear its ugly head.

Oil-stained fingers decorated with skull rings grasped one of several mason jars from a worn rucksack. Each jar was a mixture of gasoline, orange juice, powdered laundry detergent, and black gunpowder. Capped with a wick drilled into the golden lid. It was Medford's personal firebomb cocktail. He and his clan of crankheads had parked at the end of an old logging trail on Jacque Bocart's property. Tracked uphill damn near a mile. Bearing gifts. Sawed-off shotguns with the safety off. Fingers on the trigger. Buckshot in the chamber. Medford replayed how Hersey appeared in that hospital bed three days ago, eyes sewing-thread thin, outlined by the color of his meth-mouth complexion. Lips fragmented by ruts. Jagged marrow lined his gums like he'd tried to huff a stick of dynamite. But when he stuttered into Medford's ear he sounded like a drunk who had Frenched a running chain saw. "J-J-J-Jacque B-B-Bocart d-d-did th-th-this t-t-to me-e-e, D-D-D-Daddy."

Medford's black-braided hemp hair bounced against his spine as damp briars and weeds painted his scuffed combat boots. His four crankheads, Swartz, Orange Peel, Pine

Box Willie, and Toad followed behind with a full moon guiding them through the night.

They made it to the edge of a cornfield lined by three strands of braided barbed wire circling ceramic insulators connected to posts. Up on a hill beyond the fields Medford could see the kitchen lights of the old farmhouse. Swartz pulled a pair of rubber-insulated wire snips from his rucksack. Everyone watched the electric current flame blue as he severed the braided wire.

The men spread out like the wingspan of a vulture homing in on its prey. Started into the maze of cricket-chirping vegetation. A quarter of the way in, the thick-gummed scent of cannabis burned their nostrils like cayenne pepper. Orange Peel and Pine Box Willie stepped toward the thick scent. Reached with their free hands. Medford huffed, "Wait, might be booby-trapped!"

The tempered steel of a long-spring trap bit into the marrow of Orange Peel's ankle. He screamed forward all the way to the ground. His index finger jerked. Buckshot from his .12-gauge peppered the darkness of vegetation. Silenced his pain.

Pine Box Willie stepped down onto a two-by-six of rusted sixteen-penny nails that replaced the soles of his boots. Heated the insides of his socks with blood. He dropped his .12 gauge. Fell backwards. Medford reacted fast. Dropped his sawed-off pump. Hefted Pine Box's outline while spitting, "Shit! Shit! Shit!"

Medford rode Pine Box to the ground in a bear hug from behind. Glanced over his shaved skull at Swartz in the September moonlight, who whispered to Pine Box, "This is gonna hurt." Swartz ripped the board from Pine Box Willie's foot.

Jacque knew he could have killed Hersey if not for Abby telling him, "But I got away from him, Grandpa. I punched him just like you taught me on the bag." He touched Hersey back. Gave him a beating. An eye for an eye.

But even after three days everything still infected Jacque's mind. He sat at the kitchen table taking in the bruises that fingerprinted the length of Abby's arm, as she guided the red crayon into the empty space between the black outlines within the coloring book. Dock Boggs's banjo on the radio picked out the tune of "Oh, Death." Avis sat opposite Jacque, chain-smoking, her pencil frame tinted by chigger bites. A head of unwashed maple-colored hair and mushroomed features. Jacque shook his head. He knew what his only child had caused to her own and it bothered her not one damn bit.

The phone rang and Jacque stood up from the table, stepped to the wall where it hung, and answered, "Yeah?"

It was his brother-in-law Blaze, all excited. "Orange Peel's little brother told Cross-Eyed Chucky that Medford and his crew are haulin' ass over to your place, Jacque."

"Tonight?"

"As we speak. They're comin' for you 'cause of what you did to Hersey."

Jacque eyed the locked-and-loaded 30-30 over his kitchen door. The cabinet drawer that held one of his pistols, a loaded Smith & Wesson 9 mm.

"It'll be their funeral."

Anna May came into the kitchen from the dining room, a hornet's nest of hair wrapped upon her head, knowing whoever was phoning this late had bad news.

And Blaze rattled, "Need me over there?"

The light above the stove blinked once. Twice. And didn't stop. Jacque knew they were either cutting the north side of the barbed electric fence or they were using a barrier to get over it. He knew they were coming.

"They're here. I'll call when I'm done. You can help with getting rid of their remains."

He slammed the phone down. Grabbed his 30-30 from above the kitchen door. Pulled his 9 mm from the cabinet drawer, tucked it down his worn dungarees. Told Anna May, "Medford's here. Grab the sixteen-gauge from above the living room door. Get a box of shells. Take Abby and Avis to the basement. Lock the door. Don't unlock it until I come back. Anyone else comes, fill them with buckshot."

Shaking, Anna May asked, "What about Billy? We can call him."

Glancing at Abby, Jacque told Anna May, "This don't concern Billy. Now get the shotgun and get downstairs."

Jacque stepped out the back door and into the yard. Followed the shadow of a tree's leafy branches for cover. Stepped over the roots. Turned. Pressed his back against the jagged bark of the trunk. Stared out into the distance. Watching and listening for any sign of Medford and his crew. Then a shotgun blast sounded from his acreage of cornstalks, followed by a familiar voice.

Jacque faced the direction from which the gunshot and cursing sounded. Smiled and kneeled to the damp ground. His heart pulsed in his fingertips as he thumbed the hammer of his 30-30 back. Fingered the trigger and scanned the edge of the field along with four other eyes.

·

Hell came quick as a flame igniting dry pasture. Pine Box Willie came jack-legged limping. Set off the motion lights that hung from the phone poles at the corners of the field. Jacque parted the silence of the night with an explosion of gunfire that lit up Pine Box Willie's side with an erupting flame. Jacque had hit the rucksack storing Medford's firebomb cocktail. Pine Box Willie was a human torch screaming for his life. Jacque extinguished an empty shell. Rifled another round into Pine Box Willie. He dropped to the ground. Rolled around like electricity trapped in a hamster wheel, his pleas smoldering like the flames that had ignited his body.

Swartz, Toad, and Medford erupted from the field with Civil War battle cries, pumping buckshot that nicked Jacque's left shoulder, forcing him to drop his 30-30 to the earth. Son of a bitch.

From the outer edges of darkness, behind the security lights, two cave-black cur hounds with vocal cords severed so they'd be unheard by trespassers came like a whisper in hell. Clamping tines into the marrow of Swartz's and Toad's calves. Stealing their wind. Sawed-offs were dropped. The curs rode Swartz and Toad into the ground, fighting and screaming. Worked their way up to their necks, making their vocal cords equal with the curs'.

Jacque stepped from the light with a soiled left shoulder. Sprayed lead had nicked and dug into the old leather above his right eyebrow. He blinked blood. Drew his 9 mm. Aimed at Medford, whose boots tossed up earth behind him as he pulled his Walther P38 9 mm handgun from his belt line. In his other hand the firebomb cocktail. And each man came forward, fighting the recoil of the trigger pull until their clips were empty.

Anna May locked the basement door. Followed the wooden steps to the bottom. Pulled the old rotary phone from the wall and dialed 911. Then the shooting started. Her heart exploded. She thumbed the safety of the 16-gauge into the unsafe position. And waited.

Into the house with firearm drawn, lights above the stove like hazard lights, Marshal Hines's voice bounced throughout the house with rushed breathing.

"Anna May? It's Billy Hines."

At the top of the steps. Behind the locked basement door she hid the trembling in her tone. "I'm here."

"You all right?"

"I'm okay. I got Abby and Avis."

"Where's Jacque?"

"Out in the backyard. I heard shooting. Men screaming."

"You stay put. Don't open that door till I come back."

Out the back door and into the yard, bright quartz lights lit up the lifeless outlines of the beaten, bloody, and aged gladiators. Billy ID'd them as Medford's grease-wired cronies.

Swartz was spread out on the ground with his neck gaping. Mangled. Dark wounds up and down his outline mirroring Toad's. Pine Box Willie's frame sat smoking where the field met the grassy yard. Billy nudged the two dead curs with the toe of his boot. Each had their ribs parted by bullet holes. He shook his head.

"Damn waste of two good hounds."

Billy hadn't ID'd Medford, Orange Peel, or Jacque. He scanned the field's edge. The yard. Boots caught his eyes at the edge of the quartz light. He approached the boots and saw they were attached to a smoldering frame. The scent of another ignited by fuel: Jacque.

Billy knelt down over him. Wrapped two fingers to the pulse of Jacque's greasy black wrist, chewed by buckshot and flame. What Billy felt was barely a beat. Fighting tears for a man he'd known his whole life, his gut knotted up like twine. Bubbled. Boiled over. He vomited on Jacque. Caused his flesh to sizzle.

Billy wiped the yellow bile from his lips onto his sleeve. Pulled and keyed the radio from his side. "Donna, we got a bloodbath out here at Jacque Bocart's farm. Bocart's been grilled. Barely breathing. There are three dead. I repeat, one barely breathing. Three dead. Gonna need an ambulance. Whatever reserve unit—"

An empty sawed-off swung like a ball bat at the back of Billy's skull. Combat boots stepped fast from behind the tree. The silhouette blended into the field. Disappeared into the September night. Billy lay on the cold earth and Donna repeated, "Billy? Billy? Billy?"

It had been ten years since the long potholed drive colored red and blue with the lights of reserve units. The ambulance and state police. While the girl, her grandmother, and mother watched from the basement window. Then they rushed up the stairs and into the unknown madness of bloodshed that decorated the backyard.

It had been ten years since Jacque had been released from the hospital's burn unit to Harrison County Corrections. Since the state had offered him a plea bargain in return for the story of what had provoked the loss of life on his property. And who had disfigured him. He told them he had no recollection of that night or the events that unfolded. He served time but passed away before his sentence was fulfilled.

It had been ten years since Billy Hines had been forced out as town marshal and replaced by one of Elmo Sig's lawless deputies. Who turned a blind eye for cash from a father and son who were transporting meth throughout the poverty-stricken county's veins and the surrounding counties' arteries.

But now, seated in the rusted Chevy four-by-four, the girl nodded at the aged outline seated next to her and whispered, "It's time." She stepped from the Chevy with her hair pulled tight into a ponytail, the .45 gripped in the gunpowder-burned palm of her right hand. The busted soles of her boots cut through the knee-high weeds. Across the chewed-back-road pavement. The outline sat in the four-by-four, watching her walk through the gate of the rusted fence that housed the skeletal remains of vehicles decorating acres of red clay. To the outline she appeared like a king cobra with her stitched softball shoulders, V-shaped back, and hourglass waist beneath the full moon's glow.

She stopped in front of the rusted tin building. Listened to the sound of an air-powered drill zipping lug nuts from axles. The smell of motor oil and gasoline fueled the blood-lust that had been circulating throughout her frame for the past ten years. She stood remembering all of the times the aged outline had picked her up from her great-uncle's. Then he and she'd park across the road at the abandoned farm and sit studying the father and son.

Placing her eye to the crack of light in the tin door, she watched the son with a pearl-white eye. A head of blackish gray hair. Oily and stringy. He zipped the air drill and she remembered the ten fingers. How they had forced bruises up and down her ceramic skin as she pleaded, "STOP!"

Behind the son sat the father on a bucket, gray strands braided down to the chain of his leather wallet. He'd stretched-taffy arms, pitted and ripped by buckshot. Lifting a coffin nail to his lips.

The girl thumbed the hammer of the .45-caliber Colt. Then the safety. He thought he'd gotten away with what he'd done ten years ago. He'd been questioned. Had an alibi. Then he was forgotten when her grandfather wouldn't talk.

But when the girl swung the tin door open none of that would matter. Because she was carrying on the wisdom. And watching from the four-by-four, Billy Hines could forgive himself and her grandfather could rest in peace after his granddaughter pulled the trigger, just as he had that night ten years ago, until the clip was empty.

TRESPASSING BETWEEN HEAVEN AND HELL

Everything exploded like flashbulbs across the top of an old Polaroid camera in Everett's mind as he stood scrubbing the red from within the cracks of his hand's life line. Beneath his thick black-rimmed glasses, he squeezed his blood-sprayed eyes closed and fought the voices of the dead. Remembering his headlights cutting holes through the darkness above the gravel, rounding the wall of trees that lined each side of the road dividing the land on one side from the river on the other. And the frail outline of color attached to a small frame that thudded and disappeared beneath the truck.

Tires locked up over the gravel, Hank Williams blaring "I Dreamed About Mama Last Night" from his truck's cassette player. He opened the door, inhaling the dust that polluted the night. Tossed his empty can of Pabst Blue Ribbon into the bushes.

Behind his truck, he kneeled. Palmed the neck that was trading warmth for cold. Time turned back in his mind to a war he had served in overseas and the screams of a man in his platoon, Private Dubious, whose words echoed throughout his head: "Stop the pain! Stop the fucking pain!" He couldn't separate the voices and the memories from his everyday living.

He took in the shape of the boy on the road glowing red with the truck's taillights. Everett had more than a few beers in him. He wasn't about to go to jail because someone couldn't keep an eye on their own. Letting the boy run rampant in the valley on everyone's land. Land that people had worked to pay for, take care of. He shoveled his arms beneath the boy's body. Carried it to the riverbank, listened to the water's current. Thought of how the boy's mother was a pox on his valley with her on-again off-again lifestyle of drugs and jail time. The home she lived in had once been a well-maintained white wood-sided cottage with blue shutters. A shiny tin roof. The previous owner gave it a fresh coat of paint every spring. The shutters were now rotted frames outlining the cardboard that had replaced the broken glass.

Everett told himself he wasn't going to jail, to lose what time he had left. He'd already lost enough.

An explosion rang through his mind and out of his ears. He could smell the smoke, feel the flecks of hot earth pelt his face, and that vision of Private Dubious was no more.

Everett heaved the boy's outline into the sludge below him. Listened to the splashing of the body. He started to turn to the idling engine but noticed a stringer of fish lying in the gravel, picked them up knowing they belonged to the boy, threw them into the bed of his truck. Got in. Grabbed a cold beer from his cooler on the floor. Put his truck in drive.

At home, Everett rinsed the powdered Clorox from his hands. It had started out white but turned a pink foam. He shut off the steaming water. Grabbed a towel from the stove. Thought of the war he'd served in. The men he'd watched die.

·

Deputy Sheriff Pat Daniels stood shaking his head, watching the boy being pulled from the green river. He wondered why God sometimes took the simple and innocent, let unexplained evils of the world live on.

The boy's body resembled an overcast day, with lost milky eyes and violet lips, as they loaded him onto the gurney.

The night before, Pat had been working late at the station when dispatch connected him with Stace Anderson. She had filed a missing persons on her boy, Matthew. He hadn't come home from fishing. Said she'd walked the valley road looking for him, asking every neighbor with a house light on if they'd seen him. No one had.

At first, Pat thought the boy had been wade fishing. Fallen in. Drowned. But after County Coroner Owen and Detective Mitchell took in the details of major trauma, the broken ribs and femur, they concluded it wasn't a drowning but instead foul play.

"We gotta keep a short leash on this, Pat."

"I aim to keep this hound in her pen. Media gets ahold of this, it'll get ugly."

"How the Galloway interviews go?"

When Pat first arrived on the scene he'd interviewed Needle Galloway and his son Beady. They'd been crappie fishing after church that morning when they came upon the body.

"They're innocent as the Virgin Mary."

"You ready to break the news to the mother?"

"If Chaplain Pip ever gets here."

"Surprised the mother ain't down here wondering what we're up to. You say she just lives up the road?"

"About a mile and a half in the widow Ruth's old place. I take it you ain't heard much about the mother?"

"Don't know a thing, this is your neck of the woods. Why?"

"She's in and out of jail and rehab. One time she skipped from the hospital after a meth lab exploded into a house fire."

"The one down off of Lickford Road a while back?"

"That'd be the one. When she was caught the judge gave her community service and probation."

"Figures. Well, I done contacted the sheriff, let him know it looks like foul play. Think she could've killed the boy?"

"If I had to guess I'd say no. Aside from being a meth addict she did try to be a good mother."

"What about insurance money?"

"Gal like that, can't hold a job any longer than she can stay clean, she's lucky if she can keep her light bill paid."

"What about the father?"

"Nelson, he ain't been the same since Stace got hooked on that shit. Went back on the sauce, divorced her. To be honest, that boy was all he had left."

"See how she reacts when you give her the news."

"What's your theory on the boy's death?"

"He's hit by a vehicle sometime last night and for whatever reason someone decided to dump him in the river."

"Well, Stace'd be lucky if she could hold a Whopper from Burger King with two hands. Let alone carry a body."

"Telling me she's frail?"

"Frail would describe her as muscular. Last time I seen her she was POW thin."

"What about a boyfriend?"

"None that I know of."

"Don't your brother live down this way?"

"Yeah, but I ain't been down here to visit since he near cut Sheldon's ear off."

"I heard 'bout that."

"Lord God, shoulda seen the blood. Look like he had a bird wing sproutin' from his head."

"Lucky Sheldon didn't press charges."

"Lucky's ass, if the county prosecutor got wind of it he'd be in jail."

"Seems hard to talk to sometimes when I see him in town."

"More like all the time, why I don't visit much, he's gotten worse."

"Probably like being a cop, see some bad shit that stays with you no matter how much time passes."

Everett emptied his beer. Visited a time before. Remembering the words from Preston's lips when he shook a cigarette from his pack that morning. He remembered how the cigarette was dry. Unbroken. How Preston's stubble complexion was mapped by the heat of the jungle with beads of moisture. How the platoon stood in early morning silence, everyone keeping watch. Preston's green helmet tilted on his head; his eyes looked itchy with hay fever but it was from a lack of sleep. He sparked a match, brought an orange heat to the cigarette's end and said, "If it ain't wet, it ain't broken."

Preston led the men through the stillness, cigarette smoke clouding into the air above, when the explosion of gunfire dropped everyone to the ground for cover. Only Preston dropped because he'd found his end.

"Ready for another Pabst, Everett?"

Everett came back to the now, blinking. Followed the folds of flesh up Poe's neck to his worn leather jawline, his parched lips with a hint of chalk-white spittle in the corners.

"A what?"

"Pabst? You want another one or you switching back to Natural Light?"

"Give me another Pabst, tired of drinkin' that deer piss."

Poe was a lanky man with faded rebel flags and green skulls that used to be black tattooed up and down each arm. He spoke with a smoker's cough as he bartended at the Leavenworth Tavern, a local bar that sat down along the Ohio River. A place Everett drove to be alone with himself and this hell that had plagued his mind for thirty-some years.

Behind Everett, Nelson Anderson sat off in the far corner with his cherry-stained eyes staring out the tinted glass window, sulking over the wife that left him for meth addiction some time ago.

Nelson and Everett were the only regulars until the entrance door opened, flamed the bar with sunlight. Everett watched the dark figure's reflection approach in the barroom mirror in front of him. The figure sat down on the stool beside him.

"There was a mess of police and an ambulance down your way, Everett."

"So what are you tellin' me, Merritt, that maybe I should take the long way home?"

Merritt had served in the Marines during the Vietnam War, never saw any action, but guarded an ammo dump off the coast of Puerto Rico. He frequented the tavern several times a week just as he did the valley of Blue River Village, where Everett lived. He gave Merritt permission to fish across from his place down on the river. In return Merritt allowed Everett to hunt, day or night, on the wooded farmland his family had left him after passing.

Poe opened the chrome cooler, pulled out cans of Budweiser and Pabst. Popped them open. Sat one in front of Everett. The other in front of Merritt.

"Shit, don't keep us in suspense, what's going on?"

"All I heard is Needle and Beady Galloway was fishing this morning. Found a boy's body in the river."

There was the scraping of a chair across the floor. Then the voice of Nelson Anderson. "You say a boy's body?"

Merritt had gotten his first swallow of Budweiser. He turned to Nelson's already reddened whiskers with recessed eyes the color of an eggplant. He fought back the bubbles. A numbness expanded up and down Merritt's spine. He'd not noticed Nelson when he entered.

"That's just what I heard from Virgil MacCullum."

Poe added, "He is the only boy in the village."

Setting his Budweiser back on the bar, Merritt inhaled smoke from his Camel. Watched Nelson rush out of the bar like a kamikaze pilot.

Merritt shook his head.

"Shit, didn't even see Nelson when I come in here or I'd have maybe thought before I started yappin' my jaws. His ex–old lady lives down by you, Everett, with that boy of theirs."

Everett watched Merritt pull the Camel from his lips, the smoke trailing like a smoldering fire, deliberate and ghostly. Everett pushed his thick black-framed glasses up his nose, exhaled. "They found the boy." He turned his head oddly and in a sad raspy tone mumbled, "Now everthing's wet and broken."

Merritt turned to Everett, wondering what he meant. He was acting more strange than normal. "What you mean, wet and broken?"

Everett shook his head, began palming his forehead, saying, "No, no! Ain't none of your concern."

Merritt looked to Poe, back at Everett. "Concern? You ain't makin' much sense, Everett." In Everett's mind, he was back in the jungle, where he hunkered down, explosions zipping past. Earth rumbling with mortar fire. Preston laid out, his skull peeled open and scattered. And Everett felt that same way now as he did then. The fear of the world around him becoming unbalanced.

Confusion wrinkled Merritt's cheeks into his eyes.

"Everett, you okay?"

Everett snapped back to the haze of the bar, waved his right hand up into the air.

Everett glanced at the grain of the bar, his sweating drink, glanced beside him, and said, "That boy was slow as an inchworm. Everyone in the valley warned his doped-up mother about his running loose up and down the road, fishing from our property. It was a matter of time."

Merritt and Poe glanced at each other and Poe said, "What are you trying to say, Everett?"

"That woman and boy have been a problem in the valley since Nelson sent her ass afoul."

Poe cleared his throat. Said, "Being kinda harsh, ain't you?"

Everett looked at Poe and said, "Harsh is when you's tryin' to stop your buddy from bleedin' only it don't matter 'cause he's already dead."

Pip never showed. Pat had to break the news to Stace, alone. She sat on a love seat decorated with cigarette burns and cat hair. She'd a muskrat mien, tear-swollen eyes and a body gouged by scabs. She caught her breath and asked, "Why'd a person run over an innocent child?" She paused, lost in an unfilled blank, ran her chicken-bone arm over her sunken complexion and said, "Toss them into the river just like they's a piece of trash."

Pat sat on the ratty sofa, trying to ignore the waft of unchanged cat litter, the stubbed-out smokes lining ash-trays, empty plastic cola bottles on their sides, and food-smeared dishes. All he could muster was "They's evils in people that make little if any sense, and trying to figure them out does a person little to no good."

Beside him the door swung open. Pat was ready to draw his pistol. Nelson swarmed in with light warming the house's stale interior of wrecked living. His lips moving, saying, "I heard what happened. Is it true?" Stace never stood, sat cradling herself. Raised her head up and down. Nelson dropped down beside her, wrapped his arms around what little was left of her. He reeked of booze. If a spark hit the air, the room would ignite. Pat ignored it. He leaned forward with his elbows digging through his khakis and into his knees, told Nelson, "Matthew's found early this morning."

Nelson waved a hand, said, "By the Galloways."

Pat shook, said, "Yeah." Paused and told them, "I know you're upset, but I got a few questions, answer best as you can."

Stace wiped tears, nodded.

"You and the boy had any problems, disagreements?"

"No." She sobbed with mucus dribbling from her nose. Anger thinning her tears and she said, "Why don't you ask some these ass-minded folk always judgin' me and Matthew."

"What'd you mean?"

Nelson cut in and said, "She means coulda been any neighbor lives down here. Ever' time I come to pick Matthew up someone has started shit with her."

Pat asked, "What kind of problems the neighbors give you?"

Stace inhaled for composure, told Pat, "They all paid me visits, bitchin' 'bout my boy runnin' up and down the valley, fishin' from they land." She stopped, half smiled, remembering something, and continued with "Matthew always brought home his blue fishin' stringer weighted down. Knew where all the fishin' holes was." Then her smile trailed off.

Pat looked at Nelson. "Where was you last night?"

"Hold on a goddamned minute—"

Pat cut him off. "Gotta ask, nothin' personal. Where was you?"

"At the bar, ask Poe. Was there till closing."

They all sat in a discomforting silence until Pat couldn't take it any longer and stood up. Stace asked, "You find his pole or tackle?"

"To be honest, don't even know the exact location of where he was hit and thrown in."

Tears and sniffs came from each, and she mustered, "He'd a black-and-red Ugly Stik. Matchin' tackle box. Bought it for him at the Walmart. God, how he loved to fish." Then she pulled her legs from the floor and sat on them, began to tremor, pushed her face into Nelson's chest. Created a damp spot on his shirt.

Pat had nothing left to ask, told them he'd keep them informed, let them know if anything came up. He stepped to the door, and Stace raised her head from Nelson's chest, said, "You question people down here, start with that brother of yours, Everett. He's been the worst one."

Driving down the mosquito-infested road, Stace's words dug a shelf across Pat's chest. The worst one, Everett. His older brother. The man was mean, but would he run over a child? Throw him in the river?

His brother was many things. Tortured by the memory of war. Never touched drugs. A drunk who didn't agree with those who didn't work. But kill a kid? Pat shook his head. With the window rolled down, hints of maple and walnut meshed with the fish stink of the river, streaming through with the clank and pitch of gravel. Birds whispered and Pat remembered showing up at the Leavenworth Tavern to stop a disagreement. Everett was holding Sheldon Noble down, a knee buried in his spine, hair in one hand, blade in the other. Thought Everett was gonna scalp the bastard. And what for? All because he called Everett a stupid-ass, dink-lovin' jarhead.

Rounding a blind curve, a swarm of dog-pecker gnats peppered his windshield, wafted through the window. He swatted and cursed, "Now, dammit," as the smear of a boy raced across the road.

Pat stomped his brakes. Went sideways.

"Shit!"

He put his cruiser into park. Got out. His legs went weak. His hands shook. He looked beneath his cruiser, walked around it. Nothing. He stepped to the weeds, took in the wall of trees. Blind spot. Person could hit an animal or a child. Shaken up and angered, he stared at the weeds and raised his tone.

"This is Harrison County Deputy Sheriff Pat Daniels. You in them weeds come on up outta there, got a good mind to tan your ass."

The cruiser sat idling behind him, the river's current flowed below. There was no sign of the boy, but that's when he saw it sticking up out of the weeds.

"I'll be damn."

It was a scuffed black-and-red Ugly Stik fishing rod. The reel was busted. A few of the eyelets were bent. He stepped deeper into the green and tan strands of foliage, and his boot thudded against something. He reached down and picked up a black-and-red tackle box.

Pat surveyed the weeds like he did during deer season when he'd shoot a deer and it would keep going on adrenaline, leaving behind drops of blood. He'd use them to track it until its adrenaline ran out. But this time he found nothing. He turned to step back onto the road and saw the dented twelve-ounce glimmer. He kneeled, picked it up. It was an empty can of Pabst Blue Ribbon. The emblem glistened red, white, and blue. The colors were fresh, not faded. He put his nose to its opening. The scent was warm beer, not soured. The can was new.

He glanced around in the weeds for more cans but, just like the boy, he couldn't find a trace.

"You got one more chance to come on up out of them weeds, boy."

And what he heard was nothing more than the flow of the river below him.

"Little shit."

Pat stepped to the rear of his vehicle. Popped the trunk, dropped the rod and tackle inside. Closed it. Looked at the blind spot once more. Added alcohol to his theory, that made it even more feasible. He got into the cruiser, knowing what brand of beer his brother Everett drank, Natural Light, not PBR. That set his mind at ease and he thought he'd stop in, seeing as they hadn't spoken in a while.

Everett could still feel Poe's and Merritt's eyes engraving their pity for Nelson into his right temple. He fished another Pabst Blue Ribbon from the ice of his cooler. Popped the beer open. Tilted the can to his lips. Navigated the truck down the road. As he sucked the icy foam from his beer, anger took on an acidic form and traveled throughout his insides.

"Who's Poe think he is any damn way? Being kind of harsh, ain't you?"

Everett's truck tires tossed road as he turned down his driveway. He thought about the boy in the dark, his face red from the taillights, and he told himself, "It was an accident, let it go."

Taking another swig of his Pabst, he saw the cruiser up by his house. Turned and saw his baby brother Pat coming from up by the toolshed. Everett shifted his truck into park, killed the engine, and opened the door, taking in what Pat was holding. The stringer he'd left hanging from the rusted nail in the paint-flaked door after skinning those crappie last night. Everett bent his head back and guzzled his brew. Swallowed and said, "The shit brings you down my way?"

Pat heard Everett's question, not wanting to believe what he'd found, trying to write it off as a coincidence. He'd pulled up minutes before, sat waiting in his cruiser, saw the boy again, this time running up to Everett's shed. He'd gotten out, wondering what the hell was going on. There was no trace of the boy. Just a blue stringer hanging from a nail. The scent of rotted fish guts coating the insides of his nose as they decorated the ground.

And now Everett had pulled up, got out with a PBR in his hand.

Pat told him, "Came down to ask you a few questions. Seen a . . ." He stopped short about seeing the boy. Cleared his throat and said, "Thought maybe you's up at the shed. Seen the stringer. The fish guts. You go fishin' yesterday?"

Everett rolled the question around in his mind. The booze sloshed his words.

"Went lass night. Caught me a few crappie."

Pat blinked, saw the boy appear from nothing, run toward Everett's truck. Pat said, "The shit is goin' on?" Rushed past his brother.

Everett followed his movements, turned with Pat's steps. Asked, "The hell you doin'?"

Pat made his way to the front of Everett's Silverado truck. Kneeled down, looked for the boy. Saw specks the shade of human spotting the bumper. He swallowed and said, "Got some blood on your bumper. Hit an animal recently?"

Everett crushed the can. Dropped it to the ground, stepped to the rear of his truck, seeing how things were playing out. What he'd done wasn't going to be forgotten. Regardless, he wasn't going to jail, and he said, "No animal." Grabbed a crowbar from the truck bed, came around the hood just as Pat stood up. Met his gaze. It held disbelief.

Everett brought the octagon extension sideways. Pat raised his right arm as a reaction, shielding himself from the swing. Felt the bone in his forearm chink. He gritted his teeth, stepped away from Everett, patted his side. Unsnapped the leather holder on his belt, pulled the metal can from it. A chill had started to line Pat's veins. The pain was thick; he wanted to vomit.

Everett came forward, said, "You's my brother, but I ain't goin' to jail for that little bastard." And he raised the crowbar for another strike.

Pat pushed the pepper mace into Everett's face, pulled the trigger, and shouted, "Kinda evil has gotten in you? It was someone's son!"

"Goddammit!" Everett screamed. Dropped the crowbar. His hands clawed at his eyes and cheeks, festering with burn.

Pat's arm hung loose at his ribs, throbbing and changing shape. It felt as though it would ignite. He came toward Everett, released the mace, pulled his ASP baton. Damp fell from the burn of Everett's face as he felt the steel hammer the back of his neck and push him into his truck's hood. Behind him Pat's voice told him, "I's takin' you in for murder."

Everett shook his head, repeating the words "NO, NO, NO, NO, NO!" over and over. Tried to twist away, but his face felt as though it'd been ignited with kerosene and a match.

Pat dropped his weight against him. Everett gave in,

didn't fight as Pat pulled his left arm, then his right, to his lower back. Steel clasped around each wrist. Pat pulled his brother from the hood, led him toward his cruiser in shock as he looked up by the shed, watched the bruised shadow of a boy run and disappear.

A RABBIT IN THE LETTUCE PATCH

Ina Flisport sat like a used rag doll tossed onto potholed pavement and left behind after meeting Clay at Tuke's Bar, a rural watering hole within the backwoods of Orange County, Indiana, where she told Clay she'd left her conservation officer husband, Moon, for him. Clay stood up, laughing. "I don't wanna shack up with some whore-ass housewife. I just wanted a piece. I'm done with you."

And after two months of sharing the sheets, the affair ended. Lester the bartender stood in the bar's kitchen, running his reptile tongue over his parched lips as he eavesdropped on Ina's and Clay's words. Then Clay left. Ina stayed.

Lester dialed Kenny's number, telling him, "Got ourselves another rabbit in the lettuce patch."

Lester exited the kitchen's back door into the cold darkness. Walking around to the front door of Tuke's, he turned the OPEN sign to CLOSED, pulled out his keys, and gently locked the door from the outside, slid the padlock back into place.

Ina lit another cigarette and wondered if Moon had found the letter she'd left, telling him that thirty years of making sure his meals were cooked, his hound dogs were fed, laundry was done, and the yard was mowed were twenty-eight years too many.

She'd sit up late most nights while he coon hunted. She smoked cigarettes, played solitaire with David Letterman for company. Hoping for some form of affection, a touch, a kiss, a gesture of appreciation, something that she no longer received. Moon would come in and pretend she didn't exist. She'd decided that his taking her for granted was enough, their marriage was over.

They'd met when she was fifteen, in the summer of '73. Young by today's standards, but back then older men married younger women. She was knocked up and married by sixteen. Had her second when she was seventeen and her third by eighteen.

Lester returned from the kitchen with a cup of coffee and asked Ina, "Need another Bud Light?"

Ina glanced up from her beer through a haze of smoke, thinking to herself that Lester appeared malnourished, with his greasy hair and flesh so pale it was as if he lived without proper lighting, and told him, "Not yet."

Behind the bar, Lester stood sneering as he sipped his cup of coffee. He could hardly contain himself as he took in Ina's grapefruit-shaped breasts, tawny hair hanging above them with the finest hints of gray. He imagined his worm-like self buried within her succulent pigment, painted by the passing summer. To a rural-lowlife-deviant bartender like Lester Money, sex was an appreciated endeavor regardless of how aged a woman was. He couldn't be picky. But in his mind Ina appeared to be in her early thirties, though he believed her to be older.

Ina watched the steam from Lester's coffee rise and wanted to hit the road, find a motel or bed-and-breakfast to sleep off all the bad of being dropped like a stillborn. But she needed to sober up and she asked Lester, "Think I could get a cup of coffee?"

"Coffee?" She must be planning on leaving. He didn't need to mess up again, told her, "Sure, give me a sec." He walked back to the kitchen, pulled a clean mug from a hook on the wall, poured her a steaming cup. Pulled the small vial of liquid from his pocket. Some Georgia Home Boy. He twisted the lid off, poured the colorless liquid into her coffee. Brought the cup of coffee to her side of the bar, sat beside her, and winked as he sucked on his lime-colored teeth and said, "Couldn't help overhearing your words with Clay. He's a regular, and you mentioned someone goes by the name of Moon. I get a feller comes in here from time to time for a drink after fishing. His name is Moon. He's a conservation officer."

Ina took a sip of her coffee, not liking this salamander of a man being seated beside her. He made her feel unclean. Knowing her personal business. Her husband's name.

Lester continued with "I'd be willing to bet that man you come in with, Clay, I'd be willing to bet you and he are having an affair and the man you mentioned leaving, whose name is Moon, is the same Moon comes in here."

Ina finished her coffee. Felt her insides go limp. She'd be damned if she'd sit here and listen to any more of what this slug had to say, and she told him, "That'd be none of your business."

"It'd be a terrible thing for a husband to find out his wife was having an affair. I'd be willing to turn a cheek for a piece of your sweet stuff." Then he wrapped his nicotine-smudged fingers around her arm and pulled her into him.

Ina jerked her arm from him. Drove her elbow up into his chin. Rattled his jaw and teeth. Turned away and grabbed the first thing she saw, the thick green glass ashtray she'd been using, smashed it on top of his skull. He dropped in a cloud of ashes and cigarette butts, hollered from the floor, "Fuckin' whore!" Ina grabbed her purse, placed her feet on the bar's floor, and it hit her. The sinkhole of her insides. The rubber-band strength of her legs. The shifting angles of the room as it frayed and tilted. The Georgia Home Boy.

She struggled to the door. The locks clicked. The door swung open. Knocked her backwards. Two men with beards and oil-stained trucker caps stood looking at her. One wore a skinning knife, the other a pocketknife. Each stank of cold outdoor air, burned wood, dirty work.

The one with the skinning knife was as big as an oak tree and he told her, "You got a taste of age on you, but you is a pretty thing." Ina didn't know if it was the booze or the coffee or the butt of the gun she didn't see or feel as it made contact with her face when she tried to run between the two men. Her whole body had become a hollowed-out abyss. The last thing she heard wasn't the sound the gun made against her head or how the floor sounded when it echoed in her skull. It was the words the man with the pocketknife said that echoed through her skull: "Lester, you about let this ol' rabbit run plum out the damn lettuce patch again."

The old dirt road led to a home where a primered Firebird, a rusted Ford pickup truck, and Ina's gray '85 Toyota Land Cruiser sat beneath the big beech trees that were almost bare of their leaves. The house was nothing more than a 1,300-square-foot shingle-sided home with a leaking tin roof and a flaking white-framed wooden screen door with holes that had been patched with pieces of rolled-up yellowing newspaper. The windows were devoid of outside light, boarded up from the inside with plywood and thick plastic on the outside to keep out the cold. Dead in the center of the screen door was a chipped black plastic sign with large orange lettering: PRIVATE PROPERTY—KEEP OUT.

Somewhere inside, Ina struggled with her sight. She forced her eyes open with a sudden intake of air through her nose. Her lungs panted and cold fever outlined her body.

The air was thick with the stagnant scent of a peeled onion and the dank darkness of not knowing. It was as if the night had dropped upon her like a dead body, its weight heavy and hot with a sticky haze. Some feeling returned to her hands and she touched what lay on her. A man, passed out or asleep. What she felt of him was his slack naked torso.

Below her was a bed. Like this stranger on top of her, she was nude, with an ache in her inner thighs. Her mind and body were disoriented. Her head throbbed as she searched her memory for where and what had brought her to this place. She inhaled the scent of the peeled-onion odor, mixed with cigarette smoke, stale beer, mildew, and rotted wood. She started to push the man who lay upon her, but feared what he'd do if she woke him. She didn't have her bearings to fight back. She ran her hands along the bed, which was no more than a mattress and box spring, turned her head, her eyes adjusting to her surroundings. Outlines of clothing piled on the floor. What looked to be her jacket and skirt, some jeans with a belt, work boots, and a flannel shirt. Empty whiskey bottles on a nightstand next to the bed. Beer cans on the floor. Wads of paper. A small television with rabbit ears on a dresser. An ashtray of cigarette butts. The weight atop her had begun to snore. His arms were enormous, hanging down each side of her, his back wide, his hair greasy and scented like his body, reminiscent of the spoiled boxes of vegetables her father sometimes retrieved from the town supermarket's Dumpsters for the small number of pigs he raised behind the barn when she was a kid.

What had happened to her started to come in pieces, as if they'd been torn from a magazine, then wadded and tossed into the garbage, and now she was picking them out and unfolding them. Piece by piece. Taking in the distorted puzzle.

She'd left her husband, Moon. Met Clay at some bar to tell him. But Clay left her at that bar feeling used and getting drunk with that oily bartender who came on to her. But she couldn't remember how she'd gotten here. Wherever here was.

She glanced back at the room, wondering how long she'd been there. Her eyes worked their way up along the ceiling, which was stained with large brown splotches as if someone had slung coffee on it. Then back down onto the wall decorated by torn chunks of wallpaper that led to the thin outline of light framing a door covered in nicks and scratches. She heard men speaking in irritated tones on the other side.

"How damn much you give her, little brother?"

"A teardrop's all." The bartender's voice.

"Teardrops my ass, she's out like a blown bulb and no replacement."

"Scout's honor, Cecil."

"Lester, you ain't never been no damn Boy Scout."

"So?"

"So, your honor ain't worth a goat's sack, you got about as much sense as an empty piggy bank."

"Well, if it's empty, they ain't no cents."

"I rest my case. Now let me see that damn bottle of Georgia Home Boy you give to the ol' gal."

"Here."

"Shit fire, little brother, you might've poisoned her ass."

"Shit, that's all we need, to have poisoned a conservation officer's wife."

"A what? You stupid son of a bitch, you mean to tell me her old man's a damn squirrel cop and you knew it? Still doped her and let us bring her here anyway?"

"Why, yeah."

"You are about as dumb as an inbred hound dog. You know I've got warrants out on me. Damn, little brother. Damn."

Ina lay listening in a panic. Her insides felt like an over-trained muscle: stiff, tight, sore. She knew they'd had their way with her but not what they'd used to do it. To make her feel spooned out and weak. They knew her husband was law enforcement. Hearing the conflict in the men's tones forced Ina to believe the man she'd run out on could become a reason for her demise. She needed to get out of here, but didn't know where here was.

Ina played possum, keeping her eyes shut as the large outline got up off her. She listened to him breathing as he pulled his pants on, his belt buckle rattling. Then his shirt and his boots. Laces smacking the floor. His stopping to pull a cigarette from his pack. The flick of his lighter. The scent of butane. The smell of smoke as he opened the door, filling the room with light from the kitchen. Cecil's voice called out, "Melvin, listen to what our little brother got our asses into." The door closed.

And Cecil said, "Ain't like we can just put her vehicle on some back road, leave her behind the wheel like all the others, let her wake up confused and violated with no recall to what happened."

"Why the hell not?"

"'Cause, dumb ass, you done brought home damaged goods, her old man being a squirrel cop and all. Shit, he'll fingerprint her body, her clothing, and the vehicle. Do all sorts of that DNA shit. Find dirt from our boots or hair from one of our heads. Trace it back to us."

"That's right, that's why we got no other choice, little brother. I ain't going back to jail for some old bored housewife piece of ass."

"I guess they could do some of that blood work and find out what we give to her, maybe even who we got it from, and they'd narc us out."

"That's right, now you're thinking, little brother."

"So what are we gonna do?"

"Real simple. First thing, her car, get Luke and his brothers, who inherited Malone's Salvage Yard. They can strip down that damn Toyota of hers for scrap. They'll separate and sell it between here, Louisiana, West Virginia, and Pennsylvania."

"What about her?"

"We'll dispose of her. Need to make a call to Mr. Masonry, Nelson Dean, down in Tennessee. He can put her ass in with someone's foundation."

"That sounds a bit risky, could get caught or something." She could hear the nervousness in Lester's voice.

"Ain't got caught yet. Besides, you might have give her too much Georgia Home Boy. She might be in a coma. Regardless, we gotta get rid of her so her old man don't get nosy."

"Shit, Cecil, you're talking kind of crazy."

"You backing out on us?"

"If you are, best think long and hard about your words. I done told you I ain't going back to jail for no dumb-shit little brother who got us into this mess to begin with."

"No, no, I'm in, I'm in. Just ain't never took no person's life is all."

Lester had only done it for a piece of ass. His brothers were too big for him to handle. If he tried something they might bury his ass out back beneath the outhouse or right along with Ina. He had no other choice.

"Melvin, you go on down to Kenny's and use his phone, give Nelson Dean a call. If he ain't home, leave a message, tell him Cecil's got another squirrel stuck in the transformer. If he's home, get a price. But if he ain't, leave Kenny's number and tell Kenny to come get us as soon as Nelson calls back."

Ina lay listening, realizing she was right, the mentioning of Moon and who he was had brought on panic that wouldn't end well for her. Anxiety coursed through her veins. She thought she could feel her legs, then her feet, and she struggled up out of the bed.

The room was off balance. Her body felt brittle. Her

heart beat in rapid thuds. She had a shortness of breath, as if the room were without air. Her head reeled as her legs twitched across the cold wood. She knelt down with the room tilting and spinning. Dug through what she believed to be her clothing. Her hands struggled with her panties, skirt, shirt, socks, jacket, and shoes. Her whole body quaked as she got dressed. She felt the warm tears climbing down her face.

She looked for a window, some form of escape, but found nothing. Just the thirteen-inch television that sat on the dresser next to the door. And a flash of memory lit up her mind, the smell of a used diaper in her face and a voice laughing. "She might show you a few things, Lester."

She closed her eyes, pressed her palms into her face, and wiped the tears. Her arms tensed and shook with the hurt of this memory. She paused, tried to keep herself together, and listened to the words outside the bedroom, speaking about her as if her existence were the lowest link on the chain of life. Why, she asked herself, why had they done this to her?

She'd heard something about Melvin going to Kenny's to use the phone. She wondered who Kenny was. Then she heard footsteps. A door opening. Closing. Then a slamming screen door. Feet shuffling about in the kitchen. Then silence. The slamming of a car door somewhere. Then a loud engine came to life and slowly became more and more distant.

When the bedroom's doorknob turned, she panicked, not knowing who it was or what she'd do. Weak and light-headed, she grabbed the only thing she could, the thirteen-inch black-and-white television. She struggled to raise it above her head.

Ina exploded the television over Cecil's skull. Lester was right behind him, wedged in between not wanting to get caught and unsure about killing Ina. He felt a pinch of relief when Cecil tumbled to the floor. Until Ina came at him like a starved leper in search of food, screaming, "Why'd you do this to me?"

The fingers on both of her hands spread wide. Flashes sparked in her head as she pushed Lester backwards across the kitchen. She remembered him giving her coffee at the bar. Then the blackout. When her eyes opened back up, she stood in the room, everything slanting and twirling as hands tugged at her clothing. Unable to fight, she felt weightless as a palm pushed her backwards and she stumbled onto the mattress.

And now Ina pushed Lester and screamed, "Answer me! Why?" Lester lost his footing and his skull met the kitchen countertop's edge. By the time he hit the mildewed floor, his mind and all his motor skills were heated peanut butter. He was blinking in and out, and Ina began stomping him, remembering the tree-bark hands groping her breasts, wrenching her wrists above her head, followed by the grunts that hammered through her mind as her eyes focused on that thirteen-inch television.

Lester's frame twitched as if he were getting an electric shock. Ina's chest burned and throbbed as her air began to disappear, she thought she was having a heart attack. Pictures, tastes, and smells played over and over in her head, and Ina stopped kicking him.

Lester lay on the kitchen floor, a limp pile of blood and pale skin sheathing bone. Ina breathed hard as she struggled out the kitchen door. Anger and revulsion carried her into the yellow-and-orange-leaf-coated yard. The air was cold and Ina's heart pounded as she crumpled across the leaves and recognized her truck in the drive. The door was unlocked. The keys were in the ignition. She had started the vehicle, not knowing where she was, when Cecil exploded through the screen door, screaming like drunk trailer trash with a severed tongue. Seeing him, Ina slammed the Cruiser into drive, her heart contracting in her temples. She cut the wheel toward him as he stumbled toward the Toyota, his face blotted red like a melting candle, the fragments of the television's glass separating his features. Ina clipped him with the front fender and dropped him to the ground. She cut the wheel again, driving through the yard, slinging mud and leaves through the air to coat Cecil's twitching body.

Ina kept the gas pedal floored down the driveway of mud and potholes. The seat thudded beneath her. When she saw blacktop, she twisted the wheel to the right, tires barking onto the back road pavement.

Ina thought about the words spoken by Lester and his brothers as they discussed her like she was just a piece of meat. An animal to be slaughtered and forgotten. She felt the soreness from within, remembering more and more. She'd been raped repeatedly. She thought about the vows she'd broken, causing all of this. And tears saturated her cheeks.

Her chest ached and her vision fogged as she sped down the unknown back road that rushed beneath her truck's tires. Until all at once she thought to herself, This must be what it's like to drown.

Her heart pounded less. Her lungs tightened. She began to gasp for air. She clutched the wheel and kept the accelerator to the floor as her head began to blur. Her every breath was pain. Her chest was getting heavier and heavier, like her foot on the gas. Then the cold aching sweat trembled her body all the way down through her arms and legs, meeting her hands and feet. Her front tire hit a ditch. Then the large oak tree she'd not even seen coming head-on at eighty-some miles per hour stopped her Cruiser. She shattered through the windshield and flew out into the woods that enclosed her.

The steam of Moon's coffee cup fed the air in his kitchen as he asked Detective Mitchell, "No trace of her body?"

"Just her Cruiser smashed into that oak tree. Any reason for her being way down in Orange County?"

"None that I know of."

"You say you had an argument the night before?"

"Right."

"And you came home late after the shooting of Rusty Yates and Ina wasn't home?"

"Right. I figured she was visiting her friend, Myrtle. I started drinking to blow off some steam. Then I found this letter. She quit me."

Detective Mitchell studied the letter. Looked back at Moon. "Sorry, Moon."

Moon exhaled. "It don't make any damn sense why a person would take Ina from where she wrecked."

"Foul play."

"You mean she could've seen something she wasn't supposed to."

"Look, all county and state police know is she flew through the windshield when she hit that tree. Landed out in the woods. They found where she landed and some boot prints."

"And nothing else?"

"Nothing."

COLD, HARD LOVE

Disgust lined the burger grease that coated Carol's skin and mixed with the pain that arced through her wrists and ankles, pooled into blisters from waiting tables at Jocko's Diner. She told her husband, "Bellmont, you gotta do it tonight. Between pulling doubles and hearing that old spindle's words day after day, I cain't take much more."

After ten years of employment Bellmont had lost his job at the Brown & Williamson tobacco plant. Drained Carol and his savings, had to sell their home and move to her father's thousand-acre hog farm. They rested their heads in the old cabin her father had built next to him when his mother was ailing. And now, like his wife's, every muscle in Bellmont's body spasmed with ache, from his daily laboring on that farm, working for his father-in-law. Today he'd dug fence-post holes for a new hog pen. And Carol's disdain made the physical pain that much worse. "Maybe if we sold your car we could take that money, wager on some fights down at the tavern, win enough to stretch things out a few weeks more."

Pink flushed over Carol's cheeks and she said, "You want to sell my Iroc? That's your solution? What's next, the clothes off our backs, shoes from our feet? You just want to wait for him to die? Hope he just falls over? That ain't never gonna happen."

Bellmont ran a hand through his corroded mane, knowing Carol was right, they couldn't keep going down this road of scratching and scraping to get by. Eating what she brought home from Jocko's every evening, washing it down with a few paper sacks of his Budweiser or her Pabst. He said, "Carol, we gotta make sure our ducks are lined. We're talkin' about takin' a person's life."

Carol's back rang stiff with hurt as she rolled her blue eyes and said, "What about our life? Don't we figure into the picture?"

Fault-line cracks seamed Bellmont's forehead and he said, "Of course we do, baby, I just want us to have one together, not you visitin' me in the pokey on weekends."

A bead of moisture driveled from Carol's sparrow shade of hair, bit her eye with the lunch special from Jocko's, fried tenderloin, mashed potatoes with white gravy, flaking roll with butter, and the choice of greens or corn. She blinked it away, felt her threadworm lips crook with a caustic taste. "Don't baby me. You the one come up with this plan from all your daddy's folklore. And you been puttin' it off for months."

Isaiah McGill, Bellmont's daddy, had sketched words into his son's mind when he was a boy maturing into a man. Stories of horse dealers, fortune-tellers, bootleggers, gypsies, boxers, and wrestlers of eighteenth-century Ireland congregating once a year, bartering steins of whiskey until the unrest turned unruly and fists were traded and bodies were bruised and the Donnybrook was born.

Bellmont was going to build the Donnybrook in the

backwoods of southern Indiana. Use the soil, rock, and trees of his father-in-law's land. Do it by hand and word of mouth. He'd update his daddy's stories to the present day. Only it wouldn't be just one day, it would be a three-day bare-knuckle tournament held once a year. Out among other farmers, fishermen, factory workers, and hunters. Where working-class men still held a grasp on life. The farm had plenty of acreage for expanding, building more than one pit to fight in. Barns to be turned into sleeping quarters and training areas. Best of all, it was secluded. The problem was they needed money and the farm.

"I can't just run over and wring that fucker's neck, we have to make it look like he did it to himself."

The folklore from Bellmont streamed through Carol's mind as it had every day since he told her the stories. Giving her hope for a life devoid of struggle. And when Bellmont turned his back, stepped into the nicked hallway toward the bathroom to take a piss, steps creaked across the pine floor behind him. Hearing this, he half-turned into the clawing nails of Carol. His rhythm of thought was sheared from his mind. Carol's hands worked at his thorny cheeks. Scraped flesh like it was plowed soil. His footing slipped and, before he knew it, his head and back slammed onto the hallway floor. Carol straddled Bellmont and he gasped, "The hell is gone wrong with your brainpan?"

On top of Bellmont, the folklore in Carol's mind turned to tears, washed down her cheeks and highlighted the corners of her mouth, and she cried, "Tired of this scratchin' to see another day while that smug son of a bitch judges us like we spend our days takin' handouts. You promised me you'd do it."

Bellmont wheezed. He'd lost the wind from his lungs. He pushed one hand beneath Carol's chin, held her jarring profile and the glare of her desperation, with his other he grabbed and calmed her tilling hands, and said, "It'll be okay, baby, it'll be okay."

Only one thing could coax Carol when she was this worked up. She twisted a hand free, lifted her weight from Bellmont, reached and tugged at the zipper of his jeans.

Bellmont rocked Carol up, trying to get from beneath her, rattled her head into the wall. "Shit!" she screamed and guided herself to standing. Before he could say he was sorry, she was rubbing her head, mascara running like watercolors from her eyes, and she yelled, "Damn you!"

Bellmont sat on the hallway floor, watched Carol stomp into the kitchen, grab her car keys. She turned and stared at him, said, "Can't keep doing this, you got to do it *tonight*!"

Bellmont stood up as he watched her walk away, knowing he couldn't put it off any longer. Listening to the cabin's front door slam shut, the V8 of Carol's Iroc-Z rumble to life, tires spinning gravel against the cabin, Bellmont knew she needed time to simmer down, knew where Carol was headed, but he had no road map for the territory he was about to cross.

The past months had created one scar after the next. Bellmont and Carol had planned on having a child before he lost his job. Then, one month after moving to the farm, Carol found her mother, Aggie, laid out in the farmhouse's bathroom. Her three-pack-a-day habit had brought on a fit of coughing. Aggie lost her balance. She fell backwards. Mainlined the toilet's porcelain.

Carol's father, Jonathan, was a spiteful drunkard who had talked down to her since she'd gotten in trouble for drinking and driving long ago. Called her a spoiled whore for hanging at the tavern, lounging with the locals, and wrecking a few cars. Even after Carol cleaned her act up, met and married Bellmont, he never gave her any respect.

Before the accident, Aggie confided in Bellmont and Carol about the will and trust, how the farm had belonged to her family, not Jonathan's, and it would be passed on to Bellmont and Carol after Jonathan and she were dead.

And that's what fed Carol's imagination after her passing, after Bellmont told her about the Donnybrook. About how to get it started. The money to back it, a place to have it, the farm and its timber. Something her father would never support. Now, after months of planning, Bellmont was trying to wade the rapids a bit longer. Put off their chance at a better existence.

She fishtailed the Iroc to a stop between two '78 Fords in the gravel lot of the Leavenworth Tavern, shifted into park, thinking to herself how Bellmont could want to sell her wheels. He'd do the deed tonight if she had to tie the knot her damn self. But first she needed a sip of something stout to calm her down while she took in a good fight.

Carol clumped across the gravel lot to the rear of the tavern. Local coon hunters, farmers, and dopers gathered around the fifteen-by-fifteen depression in the ground. Sloshing beers and bourbon, they haggled and exchanged money with a man who had a pencil behind his ear, a notepad in his hand. His hair plastered across his head like Ricky Ricardo. Black-rimmed glasses arched over a fiery habanero nose with broken vessels. His moniker was Hemple. He took bets on the bare-knuckle boxing matches held every other

Friday night at the tavern. These were the places Bellmont and she would scout for the unbeaten, the new blood. They'd find them in the backwoods dives where creased bills would pass from one hand to the next, wagering on fists clattering bone until there was a victor.

Bellmont and she planned to contract a small stable of fighters, offer them a place to stay and train, feed them, travel with them to other fights. Raising the fighting purses with each unbeaten fighter, driving the bets to higher marks. Build the fighters up over the first year, spread the word about her and Bellmont's first ever Donnybrook.

Hemple nodded to Carol, and his busted woofer tone questioned her with "Where's Bellmont?"

"At the farm, spent from diggin' fence line all damn day."

Hemple pursed his lips, asked, "Wanna drop a dime on the next fight?"

"Who's favored?"

"Ali Squires."

An unbeaten bare-knuckle fighter.

"Who's he fightin'?"

"Some piece of marrow goes by Angus. Has had five scrapes, never been beat."

"Where's this Angus?"

"Standin' over yonder with that colored fella."

A black man stood with a towel tossed over the right shoulder of his thermal shirt with sleeves cut off. He whispered into the ear of a confident-faced man. He'd pallid shoulders, with lean punctures of fiber shielding his chest, arms, and abs, and several names tossed across his frame in Gothic script. Carol observed the conqueror of man: Chainsaw Angus.

She questioned Hemple, "Shit's up with the John Henry about his fighter's body?"

"They the five men he beat into a state of stillborn. Can't even sound out the alphabet no more."

Carol smirked with thoughts of a future prospect once her daddy was out of the frame. She pulled soiled clumps of ones and fives from her hip pocket, tips from work, wanting to wash the grit from her tongue. The guilt of what Bellmont and she had planned, what he had been putting off. But this was all the green she had.

Fuck it! I'll get some glass-eyed horn dog to procure me a drink, she thought, and handed the wad of bills to Hemple.

"Put it all on that Angus fella."

Beside her a voice said, "Little girl takin' a big gamble."

She turned to the ungodly shadow of Mule Furgison. He was crowd control for the disorderly. Six-six, two hundred fifty pounds. The beast was cured and carved from pure spruce hardwood. Vaseline blond hair, one eye green, the other brown, his silverback mitts hanging down to his waist, his right hand resting against the ASP baton encased at his side for backup if needed, or just a little extra hurt.

Carol ran a flirting finger up the navy blue T-shirt that covered his feed-sack chest and said, "This little girl wouldn't mind a swallow to wash down the blood that's 'bout to be lost."

With the sun setting behind him, Bellmont knocked on his father-in-law's marred screen door. Took a deep breath, knowing he had to eliminate one man's belligerent abuse to hock a better life for Carol and himself. But that didn't make the thought of it any easier to accept.

A gruff voice from inside hollered, "Down here, dammit!"

Bellmont walked into the kitchen, through the dining area to the basement door. Infirmity tugged from within.

Carol's fingernails had swelled Bellmont's cheeks. When he got down the basement steps, his father-in-law shouted with laughter. "Shit happen to you?"

Beneath the graying rafters, Jonathan sat in a chair honed from hickory as he did every evening. Several rusted hooks hung overhead where he strung up his deer, let them bleed out, then skinned and quartered them next to the table where he sat. He wore overalls and a white T-shirt wrung with five days' worth of outdoor labor around the collar and beneath the pits.

Bellmont fingered one of the swells that tracked down his face.

"Carol and me had us a disagreement."

"Guess she showed you who's wearin' the rompers of the family."

Bellmont had busted his ass for Jonathan since moving to the farm. The old bastard was always pressing buttons. Carol was right, his degradation wouldn't be missed.

"She had her a fit was all."

Jonathan grabbed the glass of hoppy liquid that sweated next to eight empty brown bottles. Tilted it to his lips. Emptied the glass. Reached down to a faded old red cooler, lifted the lid. Ice clacked as he removed another bottle, laid it on the table. Smirked and said, "Think Carol'd mind if you natured yourself a swill?"

Bellmont pulled his keys from his pocket. Thumbed the

attached Falls City bottle opener, said, "Carol ain't the boss of me. Angle me one from your pink cooler there."

Jonathan hesitated, grabbed a beer from the ice, tossed it hard to Bellmont, and said, "My cooler might be pink, but no man should ever have to placate that kinda ass stompin' from a female."

Popping the cap from the bottle, Bellmont teetered on busting it across the old man's dead-leaf tint. But he didn't wanna show signs of a confrontation, understanding how he'd go about making the scene appear self-inflicted. He said, "She didn't stomp my ass."

Jonathan opened his beer. Filled his empty glass, said, "Carol's mother, Aggie, she tried that shit on me once. Stood over the stove boilin' tea one evening after I'd bailed Carol out of jail for another DUI. Cursed me for callin' my daughter a sheet-swappin' tramp. I says to her, 'Don't think I won't come over and slap the hem from your skirt, make your skin flame and itch.' She tossed that pan of boilin' tea onto me. Near sheared the hide from my bone. I winged the kettle right back at the heifer, creased her chin. She never laid a cross word again' me after that."

Bellmont said, "Maybe you shouldn't have talked about your own blood in such a tone."

Jonathan hollered, "Aggie needed to hear the truth. Little rip had a fake ID 'fore she was legal, just to go to the tavern, bat them fawn eyes and throw that hip to ever' man with a beer tab."

"Watch your lip, Jonathan, Carol's my wife."

"Carol was a coathanger whore 'fore you come along, don't wanna think about how many lives she ended 'fore they even took shape."

Anger hardened in Bellmont's joints like arthritis.

"Ain't warnin' you again, Jon, she's your goddamn daughter!"

"Warnin's ass," Jonathan said. "Aggie spoiled Carol. Damn girl was always blowin' her coin on clothes and booze. Then wanna borrow money from us."

Bellmont walked off behind Jonathan, unable to fathom how many times he'd helped the piece of gristle kill, string, and process venison. He stared at the plywood shelving of twine, nylon rope, and an assortment of blades, pliers, and bone saws. Then up at the hook above Jon's head. Thought killing an animal was for survival. Nourishment. Watched Jonathan finish his beer. Reach for another. He didn't pour it into his glass. He took it from the bottle and Bellmont said, "Carol and me is gonna start up our own business."

Jonathan said, "With what? Two of you is broke as a two-dollar whore."

Trading his beer for cords of nylon, Bellmont worked the rope into a noose, said, "Gonna use the land you got here."

Jonathan almost spat his beer through his nose and said, "My land? The shit you talkin' about?"

The rope was electric in Bellmont's grip as he told himself this was for Carol's and his survival. Jonathan was in mid-turn as Bellmont lassoed the rope over his head, strung it up over the rusted hook in the ceiling's rafter, jerked the nylon, hoisted Jonathan up from his chair, and said, "Ever hear of Donnybrook?"

Ali feinted right. Angus twisted to Ali's left. Ali's jab reached. Angus peppered Ali's forearms. Shined the scars that pouted above his lids. Cauliflowered his ears with left-right hooks.

Around the pit, men and women shrieked. Beers and glasses of whiskey sloshed.

After the third advance, Ali was winded. Stepped back. Angus took to the angles. Scourged Ali's ribs. Got them ready for the sauce. Ali dropped his elbows, trying to protect his torso. Angus painted the undersides of Ali's jaw. Made him chew on cankered silt.

Ali's corner man hollered, "Move your ass, Ali."

Ali staggered, liquid dribbling like strings of violet grease from his lips. Angus doubled up his left and right, giving Ali the sauce just below his navel, taking his center. Ali hit the ground. Angus stoked the grill. Laid his right shin into Ali's throat, took Ali's left arm across his left knee, applied downward pressure until Ali's wrist fractured. Angus smiled down at Ali's screams of submission, knowing he was seared.

From the crowd, boos and cheers showered down on the fighters like rain.

"Wasn't even a fight," Carol said, counting the stack of worn bills. Five hundred in green. Maybe this would be enough to convince Bellmont to get off his ass and take care of business. This, and Angus. Maybe he'd be their first fighter. A big mitt enclosed her shoulder. Mule, scouring the pool-ball bulge of his crotch with one hand, pulling her tight, said, "Now you owe me a couple drinks." Carol twisted from his grasp, said, "Don't think so." She walked toward the gravel lot and her Iroc. Mule hollered, "The hell you think you're goin'?" but she ignored him.

Jonathan's heartbeat jarred his temples. Rope hairs dug into his neck. Bellmont kept his knees bent and his weight dropped as he pulled.

Jonathan huffed, "Mother . . . fuck—" The noose dammed the passage of breath from his mouth. Fingers dug between rope and throat. His face went the color of a pickled beet, his whites twined with slithers of pink vessel. Denim-covered legs kicked stiff, sweat iced Bellmont's body as he struggled to tie the rope around a four-by-four that framed the plywood shelves. He stood half shaken, walked in front of Jonathan's body. Kicked the hickory chair over. His eyes had already wheeled into the rear of his head.

Carol and he had watched the Friday-night blood feuds behind the tavern for more than a year. Watched the wagers being chalked and paid for the men who delivered the pain. Watched the booze being sold. The dope being smoked. The men and women corralling around the indented earth like feral mongrels.

In a state of intoxicated despair, Bellmont forged an idea more lucrative than a Friday-night scrapping session. Seeing all of the money that exchanged hands on Friday nights, Bellmont told Carol of the stories from his daddy, of his idea to deliver the two of them from their days of scraping by. At Donnybrook, they could charge people sixty to a hundred bucks for three days of watchin', but a fighter's fee would be around five hundred bucks. That wasn't counting the betting and the boozing or purse for the winner after three days of fighting. He thought if people wanted to sell drugs, they could but he'd get a cut of it. And they'd do it year after year, because now they'd have a place to do it.

Outside, car lights shadowed through the basement window onto Jonathan's outline. He hung from the rafter like a water-soaked towel weighing down a clothesline. His worn overalls already blotted dark at the crotch. Puddled onto the basement's creek rock floor. The smell of feces was a permanent testament on the air.

Outside, a car door slammed. And within minutes the screen door upstairs screeched open and Carol yelled, "Bellmont, you in here?"

Bellmont shouted, "I's downstairs."

Feet rushed across the floor planks. The basement door squeaked. Carol burst down the wooden steps. Bellmont turned, Jonathan's knees bumping against his shoulder; he smirked and said, "The son of a bitch done dropped his bladder but his chest is still pushin' wind."

Winded, Carol eyed her father, hanging like fresh-cut tobacco from the webbed rafter, and said, "Wondered if you was over here. Done checked the cabin. Seen the basement light through the window." She wiped a tear from her eye, realizing Bellmont had done it, the old man was near dead, and she said, "Bastard always was tougher than a cast-iron griddle. Think he's done?"

"How the shit should I know, never made nobody commit suicide before."

"Won't believe what I come across tonight?"

"What?"

"A bad piece of loin goes by Angus, handed Ali his walker for the retirement home."

"No sh—"

Out the basement window, a truck engine grew in pitch, more car lights shadowed. Gravel clanked against tires. A door opened and a man's voice hollered, "Where the shit you at, Carol McGill?"

Bellmont looked at Carol. "The fuck is that?"

"Aw hell, must be Mule Furgison."

"Shit's he doin' here?"

"Bought me a drink at the tavern."

Bellmont felt the scrapes on his face kindle and said, "Bought you a drink? You know what I just did here to give us a better life?"

Upstairs the kitchen's screen door opened.

Carol red-eyed Bellmont, said, "I'll fix it," and ran up the basement steps before Bellmont could stop her.

In the kitchen, Carol yelled, "Shit you think you're doin' here, Mule?"

"Think you gonna prick-tease me, Carol, you got another thing comin'."

Carol demanded, "Get your hands offa me! My husband is right downstairs."

Bellmont heard feet shuffle across the kitchen floor. A table scuffing linoleum. Carol screaming, "Quit it, Mule!" A palm bounced a few life lines off her skin, wilted her backwards onto the kitchen table.

Bellmont ran up the steps. Took in the mammoth shape of Mule standing in front of his dazed wife laid out like a slab of meat on a butcher's block, her knees bent and hanging over the table's edge.

"Piece of inbred hash. Get the hell away from my wife!"

Mule whirled into two fists pounding his face. Stunned, the big man fell back. His right hand pawed for the snap of his ASP's case, pulled the ASP free, thumbed the button. Extended the steel baton. Mule came at Bellmont, sledged the steel section across Bellmont's nose. Cartilage butterflied. Bellmont's legs quaked. He knelt to the floor on one knee, tongued the blood, and screamed, "Fuckin' shit!"

Carol shook off Mule's palm branding her flesh, crunched up from the table, and reached her arms around his five-gallon bucket of a neck, wrapped her legs around his whiskey-barrel waist, and rooted her fingers into his tresses and ripped at the layers. Mule grunted. His left hand pawed for Carol's head. She sank her teeth into the back of his neck.

Mule dropped the ASP. Slapped both hands backwards at Carol. Bellmont grabbed the ASP. Notched Mule's shin. Parted his knee. Mule staggered backwards. Carol released her anaconda grip, fell onto the table, spitting skin and hair.

Bellmont worked his way up Mule's torso, beat the grizzly's thighs, made his knees hinge to the floor. Bruised and oozing, Bellmont told him, "Any man think he's gonna get himself a whiff of my wife best sit a spell and reconsider." He brought the ASP down over Mule's head, rolled him into a ball of dough. Bellmont raised the ASP again and Carol came from the table, screamed, "Stop, 'fore you kill him!" She bear-hugged Bellmont. He looked down over her shoulder onto Mule's parched profile, shading into blackberries and rust.

A craving spread through Carol's frame as she tugged his face to hers, feeling the savage jolt of lips and the violent twitch of their tendons. She fingered the buckle of his pants, pushed them down to his ankles. Kicked her shoes free, unbuttoned and squirmed from her own pants. Bellmont held the length of steel in his right, ripped her panties from her with his left, keeping his eyes on Mule, who lay on his side, his ribs raising and lowering slowly. Carol flung Bellmont against the kitchen wall, locked her legs around his waist. Met the stab of his pelvis into hers as she bucked a violent teeter-totter of cold, hard love.

Afterward, they stood sheened and panting over Mule, who lay like a tree that had been chopped and derooted, pulp ebbing from his lips and nose.

Carol looked at Bellmont and asked, "Now what?"

The silence from the basement was overwhelming. It drowned out Mule's bubbling gasps. Bellmont looked at his wife, at his hands, around his new kitchen. "I'll load this piece of shit up in his truck, drive him home. You follow me, bring me back here. We get some of his bloodstains cleaned from the floor."

"We gonna let him live?"

"Yeah, most he's gonna be doin' for a while is spreadin' the word about how others ought to not fuck with Bellmont McGill and his wife."

"What about Daddy?"

"Leave his ass hangin' like meat in a cooler, make sure he's really dead. We make the call in the mornin'."

"And we start new?"

Bellmont abraded Carol's stomach, thinking about the child they both wanted but hadn't been able to have, mashed his lips against hers, and said, "Yeah, we start new."

CRIMES IN SOUTHERN INDIANA

Loss lubricated the sixteen-by-sixteen pit where four canine legs twitched muscle beneath soiled fur. Red the color of roses drooled from the teeth of Boono, a black-tan Walker hound. Puddled onto Ruby's lifeless golden cur hide. The referee declared the winner.

Outside the heated glow of the pit, Iris stood like a bastard child with a clubfoot and Elephant Man features, fighting back the mucus and the tears of his loss. He watched opal-skinned men dressed in bibs, some with T-shirts, others without, count crumpled bills to the winning bettors of Boono. While tobacco-skinned men in denim sagging below their asses traded small squares of cellophane for cash from grizzly-faced white men whose arms were graffitied up with Marksman crosshairs, American flags, M16s, and big-breasted females.

But not Iris. He was deep in the hole after his third hound, Ruby, was beaten.

Going over all that he'd lost. The wife. The morals. And now, the dogs. Five fingers lay heavy as regret over Iris's right shoulder. The words of Chancellor's broken southern Indiana tongue rang in his ear.

"Mr. Iris, looks to me you's about fifteen grand in the hole."

Iris kept his back to Chancellor and said, "Ain't got it."

Chancellor chuckled in a deep bellow and said, "Them's three words I don't never care to hear." He went silent among the hopped-up screams of unshaven, gap-toothed men swilling drinks and snorting the crystalline powders from their purchases. Knowing Iris was a renowned trainer of coonhounds, he drawled, "You got two choices. You labor my dogs under my rules for a few fights, work off what you owe, or—"

Chancellor paused, waited for Iris to acknowledge him.

Iris turned around. His cataract eyes met the pugilistic glow of Chancellor Evans, whose hair thorned up into oily intestinal nails, framed his floured skin and bristled beard. He had hubcap shoulders attached to iron-ore arms. Stood with a black shirt worn to the shade of spent charcoal. A .45-caliber Glock was tucked below his navel. Chancellor was a war veteran of Afghanistan who returned home, hating America for the war it had started and never finished. He ran guns throughout Kentucky, Tennessee, and Ohio. Had meth brought in for his family's mid-level dogfighting ring and, after all the generations before him, he was now eyeing the big-money fights.

Anger festered behind eyes split with red vein. Iris swallowed his pride and asked, "Or what?"

Chancellor smiled. His metallic blue eyes rolled down toward the pistol tucked in his front, came back to Iris as he lifted his hand to his temple, index finger pointing, thumb high like a hammer, and he said, "Or one of the Salvadorans can take ye out behind the barn, put a nine to your pan."

When Chancellor's supplier for meth caught his abandoned cookhouse on fire on Lickford Bridge Road, he'd gotten word of men who pushed a purer form of amphetamine within the small riverboat towns that ran east along the Ohio River. He approached these men and worked out an arrangement for them to supply extra muscle at the dog-fights and drugs to the locals who worked the power plant and automotive and oil factories in the surrounding coun-ties. Aging men and women who callused their grips for a wage and craved carnage. The men Chancellor approached were the Mara Salvatrucha. He conceived the MS-13 gang to be soldiers like him and his men, playing by the rules of the grotesque. And they agreed.

Iris's bones itched with fear and crashed with loss. What he wanted was to kill this savage to whom he'd gotten in-debted.

Iris sucked up his pride, leveled his tone to Chancellor. "Know a lotta faces are here to wager. See somethin' bleed. I gave 'em that. I work off what I owe. Not a penny more."

Chanellor's lips shaped into a smirk and said, "Clean that dog of yours outta my pit. Take 'im out back, toss him in Crazy's truck with the others." Iris turned, felt his insides go warm. No burial for his hounds. He made his way through the shadowed frames. Walked toward the lighted pit where Ruby's motionless shape lay as a testament to his mistake, stepped over the wooden wall decorated by the dead. Wrin-kled bills for the next round of bets were passed.

Gothic clowns morphed from Crazy's shoulders, inked into ropes down around his elbows. Daggers ripped over his fore-arms and beneath the cuffed wrists that twisted behind his back.

Crazy had been IDed as Felix Martinez, a man who worked at a local chicken factory by day. By night he networked a cocktail of mayhem, stealing, cashing out dope, and when needed transporting dead canines.

Detective Mitchell stood in the interrogation room, eyes spent, carbon hair matted against his head, a jawline of stubble. He had run Crazy's prints, scanned his sheet. Discovered Felix was an MS-13 lieutenant. Wanted for car thefts, misdemeanors, and even tied to a few malicious-wounding charges in other states. His ID was falsified.

Crazy leaned into the metal chair more than he sat in it. His black-and-white skull-and-crossbones boxers rimmed out of his loose-hanging denims, which were spotted with crimson.

Mitchell leaned down in front of Crazy. His words bounced within the eight-by-eight room of carpeted floor and wood-paneled walls as he asked, "Name Iris got any meanin' to you?"

Mitchell had been investigating the bloated hides of dead dogs scattered down in White Cloud, Indiana, from two months ago. Where a single road of gnarled blacktop led to a few fishing cabins spread out along the Blue River and the antique gas station that hadn't operated since the sixties or seventies. The dogs, dumped behind the station, had been discovered by a local.

The dog's necks had been torn out by teeth. Flies had taken shelter within their ears and nostrils, depositing larvae, swelling their eyes. The innards had begun to reek of decay. His hunch was he was tracking a dogfighting ring.

Mitchell had no leads, knew dogfights didn't happen every week, they were spread out. He had been staking out the gas station on weekends. Parked his old truck within the shadows of willow trees and waited. Headlights cut through the dew of Sunday morning. Inhaling a cigarette and sipping cold caffeine, Mitchell watched a Nissan truck putter to a stop, then reverse next to the gas station and kill the engine.

From it stepped Crazy in his T-shirt with sagging jeans and big white tennis shoes, a wool ball cap cocked to the east. "The fuck?" Mitchell muttered. "Damn fish outta water."

The young man dropped the tailgate. Cradled out several stiff shapes. Threw them down the same embankment of dried leaves and rock. Mitchell unholstered his piece and got out of his cruiser.

Now Crazy sat smelling of tainted hides, staring holes in the white-and-gold table before him, and said, "No hear of him."

The dogs Crazy had dumped had been tagged, the letters I.P. branded within the left and right inner ears of each hound. The owner's initials. Iris Perkins. A local breeder, hunter, and legend amongst the coon hunters of Harrison County. A man Mitchell's father had hunted with when he was a boy.

The dogs could have been stolen and sold. But no reports had been filed on missing coonhounds. Mitchell said, "Them dogs was killed by other dogs. Meanin' they was part of a dogfighting ring. Big fuckin' no-no 'round these parts. We love our dogs here. I wanna know who runs it." Crazy said nothing.

"Fine, your prints tell me you got forged documentation. You've a sheet that's been opened for a bit, it'll likely take you some years to close it, servin' time in prison." Crazy didn't even blink. "World's most dangerous gang, that's your title. 'Course, you do time your face and ass'll be gettin' used in all kinds of dangerous ways."

Crazy was still calm.

Mitchell said, "And they's the duffel bag of cash I found in your truck." Crazy lifted his gaze from the table, eyed Mitchell but didn't say anything. Mitchell had gotten his attention and said, "You's fucked."

Mitchell exited the room. Let his words worm through Crazy's head. He walked to the break room, refilled his takeout cup with coffee. Went over to another room and set the thermostat of the interview room's A/C to 58. Let that fucker freeze. Knowing he was from way down south, couldn't be used to the cold.

In the room, Crazy thought about how everything started thirteen years ago in El Salvador, where poverty and hunger had run cold, pained his mother's and father's guts in a driftwood shack with a tin roof nestled upon a mound of dirt and dreams of saving enough to immigrate to the States. Until Crazy found a new family, which was green script entwined with crossbones, daggers, and teardrops from forehead to heel. They hopped trains to the north. Crossed the Rio Grande. Paid the coyotes to bring his set leader, Angel, and him to the Midwest with ten other members six years ago. They'd an objective: spread out to the small cracker-ass redneck towns. Get a job with other immigrants. Blend in. Start recruiting members for the MS. Set up trafficking routes for drugs and humans.

Now he was second in charge of that family, directly under Angel. But the thieving, smuggling, and killing had taken its toll, making him question when he'd be the next statistic. He started skimming cash from the dope he and his set smuggled from another MS set who delivered by boat along the Ohio River and sold throughout Indiana, Kentucky, and Ohio. He and his homies exchanged cash from the previous sale of product after they'd gotten their cut. Loaded the new product. Sometimes cellophane bricks of weed, other times meth. Crazy drove the drugs in one car while another ran interference if needed for the conservation officers, as well as the state and county cops. Then they broke it down, cut it up for resale to the locals throughout the surrounding counties. Crazy planned to take the money he'd stolen, disappear, begin a life without violence.

Recently, Angel had formed an alliance with a local gunrunner who held dogfights, thought it would help to spread their reach deeper into the rural landscape. A cracker named Chancellor Evans, who held bouts every couple months for locals and out-of-towners. His supplier had been busted after his cookhouse found a spark and burned to the ground, or so he thought. Angel and Crazy got word of its location, rigged it to burn to get more meth territory. As an added bonus, he helped sling amphetamines and provided some of his clique's extra muscle for Chancellor's fights. The deal Evans laid on the table was simple: supply the narcotics and get a 30 percent cut on his take. Angel took it. Crazy was drafted to dump the losing dogs, only tonight he'd planned on dumping the hounds and disappearing with the money he'd been skimming over the months, piling the cash up and hiding it in the spare-tire compartment behind the seat. But tonight the cash was sitting next to him because he was planning to run away, start over, and the cop came out of nowhere.

He'd been sitting for what seemed like hours. The joints of his arms and legs ached, his skin pimpled. He was cold and stiff. He wanted out.

Mitchell entered the room with a steaming cup of coffee. He sipped it. "Ahh," he said, "somethin' to take the chill out."

Crazy sat up in the chair, shivering.

Mitchell eyed Crazy, remembered the dogs: one golden, one fudge, and one raven. But what Crazy had dumped was chomped and clawed into Chiclets of red. Necks busted with gums smeared and teeth filed to points. Hinds and fores sprained and broken.

Crazy sat silent, inhaled deeply, exhaled.

Mitchell took in Crazy's candy-corn scars, knife wounds. And his eyes, bottomless pools of unknown savagery. Mitchell sipped his coffee. Crazy wasn't playing hard, he was hard. Mitchell wanted to get inside Crazy's head. Try to flip him. The dogs weren't going to work. He thought of the way Crazy had looked up from that table when he mentioned the cash and he said, "Shame, all that money you had. Know what happens to it? Twenty percent automatically goes to Uncle Sam. The other eighty goes to the department. Buy us new equipment."

Crazy's sight was burning when Mitchell said this. All of the work he'd done. Time and risk taken to not get caught. And Crazy said, "Muthafucker."

Mitchell smiled. "Not only do I got your money, I got your plate number, know where you work and sleep."

"That money belong to me."

The bag had been sitting on the seat with a change of clothes, deodorant, and soap. His Nissan had a near full tank of gas. Was Crazy stealing from the hands that fed him? Plannin' to run away with money earned from the dogfights?

It was a long shot but Mitchell would take it. He threw out his lure and said, "Bet it belongs to your set, your gang."

Enraged, Crazy repeated, "Belong to me."

Mitchell said, "What's it worth to you?"

"Worth?"

"Yeah, what would you do for it? I could get word to your gang, let 'em know you're dirty. Cut you loose and see how long you last."

The chill in Crazy's bones was breaking him down. He wasn't afraid of Angel anymore, Angel was going to come after him anyway once he left, but he'd risked his life over the course of a year skimming that money and this pig was trying to make him walk the coals.

Mitchell told him, "You give me names. Locations. Maybe we can work somethin' out."

Somethin', Crazy thought, meant ratting out Chancellor, whom Crazy had stolen some of the money from. The rest he'd stolen from the MS. If the MS or Chancellor discovered he had turned rat, he'd be hunted and maimed. He was standing on a cliff with a bottomless drop.

"I say anything I'm dead man."

Mitchell had him and said, "Waive your rights, turn informant, get me what I need, I get you assurance and relocation."

Crazy said, "Relocation?"

"Federal protection. New name, job, home in another state, but you gotta give me everything you know."

If Crazy wanted out, this could be his only chance. Staring through Mitchell, he said, "What about money?"

Mitchell hadn't turned it in as evidence; it now belonged to him. He lied, "See what I can do."

And Crazy said, "Orange County, me and my set sling

dope at dogfights, help muscle the crowd. I dump dogs who lose."

A cannon sounded in Mitchell's mind when Crazy said dope. Mitchell asked, "That where the money came from, dope?"

"Yeah."

"The fights, the dog ring, who runs it?"

"Man call himself Evans."

"Chancellor Evans?"

Crazy pursed his lips and said, "Yeah."

Chancellor Evans came from a long line of backwoods gunrunners and dogfighting. Had a lot of reach even with the law enforcement in that county, hard man to bust, paid a lot of people off, rumor was even the cops bought and sold from him. But mixing with the Mara Salvatrucha? God-damn, every cop had been trained to know their story. Immigrants who came up from El Salvador to the West Coast in the '80s. Got harassed by others. Formed their own gang to fight back, to survive. Eventually became the most vicious of all gangs, and why? Because we busted them, housed them in our prisons, where they were schooled in savagery. They didn't just kill men, they'd disembowel them, hang their insides up like party decorations. Taught their new tactics to others. Were now street soldiers for the cartels of Mexico, and those guys were even scarier. They had embedded themselves within most major cities and now were showing up in the heartland, as Crazy's presence attested. They'd all heard about it, knew they were coming. Mitchell knew the Mexicans all worked down at the chicken plant, but Crazy was the first real-life MS-13 gangster he knew of who'd been in custody in all the surrounding counties.

This could be a big break for Mitchell, a promotion.

"How the hell the MS get hooked up with Chancellor?"

"We, the Crazy Blades, we get word that Chancellor need meth to sell during fights, Angel wanna spread our trade deeper."

"Angel?"

"First in command."

"These fights, they held at Chancellor's place in Orange County?"

"In Orange County, yeah. Never at Chancellor's."

"How often?"

"Every so many months. Take time to set up. Secretive."

"And the dope?"

Crazy teethed on pause, ran this through his mind. The other MS set they ran dope with didn't have a problem killing cops or an MS rat.

Mitchell sensed his hesitation, leaned forward and said, "You want my deal I need ever'thing you know."

"Twice a month we meet other MS members on the Ohio River. They travel by boat. I trade money from what we sold for more dope minus our cut. Sometime is weed but most time is meth."

"Damn, we used to make all that stuff here on our own," Mitchell interrupted, mostly talking to himself.

"I don't know," Crazy said. "People say your stuff shit."

Mitchell came back to the interrogation. "The cash in your truck?"

"From crystal at the dogfights."

"You said it was *your* money."

"My money. I take it. You want me to deal, I need keep it or I become a question floating on river."

Deal? Looked like Crazy was willing to talk. Fucker had been skimming from the hand that feeds him. Letting him keep the cash was a risk, but Mitchell couldn't blow Crazy's cover, he'd have to let him take it. The dog ring he'd place on the back burner, use it after he busted the network running drugs on the Ohio River and into Indiana. The drugs would net a bigger bust, more attention for Mitchell. Another notch in the food chain of law enforcement's politics. This was big-time. Crazy needed to document his story on paper and video, the how and the who, and quick.

Early-morning sun heated the rusted tin roof of the barn where the bark and whine of caged dogs vibrated down the hand-planed walls, chipped the lining of Iris's conscience. It had been two weeks since the fight. Two weeks of training dogs from dusk to dawn. Every night he left Chancellor's farm, returning to his own mattress. Pouring whiskey down his throat, wanting to wash away his wrongs, to bring back what had once been right.

Opening the cage for Spade, Iris's arms were bruised and stiff, joints quartered by sharp blades of pain from attaching the heavy-gauge chain to the hounds, setting traps, and catching coyotes. He leashed the bluetick hound, led him out of the barn.

Iris had been a master in the realm of breeding, raising, and training a hound for hunting coon. He had retired from being a town street supervisor, keeping the sidewalks clean. Signs changed. His wife had passed from diabetes, taking one limb and then the next until she was no longer human. After burying her, he fell into a dark well of existence. Wanted a new challenge. Heard men at the Leavenworth Tavern speaking in hushed tones about fighting dogs, the battling and the rush that it delivered.

Iris forfeited everything he once knew. Got pulled in by the addiction of battle, blood, and the exchange of cash.

Stopping in front of the twenty-by-twenty practice pit, the soil turned up fine and blotted by other animals passing from this life, he bent down, hefted the hound, stepped over the thick lumbered walls colored by past kills. Training, Chancellor called it.

From a distance, he heard the cigar-voiced greeting of Chancellor. "Mornin', Mr. Iris. How goes?"

Iris ignored him. Set Spade on the ground. Was reminded of his own dogs he used for fighting. Iris filled troughs with hot and cold water, training Ruby, Ring, and Checkers to endure shock, something a hunting dog didn't need. They enjoyed the hunt, knowing they'd be rewarded by the dead coon and the affection it brought from the owner afterward, not maimed trying to win or because they lost a fight. But just like training his hounds for hunting, the fighters got walked in the morning, taken swimming in streams and ponds in the evenings. Iris also used weighted chains, attached them to his fighting dogs' collars when he removed them from their cages during the waking hours of man to strengthen their necks. Combined vitamins with loin for lean fuel, fed to them in the morning and evening. Coyotes were trapped, restrained with choke poles, led to the practice pit for the hounds to get the taste of battle and a fresh kill. Just like the one whose left hind had been disfigured from the metal teeth. Trapped this morning, now chained to the log post smeared with the graffiti of fur and innards in the pit's center.

The coyote's mangy frame tensed and twitched every

time it tried to touch its left hind to the ground, growled and bared its teeth.

The pat of boots across the dead grass lot grew in pitch and Chancellor said, "You's 'bout a stubborn ol' son of a bitch. Least you is still able to see the world flourish with all its color."

In one of the pit's corners, Iris kneeled down, kept Spade from seeing the coyote, and said, "Ain't nothin' purty 'bout what I been doin'. And just 'cause we got a deal don't mean I got to like it." He felt Spade's heart vibrating his ribs, flexing his tendon and muscle. Spade could smell the coyote, hear its scratch and whine. Iris removed the collar, held Spade as if this were a real fight. He thought about how none of his friends knew what he'd been doing. Only God knew his wrongs.

Spade growled, slumped his shoulders. His ears hung like limp tissue at the sides of each jaw. Iris moved beside him. He'd grown fond of the hound over the weeks, as it reminded him of his first hunting dog, Eddie, when he was a boy. Iris whispered in Spade's ear. "I's sorry." As if he understood the old man. Chancellor just shook his head. And Iris released Spade.

The bluetick mainlined for the coyote. Feinted low. The coyote's fur finned up across its spine. Tried to back away, stand its ground. The chain around its neck went tight, the left hind gave, the coyote bared its teeth and tried to stand its ground, and Spade went to the neck. Jerked and tugged from side to side while its claws pushed the coyote into the soil. Bawls lit up the air. Birds flew from trees and Chancellor sipped his coffee, swallowed, and said, "Be damned if that don't get your eyes puckered with glow for the rest of the day."

Iris's stomach clenched and burned as he watched this dismantling of the weak, listening to the yelps that were pleas for help the same as a human injured and defenseless against his or her attacker. He watched Spade work and part the fur of the coyote's throat until movement was gone. He knew then the difference between the hounds he'd raised and the ones Chancellor raised. Knew how he'd make things right, or as right as he could.

Eyes burned with the stench of rot. Angel's words still coursing through Crazy's head with what he'd been waiting for, telling him last night, "Tomorrow after work, we motor to the river, make a swap."

Crazy stood in the chicken factory, tired of waiting to become another number riddled across the land. Using a stainless edge he parted the dead and plucked chickens that hung from the steel shackle line. Crazy had been sneaking around. Texting. Making phone calls. Feeding Mitchell intel about future dope deals running from Illinois, Indiana, Kentucky, Ohio, and even Pennsylvania and West Virginia. Telling about the house out in the country where they cut, weighed, and repackaged the dope for resale. Mitchell had their routes on and off Highway 62. He was waiting to nail the runners and Crazy's set on the next swap down along the Ohio River—at the old lighthouse. Pull Crazy out and place him in the custody of U.S. marshals, where he'd begin a new life.

Until then, Crazy kept a standard daylight profile working at the factory. But that profile was eating him up inside. He was tense, his nerves rattled day to day, not wanting to get caught, and Angel still offered questions.

With a latex-covered hand, Crazy fingered out the bird's stringy opaque guts, splashed them into the metal trough. The night he'd got caught, made the deal with Mitchell, and put everything to paper while being filmed, he'd made it to the apartment after sunrise. Angel waited up. Wanted to know where he'd been. Crazy told him he'd been out with a female. Angel wanted to know why he didn't call or text. Crazy told him he'd lost track of time. That it wouldn't happen again. And Angel told him *no*, it wouldn't. Then Angel questioned him about coming up short; the higher-ups had questions.

The higher-ups were the leaders in the big house, prison. Word had come from the prisons, snaked its way through the states with the other sets who made the swap with Crazy and his set. Seemed their totals were a little off sometimes. Crazy told Angel he didn't know. Maybe he should question those who trade with them. Angel told him, maybe they should.

The waiting and not knowing what Angel had running through his head had become worse than knowing.

As he passed the pimpled fowl down the line, Angel's words were a repetitive jolt. It was a relief to Crazy that he'd be out soon.

The first break bell rang. Crazy let Hyena and the other workers file out in front of him. Followed behind in shin-high rubber boots and white overalls stained with the heated insides that hid his inked flesh of La Santa Muerte, Saint Death, gothic angels, clowns, roman numerals, and knife scars.

Keeping his distance, he watched the others entering the chicken factory's tiled restroom. Made sure he was alone. Texted Mitchell, telling him, *tomorrow.Swap@lighthouse*.

Crazy walked into the restroom, pulled off his rubber

gloves, tossed them into the metal trashcan. Took in the streaks of blood that outlined them as they lay piled with the other gloves.

He stepped to the marble-circled washing station, grabbed a bar of soap, and eyed his boys Shank and Flame. With bristled heads and lean, gnarled frames, they were the first two young men Angel and Crazy had recruited after crossing the Rio Grande, paying the coyotes to bring those two and ten other MS-13 members up to Angel and him in the Midwest. They had jumped them in this very bathroom. Six years ago. And now he'd ratted them all out for his chance at freedom.

Mashing the metal bar to the floor beneath the rounded washing station, Crazy pushed out a steady flow of water, lathered his hands. Then he rinsed away the stink of his labor, stepped to one of the porcelain dryers that lined a brick wall, elbowed the chrome button that reflected his body, and dried his hands. Caught Shank and Flame nodding to the handful of factory employees to get out. Footsteps and chatter exited.

Hyena guarded the bathroom's doorway.

Crazy took a deep breath, clenched his fists. Something was going down.

Shank and Flame stood in caramel-colored work uniforms, shirts buttoned to the top, with their backs to a scuffed bathroom stall. Flame rattled his knuckles on the stall door. Beneath the door boots dropped from standing on a toilet to the floor. The door swung open. Crazy serpent-eyed Angel, taking in the pitted and scarred facade that highlighted their past. The bold letters MARA across his forehead, bleeding into teardrops down his left jaw. Angel held the duffel bag of cash Crazy had hidden in his truck. Angel tossed the bag across the grouted floor at Crazy and tongued a question. "Why you do this, Crazy?"

Crazy didn't blink. His insides iced over. "Do what?"

"Don't play me for stupid. Know how much cash is in there? More than the higher-ups know about."

Crazy ran his hand through the white suit and into his pocket, thumbed the far left button, number one. Mitchell's number. Shit was about to hit the fan.

Not wanting to be punked, Crazy said, "Tired of this never knowing. Want a life of 'gevity without worry of when it end."

Angel chuckled. "You become wormlike. American bitch."

Crazy felt the other's eyes puncturing his frame from every direction with a zillion ice picks. These guys, his family, they wanted to fillet him, feed him to Chancellor's dogs, and he said, "No, I am Salvadoran. Want to one day become elder Salvadoran."

In El Salvador it was about belonging to survive. Here in the States it was about separation by the language you didn't speak, clothes you didn't wear, and cars you couldn't afford. Trafficking drugs gave you all of that until you realized you were a number waiting to be replaced by a new one.

Angel was granite-hard. "Me, I am *primera palabra.* You were *segunda palabra.*" Angel was the first word, Mara, and Crazy had been the second word, Salvatrucha. The first and second in charge of their MS set, the Crazy Blades. Angel told Crazy, "But now you are *el ladrón.*" The thief. "Filch from the hand that accepted and nourished you. You know how we deal with a thief."

Ladrón. They were just here about the money. They didn't know about his deal. From his pocket came the echo of a tiny voice, "Felix? Felix?" Crazy's alias.

Angel glanced at Crazy's hand in his pocket. Could hear the voice. Watched Crazy pulling the phone from his pocket. Who did this bitch have to call?

Angel's face was a rumpled hide as he gritted his teeth and said, "You been green-lit by big homies. You're dead."

Into the phone Crazy shouted, "Chicken plant!" and pivoted to get his back against the wall.

Shank, Flame, and Hyena swarmed Crazy like sharks to a raw slab of beef. Flame feinted right and double-jabbed a point into Crazy's right shoulder. Pain ran red. Crazy grunted, dropped the phone, reached and gripped Flame's ear, pulled him face-to-face, let his teeth taste the cartilage of his nose. Flame screamed like a bitch. Crazy wrestled the blade from Flame's hand, sliced across Flame's eyes, halved them into a permanent state of blindness. Flame's knees dropped onto the floor, with both his hands patting the moisture that poured from his chewed nose and cleaved sight.

Shank lunged. Crazy twisted and dug the serrated piece of steel he'd pulled from Flame into the meat of Shank's left hip. Pulled it free. Shank winced, and Crazy swiped his edge across Shank's elbow flexer. Vein, tendon, and ligaments ruptured. Shank jerked, stepped back into Angel. Dropped his blade to the tile, palmed his wound.

From behind, Hyena roped a piece of braided cable over Crazy's head, noosed it tight across his throat. Lifted Crazy to the balls of his feet. Ripe-faced and gagging, Crazy staked his knife into Hyena's right thigh, over and over, tenderizing the muscle. Hyena released the cable, dropped backwards onto the tiled floor. The knife stuck in the flank of his leg. He chewed on the sting and burn, ripped the knife free.

Angel came with a jagged blade, divided Crazy's jaw just below the ink of a double teardrop, and said, "In the hospital." Crazy staggered backwards, shoulder burning, and fingered the wet from his face. Angel parted Crazy's chest and said, "In the jailhouse." Crazy pressed both hands to his chest. Angel's eyes branded Crazy's as he pressed forward. Crazy caught movement on his periphery, and a smudged body of brown came from his left, rooted a jagged piece of steel up into Angel's kidney, twisted it from side to side until it broke from the handle. Hyena said, "Or in the grave." The three destinations of an MS member's life.

Angel winced in surprise, dropped his blade, and glanced down in horror at Hyena, mouthing, "Why?" Hyena said, "'Cause I want to be the first word. Not the second if I ever get released. I want my schooling on the inside, no county time, state time."

Crazy glanced at the bag of cash, what started all of this, grabbed it, and moved to the restroom's opening. Hyena looked up at Crazy, knowing he couldn't stand up and stop him from having something he'd never get, a chance at freedom, but he knew if they ever crossed again, he'd kill him. Hyena was ready to graduate to the next level, prison, where he'd get his stripes from the higher-ups, and if he ever got out he'd be a god on the streets. He pulled Angel to the tiled floor, looked to Shank, and said, "We finish him." They swarmed Angel.

Crazy stood in the doorway holding the money, his body floured by the moisture of his wounds, his heart still pumping with shock, watching Hyena's fingers dig into Angel's head, listening to the repetitive crack and give of Angel's skull slamming into the bathroom ceramic. Crazy remembered that in El Salvador, after the jumping-in he had to seal his initiation, spill someone else's blood. He remembered watching a rival clique member steal a hen from a villager. Holding it upside down by its yellow-clawing hinds, he ran. Unseen, Crazy followed the rival to a yard knotted by cinder and soil, where he heaved and smashed the chicken's head against the earth, stomped a foot down on its head, ripped it off like a rubber Halloween mask, and tossed it into the dirt. Crazy pulled his knife free, came up behind the rival, slashed through the cartilage of his Adam's apple. Watched him wobble and stumble to the ground like the bird with its bloody knob of bone in place of its face, thrashing the earth until it bled out.

And these men weren't even rivals. Just more numbers.

Flame lay on the floor, moaning, the whites of his eyes divided and saucy. Before Crazy turned his back, he traced the four points of an imaginary crucifix over his body, bowed his head and asked forgiveness from La Santa Muerte. Then he stepped out of the restroom. Into the chaos of men and women who looked like him but were nothing close. Down in the distance he saw a man running toward him, T-shirt, black ball cap with bold white letters that spelled POLICE, his weapon drawn. An aging face of worry. It was Mitchell. Crazy lowered his head, blending in with the other workers who were fleeing to the parking lot, where he'd find his sovereignty.

In the restroom, red rivered from the bodies of Shank, Hyena, Angel, and Flame. The only chest that wasn't rising was Angel's.

The bell rang. The break was over. The men who survived knew their working alongside the other immigrants would no longer camouflage who they were, the Mara Salvatrucha. That they would go to the second stage toward their destination in this life, the state prison, where they would become initiated with new rituals and rules that differed from those in the county lockup. On the outside more numbers would step up and take their place in this unending ecosystem of violence. But one would get a second chance, a fresh start with a sack of cash, while Mitchell stood in the bathroom, realizing he'd fucked up.

Iris had reviewed it a thousand times. He rested one hand at his waist, beneath his untucked flannel, gripped the .40-caliber H&K, wanting to right his wrongs.

Standing in Chancellor's barn, a red-and-silver gas can lay upturned. The wood floor creaked beneath the weight of his boots. Strong hints of fuel mixed with the sour scents from the shapes and the weeks of their training. Each dog lay within the steel cages, muscles etched and carved like stone beneath their hides of white and black, as they waited to take their turn. Being muzzled and leashed for another day of training. Iris shook his head, wishing there was another way.

He pressed the pistol into the cage closest to the barn door, having calculated the outcome. Five dogs. Caged. Men at least a hundred feet away down in the house. Some sleeping, some hungover. Behind him was a hay floor and the horse stalls. The route he'd taken into the barn this morning. Parked his truck out back just in case he got that far.

His ears would be ringing after the first shot. Whether he'd live or die mattered little to him, only that he righted what he'd wronged with this Chancellor, who was more savage than human.

Iris had always been a man of his word but his word didn't carry much weight anymore. He pointed the pistol at the first dog, Archie. Said, "Forgive me." Looked into the carnage-filled brown eyes with a cold nose. Iris pulled the trigger. The other dogs jerked and growled. Skull and brain pasted through the cage onto the neighboring hound. He moved to the next, trembling, pointing the pistol and pulling the trigger. He did this until he'd reached the last one, Spade. His hearing full of static, he felt a man enter the barn. Iris took in the profile, unlaced boots and blanched jeans, shirt-less with an eagle atop the circular world and an anchor behind it inked upon his chest, a pistol in his right hand. Chancellor's face cringed the shade of mashed cherries, see-ing his dogs splayed about the cages, one after the next. He lifted the Glock at Iris, screaming, "The shit you done, you ol'—" Iris lined up his pistol with Chancellor's chest, tugged the trigger, and ended the world that had branded his heart with inhumane ways. Chancellor breathed his last breath and dropped to the wood floor.

Shaking, Iris tucked the pistol into his pants. Grabbed the leash that hung from Spade's cage, opened the door, hooked the leash into the dog's collar. The tongue came soft against his knuckles and Iris said, "I make it outta this, you might be salvageable." Iris hurried to the rear of the barn, where the stalls lined three openings for horses. He led Spade through an opening, reached into his pocket and pulled from it a book of matches, scratched one against the sandy strike pad, and threw it into the hay. Watched flame ignite the fuel he'd emptied onto it earlier.

Spade sat next to Iris on the front seat of the Chevy Silverado. Iris fired the engine, shifted into drive. Stomped the gas, throwing soil and rock, navigating down the gravel drive, the barn lit up behind him, he passed the pit on his right. Out in the distance to his left sat the old Dutch Colonial brick house where men stumbled out through the back screen door half dressed. Iris kept driving. Turned onto the county road, glanced over the field and acres of cedar, saw the smoke rising above the land. He reached over and rubbed Spade between his black ears, not knowing where he was headed, but knowing he wouldn't stop until he was several states shy of the crimes in southern Indiana.

ACKNOWLEDGMENTS

I'd like to thank my mother, Alice Weaver, and my father, Frank Bill Sr., for filling my upbringing with stories and a wealth of life experiences. Greg Ledford, who told me, "You got talent, don't quit." The night shift friends: John, George, Larry, Kirk, Tim, and my chief, Greg. Randy, Daryl, and Ted from the warehouse. Glen, Gary, John, and Harvey from maintenance, and all of my other union brothers. Denny and Matt Faith, you've been there from the start. The Law Dog Donnie Ross for all of the support and friendship over the years and for answering questions about police procedures: you're like a big brother and always will be. Zack Windell, friend since birth.

The families: Gayle and Israel Byrd, Jamie and Amy Pellman, Terry Crayden, Sharon Crayden, Brandon Crayden, Jessica Chanley, the Trindeitmars, the Muncys, my aunt Trudy, Aunt Becky and Uncle Dennis, Uncle Jack and cousin John. Marly Thevenot Howard. Julie Bill. Allison and Marisa Faith. Pete and Suzie Hardsaw. And Myrtle Bill, you made it to 101 years young, you are dearly missed by all. Thank you all for your support.

Allison (Lady D) and Todd (Big Daddy Thug) Robinson at *Thuglit* for those first-time edits. Anthony Neil Smith, a true friend and the editor of *Plots with Guns*, who has published many of my stories when nobody else would. David

Cranmer and Elaine Ash of *Beat to a Pulp*, thanks for giving me the time of day. Aldo Calcagno, thanks for everything, Crime Dog. Gary Lovisi for putting my words to print. Tony Black at *Pulp Pusher*. Jedidiah Ayres and Scott Phillips for inviting me to the first Noir at the Bar: thanks, guys. Kyle Minor for all the advice and late-night support. Other writers and friends: Keith Rawson, Kieran Shea, Greg Bardsley, John Rector, Steve Weddle, John Hornor Jacobs, Dan O'Shea, Joelle Charbonneau, Victor Gischler, Christa Faust, Roger Smith, Craig Clevenger, Rod Wiethop, Anonymous-9, Rhonda Abbott, Stephanie Stickels, Thad and Dana Holton. Mary Cunnigham, still an aunt at heart. The Griffee family. Kjell Kristiansen. The Reed family. And everyone who follows me on Twitter, Facebook, and Frank Bill's House of Grit.

Donald Ray Pollock, thanks for all the advice, friendship, and support. And to my super-talented agent, Stacia J. N. Decker, and the best editors this side of the United States, Sean McDonald and Emily Bell: no one works harder, you've made my prose that much stronger. To my publisher, Farrar, Straus and Giroux, thank you for taking a risk on me.